ES

E

P

1

THE INSOMNIA MUSEUM

LAURIE CANCIANI was born in 1986 and grew up in Bridgend in South Wales. She battled with a brief but crippling bout of agoraphobia when she left school and rediscovered her love of writing and reading when she was in her early twenties. She received an MA in Creative Writing from Bath Spa University and *The Insomnia Museum* is her first published novel.

THE
INSOMNIA
MUSEUM

LAURIE CANCIANI

An Apollo Book

This Apollo book was first published in the UK
in 2018 by Head of Zeus Ltd

975312468

A catalogue record for this book is available from the British Library.

ISBN (HB): 9781788541763
ISBN (XTPB): 9781788541770
ISBN (E): 9781788541756

Typeset by Adrian McLaughlin

Printed and bound in Great Britain by
CPI Group (UK) Ltd, Croydon CR0 4YY

Head of Zeus Ltd
First Floor East
5–8 Hardwick Street
London EC1R 4RG
WWW.HEADOFZEUS.COM

For my mother Jayne Canciani

For Dom, always

For Jen, my fierce ally

This book is dedicated to Brian and Marilyn Richards,

who would've loved it.

Quick Slow Time

THE MAN PULLED the feathers away so he could get a better grip on the head. The girl sat next to him with her arm around his back and her eyes turned towards the hard work in his lap. She tried to follow the fall of the painted feathers as he plucked them one by one by one from the bird but they were caught too quick by the wind that broke through the letterbox and billowed against the wallpaper and settled into the darkest corners of the room.

Your hands are shaking, Dad.

The cuckoo clock was old. Its doors were warped and the nails that held it all together were forced in at crazy angles. He picked the black varnish off his fingernails and blew out and lifted the clock and placed it in his daughter's lap. It was an effort to bring the thing home.

It was a struggle to drag away parts of the world and think on them and the cutting and changing that must be done and it was hard to make the difference. It was an effort to do much of anything. Recent weeks he had fallen far into the chase again and his eyes gleamed like polished black eggs.

She teased the metal arm out through the doors again, locked her knees around the painted house, pulled the bird from its bed and held it between her legs. He smiled as she grabbed hold of the cheeks and twisted the head back and forth and all the way around until the skin creaked.

You're doing it.

I know I am.

Ignore the broken eye.

I am.

Don't let him scare you.

I'm not.

She drove her fingernails into the hole that had split the side of the bird's neck and she hooked the head and pulled. The stitching drew back through each needle hole like a retreating snake and the head popped and ripped and the insides exploded out and then the whole head came off in her hand and the clock dropped from her lap and landed on the hard floor with the bird stuck headless on the end of the rocking metal arm.

Her father worried himself into more itching and scratching and shifting when he saw the blood welling where the beak pierced the skin on her palm. She didn't like blood. She swayed when she saw it and grabbed hold of her stomach that had started to fold. He took the head and dropped it into one of the boxes and ripped the bottom of his black tee shirt and wiped away all the blood with the cloth and tied it three times around her hand until it was sopped and the sickness was righted.

She looked at him and he looked at her. The sound of the world was coming up through the plughole in the kitchen sink and echoing deep in the walls. There was a long howl. A siren. Dogs. Rain. Then the wind came in again and bobbed the head of Plastic Jesus who lived happy and useless on top of the broken Hi-Fi.

I'll do this next part.

I know, Dad.

I always finish everything off.

You do. You're good at that.

He pulled the small house onto his lap again and tweezed away the last of the wire and sponge and string that stuck out through the hole in the neck. The light spilled through the boards in long thin slats. She picked up the new head he had found that morning while he was out looking for white rabbits. Or looking for Mum. She looked at the head.

3

It was made of plastic with fat pink lips and large blue sparkling eyes and blond hair that was curled around a lovely broken neck.

He took the head and held it against the hole in the neck of the bird and pierced the plastic with a needle and threaded string in and out and down into the empty chest cavity and back up again. He pulled the string tight and threaded it back through a loop and then out again and through another loop until the head was pulled tight to the body and the plastic face sat against the feathers as though it had been sitting there all along.

Oh Dad, it's good.

He sat back and wiped his mouth with the end of his ripped tee shirt. They both looked at the work. Then he looked at her and kissed her face. His lips were dry.

Let it be, he said. It needs to get used to itself again.

What if he doesn't like himself anymore?

He doesn't have to like himself.

Why?

He just needs to accept that there's no changing anything.

He pulled the clock to his chest and took a screwdriver from the arm of the chair and twisted it into the clock face that sat above the small doors where the creature was learning to be different. Somewhere outside something chimed and turned and the wind made an ache. It felt as though it had come from a long way away. Dad hummed a song from the seventies. She watched his mouth close around the sound and open again. He cranked the back of the clock and the hands spun around and around and settled crooked on a number. He brought a carrier bag of rusted nails and metal treasures from a box and fished in there for other numbers that he had ripped from other clocks in other houses that she had never seen. He pulled out the new numbers one and two and three and pressed them against the clock face and nailed them in place next to the digits that had been there since the clock was made in nineteen eighty something. He polished the numbers with his fingers and stuck his screwdriver into the middle of the clock and then he listened at the little doors for the sound of.

What are you listening for?

He looked at her and she looked at him. He moved his face aside and slipped his hand around her head and pulled her to the little doors and hushed her lips with his fingers. She closed her eyes. She heard it. It was the beating heart of the bird.

Dad pointed to the numbers.

This one is a six, he said.

What's that one?

A four.

And that?

Two.

This?

Fifteen.

Dorothy Gale was paused on the TV watching everything with sad homesick eyes. She turned back to the clock. She asked again and again what the numbers were and she closed her eyes.

This one?

Two. Three. Four. Twenty-six.

I can't do it.

Yes you can.

I wanted to learn to read.

Telling time is better. It's more useful.

Why?

Just listen.

He pointed to the numbers and talked about the hands and the clock face and the bird with the new face that would come out every hour if it was ready to be good and every five minutes if it felt like being bad. Depends on the clock. He told her that quarter past was as good as quarter to but not as kind as half past and he told her that there were thirty-nine hours in a day but the nights were shorter and that's why they didn't need much sleep.

There's too much work to do.

I know.

He stepped away and fell back onto the settee and pulled his silky black hair out of his eyes and looked at the ceiling. Then he rummaged for she knew just what, and fell back into the long chase. He looked up and opened his mouth and sighed.

She kissed his cheeks and turned back to Dorothy who had been talking to her these last many days. She rewound the tape. Played it again. The video was old and the player was lazy and the tape chucked the film around and it stopped and started on the TV just like thoughts.

Look at my hands.

I see them, Dad.

Dorothy sang and the light through the slat shifted and spilled over the boxes of junk and stacks of newspapers and table legs and rails of old stamps and clothes and marble topped furniture and typewriters and old chipped cups and damp patches working up the walls and screws and piles of outside and her own face, too, that was fixed upon the dusty TV screen. The room shrank. Her hand throbbed under the tight threads of tee shirt. A little seed of claustrophobia was planted in her head and she sat in the middle of the room in the last of the light. The sound of the world was gone again and in an hour the bird would come out of the hole and squawk. And then there would be only the quiet and the dark and the man who chased rabbits and Dorothy and the bird and the nodding Plastic Jesus and all the junk in all the world broken apart and pressed against the walls of that lovely insomnia museum.

The Insomnia Museum

WHEN ARE WE going to be done?

Done with what?

Changing everything.

The world is big.

I haven't seen it.

That's because it's not ready for you yet.

I love you, Dad.

I'm glad you do.

Do you love me too?

I love you more than all of it. And. I can't think.

The sun peeped through the boards and cut her body into quarters. She played the tape and watched how Dorothy stepped from her dusty farm in Kansas to a world of Technicolor. Dad sat down on the settee and rolled her a smoke and lit it and she took it and smoked it and blew it all to the ceiling that was covered in waves of dust and spider's webs. Dad straightened up on the settee and he leaned forward and scratched his forehead with the cigarette in his hand and the light zigzagging.

I'm going out again.

She looked at him. He was thinner than he had been and his skin was covered in blotches that worked their way from the medicine wounds in his arms to his neck and cheek and circled his fat lovely eye where he had recently begun to inject. She never liked it when he left her. She turned her body to his and picked at the holes in the carpet.

Why do you need to go?

I have to go and get more junk. If we bring in what's on the outside and work on it we can make everything better. I'll look for Mum too, if you want.

I don't want to see her.

I'll go looking for white rabbits then.

When she was five or six he boarded up the windows of the flat and locked the front door and began to bring home boxes of junk that he piled in towers that stretched from the carpet to the webbing and the lampshades that were blackened and yellowed by lovely smoke. In the rooms the towers grew and lined the walls and seeped into the middle and each room became a maze of junk and mess and artefacts stolen from the houses of others. She looked at the picture that hung between the boarded windows on the back wall of the living room opposite the bright TV screen. The picture was of an old woman with a severe face and grey hair and a smile that pulled her lips past the gums and teeth.

She asked him who the old lady was when he brought it here those months ago.

I think she died. They were clearing out the house and I pretended to be one of them and I walked in and looked around for money or whatever. That picture was hanging on a wall in the bedroom. I couldn't take anything else. I wasn't myself. She looked at me and I looked at her and I took her off the wall and hid her underneath my coat and I left and brought her here. Nobody wanted her. Don't you think that's sad?

He made a workshop in the attic with wooden tables and vices with two plates that twisted and screwed and held whatever junk he wanted to change. He took the junk out and brought home more and more until the walls were lined with phone books and magazines and newspapers that she couldn't read and plastic jugs and pictures of families she would not know and metal taps and table legs and street signs. There were street signs everywhere. They were all different and the letters were big and small and spaced apart and scrunched together and she lifted one and looked at Dad but he had fallen too deep into the chase and his eyes were searching for God in the back of his head. She looked at the signs again. Kansas, they said.

Dad stuffed carrier bags into his shoes because he didn't want the rain to get in. He took one shoe and looked inside and pushed the carrier bag in and turned the shoe around so that she could see. She looked at the holes in the bottoms of his shoes and she saw the white plastic pressed against the hole and she stuck her finger in and told him that it was good, Dad. It looks dry. Fine. He did the same in the other shoe and slipped them on his feet and she could hear the crackle of the bag and then nothing when his feet were flat against the sole.

When will you be back?

He stood up and went past the boxes and took the clock from the mantle and brought it back to her and pointed at the hands. He told her he would be back when this hand was. And the other hand was. About two hours and forty-five minutes and if the mad bird doesn't keep the right time he'll take off its plastic head.

Don't do that, Dad.

He kissed her face and asked if she would get to work

on the jewellery box that had no dancer and she told him that the music always made her feel sick. He went into the kitchen that was at the other end of the living room and separated by a washing machine and a unit and a stack of antique walking sticks that always tripped her when she walked by them. He filled a glass with water and came back again and handed the glass to her and told her to drink the whole thing whenever she felt the sickness come.

I will.

Good.

How long will you be?

I told you already.

I just want to make sure you remember it.

He put on two coats and lifted one of the hoods and he went out of the room and into the hallway and slipped past the stacks and past the ladder that went to the attic and then he went off into a place she couldn't see. She heard the click and she smelled the wind and then she heard the bang when the door closed then the whole place changed as it always did when half the life was gone.

Keeping Sound

DAD HAD BEEN gone for six hours.

He used to read to her before his vision started to go, before he started seeing silver worms where there was only a doorway or falling ribbons of wallpaper. When he told her about the worms, she told him that she could feel moths in her head and sometimes they gave her a nosebleed that lasted so long she thought her whole body would drain out and fill up the bath. He looked at her and blew the smoke out of his lungs.

Yeah but mine are real, he said.

He had been gone for six hours and she had missed him all that time. She worked on the jewellery box and watched *The Wizard of Oz*. She picked up the box and looked at the bottom and she shook it. There was a rattle that Dad had not noticed and she thought on that. She shook the box and stuck his screwdriver into a hole at the bottom and flicked the end and the bottom came away and something fell into her lap.

It was a round black tube with a gold ring around the middle and it was small enough to almost roll through the hole in the wooden floor beneath her. She caught it before it fell and she took it in her hands and looked at it in the small light that had crept in through the boards sometime during the last mad hour. She looked at the tube for a long time. Smelled it. Bit it. It smelled and tasted like plastic and there was a crack near the gold ring that she got her fingernail into and pulled and then the tube came apart in her hands.

Inside one half of the tube there was a red crayon and when she twisted the plastic base the crayon rose up and twisted out.

She went into the bathroom where the tiles were falling down and plaster was showing and there was a black garden growing along the wall. She turned on the light that hadn't worked for years and years and she turned it off again. Sometimes she forgot what time it was. What year. Sometimes she thought she was five or six again and the halls were clean and the lights were working and the windows were full of light. Sometimes she forgot that he had become an old man. She thought of the way his face changed and she felt. Something. Guilt. It was as though she had grown up too quickly and stolen the years from Dad and now that she was a woman, seventeen, he was old and pressed up against the ceiling, dangerously close to being as old as he would ever be. Sometimes she looked at him. She stared at him for. And then she was weighted to the threads in the carpet. Once death was done with him it would look at her and she would not be ready to look back.

She twisted and untwisted the lipstick and watched the red bulb rise and fall and she tapped her finger on the tip and saw how her skin sponged the colour. The tap in the bathroom had been broken for two or six or eight years. One tap ran constantly with thin brown water and the other ran clean water that steamed and dribbled and came out too hot and too fast. She fitted the plug into the hole and let both taps run at the same time and the water rose in the sink. Steam came. Her face sweated. She closed the bathroom door like he always told her not to do and she brushed the hair out of her face and looked at the mirror that was attached to the wall by a metal fist. She poked her tongue through the gap in her teeth that she had got when she chewed on black jacks and pieces of rubber she'd pulled from a tyre.

She twisted the tube and slipped the lipstick up and turned it towards her and looked into the mirror and stopped breathing and stopped her heart and concentrated on the bright colour and she patted the bulb onto her lips. She looked at herself.

She dabbed the colour and then she pinched her lips and slicked it from side to side until her whole mouth was as bright as poppies. The mirror sweated and she turned the water off and she wiped it with the sleeve of her father's tee shirt and she looked at herself standing there. Sometimes Dad watched these black and white films with women who danced with men and waved to their sisters and pulled children into their skirts and powdered their faces and looked right into the camera and smiled. She smiled as she remembered them smiling. She thought about her mother. She brushed her hair with her fingers and let it fall in front of her face a little and she tilted her head back and pressed her lips together.

She hid the lipstick in the back of her jeans and washed her hands in the muddish water and she went into the living room to rewind the tape and set it to play again and she made dinner even though she was distracted by the look of the lips in the toaster. She chucked a bowl of beans in the microwave.

When the bells rang she opened the door and the chemical smell came up and she poured the mess over toast and dropped the empty bowl in the sink. She heard a sound. It started small. Then it came all at once like a machine working in the sink pipes. She took the bowl out of the sink and got up on the counter and put her ear to the noise and held her hair out of the wet base and listened. She closed her eyes and the sound filled the museum.

There had always been noises outside. Dad used to play the music on the Hi-Fi loud and he used to dance and rock his head. He raved. Smoked. She listened to the music and didn't hear the other sounds from outside the flat until Dad had fallen too deep into the chase one day and hit his head against the Hi-Fi and broke the player. She heard it all while he was sleeping. It was noise without meaning. It was the outside. There was drumming from the pipes in the walls. There was a vibration. A machine. Then there was this piping sneeze that came up from the belly of the earth. It was all from that other place that was behind the rain and in the sky.

She listened to the sound rising in the sink and she pushed her ear to it and the noise of outside travelled up the pipe. There were the bells that she had first heard when she was seven or eight and no longer wanted to forgive her mother. Chiming. Rattling. The noise was like pennies in a bag. She stood on the counter and opened the door of the cupboard that was already broken on one hinge, and she took a jar from the back and emptied the vinegar into the sink and then she pressed her ear to the noise and opened the jar and let the sound rattle into the glass. She closed the lid. The sound of chimes was inside the glass and the noise of the world died away in the sink.

She listened hard to make sure the sound wasn't just the rattle in her own head and then she got off the counter and ran to her bedroom which had been full of junk and her own baby clothes and shoes and pictures of pretty women and men cut out of magazines and stuck to the wall. The picture she made was of the world. There were dogs. On the ceiling were a hundred and forty-six paper dolls that held hands and hung in arcs above her mattress. In the wardrobe there were stacks of clothes that didn't fit her anymore and some others that Dad had brought home that were too big or broken on the zips and buttons. Underneath the pile of clothes were the jars.

She picked one up from the back and looked at it but didn't unscrew the top. There was still a little jam on the base where she had scooped the insides out too quickly and had forgotten to fill it with water and shake it and drain everything out. She put the jar into the back of the wardrobe and closed the door.

Then everything was quiet. She played the tape and then she rewound it and played it again and sat with her beans and the mad bird that bashed its head against the wood and told her that it had been hours since she had last seen Dad. She looked at the clock. It rattled and ticked. Dad was probably out looking for Mum or for rabbits. I don't understand what life is, he always said. But the white rabbit can tell me.

She played the tape. Plastic Jesus said that Dad had so many secrets and she was one.

Dorothy

SHE HAD SEEN *The Wizard of Oz* over ten thousand times. But never to the end. Whenever she watched she pressed the stop button and then rewound the tape all the way to the writing at the beginning and the dusty orange and grey tint in the sky and she played it all again. She never really wanted Dorothy to go home.

She paused the tape and rewound it once more and played it again. She struck a spider dead with her fist because she felt like being bad. The jewellery box was all patched up and fixed with a new dancer that was made of wool and wax that she carved out of a candle just after she saved the noise in the jar.

Then the door opened and closed. It took Dad a long time to come into the living room where she was sitting in the green TV glow. He had been gone for the whole night. She heard him locking the front door and he came and stood in the hall looking into the living room and he wiped the winter out of his face. He looked at her. His eyes were raw from rubbing and his chin had grown those little whiskers that always made him look dirtier and older than he was. She paused the TV.

Did you find it?

What?

That white rabbit.

I found. I don't know. I'm tired.

He went back to check the lock and then he came into the living room and went into the kitchen to lean on the counter. He looked at her and stared long and deep into a place in the corner that was too dark to see.

What's the matter, Dad?

I don't know, Love.

Have you been crying?

She played with her little finger while he filled a glass with water and drank it all and filled another and drank that. Her little finger was the ugliest part of her. It had no fingernail. It was ripped and scarred and twisted up on the end like potato roots all twined together. She couldn't remember how she did it. All she could remember was how it felt. There was the pull and rip of the nail and the throb of the end and the blood from the torn skin and sometimes it made her sick to remember. Sometimes she went into the bathroom and lay down in the bath so that she could think on the rattle of the pipes and the twisted finger and Mum who had been gone for such a long. Once she put her toe up the tap to keep the dripping from wrecking her brain and she heard a different noise down the plughole. She sat up and looked down at the black hole and she rubbed the twist and she heard a crash and then she heard a cry and a scream. And nothing.

Why have you been crying, Dad?

He rolled a smoke and came into the living room and gave her one and she looked at him and he looked at her.

Later he held her hand and he told her that he went away yesterday and thought about not coming back. I'm sorry for that. I'll never think that way again. I'll never do that again. I'm your father and you are my daughter. Look at my hands. Sometimes I go to sleep and I wake up in the middle of the night and I look at my hands in the light and I can't figure out if they're mine.

He blew smoke.

You know somewhere near this building there's a beach. Did you know that? There's a beach about twenty minutes down the road and there's sand and rocks and fish and the smell of chips and fried sugar and kids run around with the sunlight on their backs. There are waves. They bring the water in and take the water out again and the air smells fresh and salty and the salt gets into your skin and dries you up. The sea gets to the core of you.

Can we go there one day?

Where?

The sea.

You don't remember. You've already been.

He was asleep on the settee and it was sometime in the dark morning. Every time the bird bashed its head against the walls of its wooden house she turned to watch him stir and mumble.

What did you say, Dad?

I saw a woman on the bus. She was looking out of the window and watching the world go past. I was talking to my mates. I wasn't doing anything. I didn't. I don't know why. Mum. It was. The bus was full and going along that long road and the woman looked straight ahead and smiled. Everything was quiet and good and all right and then.

Then what happened, Dad?

Then she screamed, Mum. For so long with her fists raised. Why did she do that? I don't know what I did wrong.

Why would someone do that? It's all. Why would someone scream for no reason?

She stroked the back of his head and smoked until she coughed.

She went into her bedroom and sat down and opened the wardrobe and lifted off the pile of clothes and she took each jar into her hands and twisted the lid to hear the noise of the world again. It was like stones shaking in a cup and falling down a long set of stairs into what was quiet and dark and far away. It was just like the sound of Dad's rough voice. She scratched the place just between her breasts where a drop of sweat had rolled and she tried to think on the place that Dad talked about before he fell deep into the chase. The sea. Sand.

A cigarette burned on a pile of plastic toys and when she picked it up the plastic softened and stuck to the tip with white fingers that stretched up but would not let it go. She licked her fingers and pinched the burning end of the cigarette until it was dead.

I Know I Have a Heart

HE DIDN'T WANT her to wear the lipstick.

In the attic there was a cage that sat around a bulb of light that hung down from the ceiling. Over years the cage had slowly filled with cobwebs and tiny spiders and when she shook it everything crawled out and snapped and drifted like hair in water. Dad stood behind one of the stacks working his hands raw on a gas tank that he told her he wanted to be a carousel.

Good job, Dad.

I think it is.

Will you be taking it back out there today?

I thought you would want to play with it first.

Well.

Well what?

I don't want to play with anything anymore.

I thought we could play together.

I don't want toys anymore, Dad.

What do you want?

When can I go out there with you?

Where?

Out there. Outside. With the sea.

When I'm done changing things.

He worked his knuckles into his lower back and raised himself from the chamber.

I don't like it when you put that stuff on your face. You're too young to wear lipstick and you're too young to go outside. It's dangerous. There are tribes of men and there are big dogs and big women who want to make you their daughter. You think you know but you don't. Look at my hands. Don't they look to you like the hands of some other man?

She left the room and went down the spiral stairs that he had made out of she couldn't remember what. Plastic Jesus nodded his head.

When she was done with the soup she looked at her face in the spoon and put the lipstick on and tilted her head back and pressed her lips together.

There was a black mark on the back of the spoon. It ran from the silver oval and down the handle and it wouldn't come off when she scraped it with her fingernail. She looked at it and saw that the mark was not on the spoon but somewhere above her. It was on the ceiling. She looked up. The mark grew like a black rose from a crack in the ceiling and spread out to where the cable descended and held the lit bulb in place. She stood on the settee and took the TV remote in her hand and used it to clear away some of the dusty webs.

She got down off the settee and looked at the mark. There were three black flowers that grew in the flaking plaster and they were growing into cracks and they were all split by a larger crack that ran between them and onto the wall. She threw a set of plastic keys on a ring to the ceiling and some of the plaster came away and all the black flowers began to bloom. She watched.

The post came through the letterbox at quarter to fifteen and she waited next to the door to listen to the sound of the man walking around on the other side. The man pushed the letters through the metal mouth at the base of the door and between the black plastic bristles and straight into her lap. She picked the letters up in a bunch and held them to her face. She held them one at a time to the light and then she brought them to her nose and smelled them. Each corner. She sniffed the glue on the envelopes and she smelled the ink that she couldn't read and the fat red writing that had grown bigger and angrier over these last few days and she smelled the oil on the fingers of the man. She smelled the whole world. Everything. Dirt. Grass. Sky. Water. Bricks. Streets. Light. All. She smelled it all on the back of the letters and leaflets and she smelled it in the air that had slipped through, for a second, from the outside.

If I Were King

SOMETIMES WIZARDS ARE just old men who make up stories. She always paused the tape when it got to that part. She always leaned forward and looked the wizard straight in his eye and tried to make sense of him.

It was raining beyond the boards. She heard it spitting fast against the metal and concrete and wood on the outside and she heard the sound it made when it filled up all the little holes and bends and openings until they burst and drained out. She imagined the outside as one great and complex surface. It was raining inside too. The shower was on and water spat down to the bath where she was sitting with the water in her face and her hair twisted up around her shoulders holding Dad against her chest. Both of them had been here before.

Wake up, Dad. Come on.

She pushed herself forward and raised him up and pulled the wet hair out of his eyes and tried to feel the heart. There was nothing. She called him and then she pressed his chest and opened his mouth and banged her wrist on the side of the bath until it was red and sore. The veins throbbed. Dad slipped again and she pulled him up and above them the showerhead rattled and clicked and the pipes whined and the plug gurgled. She touched his face and held him once more and pressed his chest with her hand and rubbed his windpipe and held his hand until she heard it. The thump.

Come on, Dad. Come on.

She knocked on his back like a door and listened there and the machine inside him worked and turned and ticked like the clock on the mantle. He opened his mouth and opened his eyes and his one big eye rolled back to the front and he went forward on his hands and knees.

It had got deep into his bones, he told her. He felt the rabbit kicking inside his head.

Look at my hands.

They're good hands, Dad.

She helped him get to the living room and then she walked with him to the settee where he lay down and didn't get up again. She took Plastic Jesus in her arms and asked him a question and then she shook him and put him down on the Hi-Fi and watched the head bobbing.

What should I do about Dad?

Who knows?

You should.

Not if you don't.

It had happened before. He had been out chasing rabbits when she was five or seven or eight and he came home and stood in the middle of the room and walked from here to there and talked about nothing fast. He said that the rabbits were getting smarter. He paced and talked and told her that he'd made a trap in his head but the rabbit would not bite.

He wanted to talk about Mum.

Talk. I think I'm dying.

I don't know what to say.

What do you remember?

Mum.

I loved her a lot.

Oh Dad.

She loved me and she loved you.

Well.

Which one is your favourite?

I don't.

Who is your favourite character?

Dorothy.

Your Mum liked the Lion.

I used to sing all the time, he said. Can you believe that? I used to sing for people and so did your Mum. She was a wonderful singer.

Dad.

She went back to watching the TV and she leaned over and put her head into his lap even though he always told her she was too big for it now. Plastic Jesus nodded and the sound of outside began to come again. She would not talk of that time that she remembered from way back before the windows were blocked with wood. Dorothy would not hear of it. Mum was gone and Dad was there and the claustrophobia that always came to sit in her throat didn't come to her then. That day was good. Kind. She would not think on Mum who had murdered her twice. Dad didn't want to remember and neither did. She only remembered watching her mother's face that was turned away and covered by the dark and then she remembered the sound of her father. Shouting. Crying. And.

Dad.

Yes?

Nothing.

Crushing Poppies

SHE WORKED. At the edge of the attic was a book of poetry that he'd brought home with him when she was young and wanted to read. He came home smelling of vodka and poppies and chemical spray and he used the wall to keep him upright and laughed like the joker drawn on the playing cards. He showed her. He read a poem called Silver by Walter de la Mare. When he was done he sat back against the settee and told her that de la Mare means of the ocean.

Do you remember the sea?

She looked at him.

Why are you laughing? Do you remember the beach that day?

It's so funny.

What is?

Walter de la Mare means Walter of the sea.

So.

It's so funny?

Why?

Because Walter is a fish.

She had been working on a plastic toy that made animal sounds when she heard the banging from downstairs. It rattled the cage around the light. Dorothy shouted for her to come down. She went from the desk with her arms out searching the dark for ways through the boxes and the blank street signs and the childish games and the stacks and stacks of magazines and pictures of other families. She pulled herself through it all and went to the top of the staircase and stepped down and looked through the steps to see him at the front door.

He looked at her and she looked at him. He killed the itches on the back of his neck and his swollen eye bulged green and sad in the dark and his shoulder was pressed against the frame and the light from the segmented glass above the front door cut him into shards. She stepped down and stood in front of him. He wouldn't look at her.

Dad.

Go away.

What are you doing, Dad?

I'm. I don't know. I'm leaving.

Where are you going to go?

Away. I'm. I have a big mess in my head. I.

Come here, Dad.

No. No. No. No. No. No. No.

He cried. She cried.

Dad.

I can't do it.

Do what?

I need. I'll be good. If I could just chase the rabbits one last time I could empty the mess from my head. Then I'll be good. I'll be right. I can stop the damp from climbing into bed with me. For just a little while.

You told me not to let you.

I was just. I was lying about that. Look at my hands.

I'm looking, Dad.

I. I don't. I can't.

What do you want to forget, Dad?

He looked at her.

You only want a little bit, she said. The world is black and strange down here and you only want to go to the place that nobody else can see. You want to have courage and love and the mind to do it all and you never want to go home again. But Dad. You have to stay here. You have to stay home. Because. Look at me. Look at my hands. Dad, I'm home. I'm home. I'm home.

Drowned Fish

THEY LIT CANDLES in the living room. The candles were kept in a box underneath the sink. He collected them from rubbish bags and other people's homes and they were always handy when the man behind the desk decided that Dad wouldn't have money for a little while.

What man behind the desk?

I hope you never know.

Is it the taxman?

Almost.

She held two candles in her fists and stood behind him and leaned in with the light while he was looking for the fish tank.

He lifted the fish tank onto the counter that separated the living room and the kitchen and she stood holding the candles that had begun to drip hot wax onto her thumbs. He took the candles. The fish tank was old. She remembered when he'd brought it home with all this clear packaging around it and a card that told them how to set it up. She helped peel off the packaging and fill the bottom with coloured stones and set up little trees that swayed in the water. He told her it was a present and she asked him what she was going to do with a box of water and some trees and funny smelling sand. That's when he brought home the fish. They lasted only two days before she.

Since then the tank had grown cloudy and dirty and there was a layer of green that stained it halfway up and went all the way around. He moved some of the stones that had been shoved into a lump and he smoothed everything with his fingers. He pulled out dead trees and turned the stones around and the dust climbed his hands and turned them as pale as the little moons inside his fingernails. He slotted the candles into the little grooves he had made and he lined them up like fat glowing soldiers two by two down the length of the tank. There were eight candles inside the tank when they were done and two on one side of the room and two on the other and one in the hall that was planted in the back of a small metal train that sat on one of the steps and one in the bathroom set on the back of the toilet that had been a pillow for his head so many times these past few. He smiled.

Remember the fish?

I don't want to talk about that.

Do you remember it though?

Yes. Be quiet.

The glow of the candles beat through the tank and fanned its fingers and it was mossy green. Dad pulled the bird from the mantel and opened the doors and stuck a screwdriver in. He pulled the hair out of his eyes and scratched the black and grey hairs on his chin. She stood in the green glow and watched him while he worked. The bird screamed and cried murder murder murder as the screwdriver went deeper. On the TV there was.

When are you going to fix the screen?

What?

She pointed to the TV.

I don't know, he said.

Why don't you know?

He looked at his hands.

Dad.

I can't think about that now.

I want to watch it. I can't be without it.

Do you remember the fish?

Be quiet about that.

Do you remember the fish, Anna?

Yes, Dad.

I thought it would make a good pet for you because a fish can't run away like a cat or a dog and you always seemed to be afraid of dogs anyway. Fish are easy. You don't have to feed them that much or that often and they ask for nothing more than that. You just keep them in the tank and keep the water as clean as you can and let them swim in the box around and around. Easy. I thought you'd want company when I went out, you know, and I thought you could talk to them. They were such pretty little things with that black stripe and those big eyes. Do you remember?

Yes, Dad, I remember. They were little and so was I.

Yeah. You were little once.

I didn't mean to do it.

I know. You shouldn't worry about that. It was my fault. I left them here and I left you alone with them and I didn't tell you everything you needed to know and you were so prone to being stuck too much in your own head back then. I couldn't. It was my fault. You thought you were doing something good.

I took him out of the tank and I let him dry in the sun. I thought that maybe he didn't want to be in the box.

But what happened when he left the box?

He drowned. He drowned because he couldn't breathe.

So, I think you should walk towards me, Girl. I think you should come and sit down really close so I can take you back into the living room again. I think you should stop crying and you should look where you are. I love you so much. I don't want to see you drown. I want you to stop what you're doing and I want you to sit next to me so close and nice. I want you to see what you're doing. I want you to look where you are. I want you to take your hand from the handle of the door.

She looked at him and then she looked at her own feet that were pressed against the rolled up carpet that lipped up over the bottom of the front door where her heels were tucked. A cold wind came around it and moved like fingers in her hair and along the ribbons of wallpaper and dusty cobwebs and boxes and through everything stacked along the walls of the insomnia museum. Even his hair stirred above his head.

Anna.

What?

Don't go.

~~Somewhere Over the~~
Somewhere Else

SHE STOOD WITH one hand on the handle and.

Dad was crying again. Fuck's sake.

Look at your hands, Dad, she said, and she liked the grown up in her voice. They're the loveliest two hands I've ever seen because they belong to my father. Don't cry, Dad. You're not to blame.

He stood up and he killed the itches on his arm and on the back of his neck where there was a blooming rash that had got worse this last hour.

She thought about it.

If you loved me as much as I loved you I don't think we'd be here.

What does that mean?

You know.

I love you.

I know.

I want to keep you safe?

There's no life in that.

There's no life out there.

There's more life in the space behind this door than.

How do you know?

I can see it.

Where?

I can see it all over your face, Dad.

I'm just scared.

I know. I am too, but I think that when I'm scared I feel most like I'm living. I think I have to be scared. I can't be protected. I have to go away. I have to be more than you and me.

Don't go, he said. Wait. Wait until you're a bit older. I'll teach you things about out there that you're going to need. I'll let you go when the time is right. I promise. If you go now you'll die.

Dad.

Daughter.

You don't see it. I'm dead already. Nothing moves on. There's no time because you taught the bird not to tell it. There's no reading because I don't know how. I sleep, I eat and I live right next to you on the floor and I wait for you to come home and we fix things that don't need fixing and all for what? What does it mean? I'm dead, Dad. I've always been dead because I never started living.

They looked at each other. Dad had stopped crying and she had opened the door enough to smell the air on the outside and to catch noises that she had never heard before. There were chimes and a buzzing and a revved up machine and a catching sheet of metal and the barking of dogs and the voices of other people. Clear. Loud. There were others and they fought and played and spat and there was swearing. There was the word fuck shouted a million times over and over. There was nothing more to say. Dad had stopped being Dad long enough for her to see that he was only a man. He was an old man with blooms on his skin and bad teeth and a beautiful face and tired shoulders and he stood apart from her, like a stranger.

I love you, Dad, she said. Thank you.

She didn't leave for a while and when she was ready she closed her eyes and let her thoughts rest awhile on the bodies of the moths in her feet. Her feet were bare. The thoughts beat like drums. She looked at them and thought that she would need shoes and she thought on that and decided that she would need socks and a coat but she had none of those things because there was never any need for them. Thoughts of Mum came next. She thought on Mum and she thought on the fish and there was a knot in her stomach that twisted and she knew that the bad blood had started. She cried but she didn't know why. She felt the cold air and she listened to the noises and she shivered and threw her hands over her face.

You can come home now, he said behind her.

I can't. I can't go back but I can't go on either. I don't know where the fuck I am. I'm. I don't. I can't. I'm hurting so much. I'm on fire and I can't put it out. What's wrong with me? I can hear the ringing. Can you hear that? What is it? Is it me? What am I waiting for? I think it's the sound of living going away. I think I'm.

I can hear it too.

She closed the door a few inches and she turned to look at him and he was searching through the piles packed up along the walls. He threw his hands in front of him and he dragged the stacks of nineteen seventy-two and nineteen eighty-three whatever magazines down in great clumps that fell in a wave by his feet. He tore at the flesh of the house and wiped his eyes in the paper that he ripped from the walls. The dust came down like that painful snow from the. She heard the head of Plastic Jesus nodding on the plastic neck and she heard the glass jars in her bedroom all singing with the long captured noises from years gone by. The ringing grew louder as he turned over all the mess he had collected and stacked and the museum whined as the weight was moved from one place to the next. In the living room the black roses bloomed on the ceiling and crept over the lip of the doorframe to the hallway and the little descended light.

I know it's here. We used to have one.

One what?

Where did I put it?

I remember something.

Can't go far. Nailed down. Red.

I remember something.

He searched until he found a black thread between a stack of thick books and a box of empty video cases and old remote controls with missing buttons and black tape that went around and around. He pulled the thread away from the wall and held it in his hands and yanked it over the fallen mess and followed it. She came away from the door and stood in the hall but she didn't let go of the handle.

What is it, Dad?

Never you mind.

Dad.

Think on the noise and let me know how loud it gets.

Okay, Dad.

She stretched from the door and left her twisted little finger holding the handle and she watched Dad as he moved along the stacks kicking and shoving and praying that the ringing wouldn't end. Sober. Sober. Sober. He pulled on the string and twisted it around his fist and pulled again and a pile of boxes came down from a tall stack next to the bathroom door. He stopped. They were both still. He looked at her and she looked at him and she didn't leave the handle but stretched as far back into the hall as she could without letting go.

What is it, Dad? What's that on the wall?

It's the phone.

She couldn't remember the phone from her girlhood but in her head she knew there would be a voice trying to speak from a plastic mouth and a place to listen and buttons to push. The phone was nailed to the wall and covered in dirt and dust and when he put his hand on the handle attached there by a spiralled cord something black and small ran from a crack underneath it. She stretched. Watched. Dad looked back.

Answer it, Dad.

Come into the hallway.

Answer it.

Come back home.

It's going to stop.

Come in.

She stepped into the hall and closed the door behind

her and felt the cold air die away and the staleness and the heat and the heavy dark return. The little light above the door made a crown on the top of his head. The noise from the outside was muted by the wood and the walls.

Pull the handle, Dad.

Dad lifted the handle and turned towards the little black box with the numbers and the chimes and the voice that she knew would be there. He pressed it to his face and he rested his hand on the wall and he pulled the hair out of his eyes and he talked.

Hello. Yes. What? No.

He looked at her and she looked at him. His hand pressed on the top of his head and his face twisted and his eyes darted from the phone to his hand to her where she stood in front of the door. He sobbed into the back of his hand and chewed on the inside of his cheeks. His breath caught in the hollows of his throat.

He nodded but said nothing and then he talked with a high trembling voice and said okay. Okay. I know. Yeah that's fine. I can. Um. I'll do something. I. I don't know. Could you help me do that? I don't think I can stand there and say those things when. Yeah. Okay.

He returned the handle to the black box and he looked at his hands that were holding out some imaginary thing in front of him. She let her little finger slide off the handle and she stepped towards him and he threw his hands over his face and she pulled them away. He looked at her. His eyes were dewy and pulsing and he cried like a boy with his bottom lip trembling and his eyes fighting to turn away. He slipped to the floor and she went down with him and kissed the sweat off his head and wiped his eyes with the end of her tee shirt.

What's going on, Dad? What did it say? Please talk to me.

He looked at her.

What did it say?

I can't. I. Um.

What, Dad?

Your Mum died.

Your Little Dog Too

HE WOULDN'T TALK.

The door was closed and the world and its tired little noises went on exactly as they had before. He sat on the floor with a deck of cards in his hand that he had fished out of some box when she had not been paying attention. He shuffled the cards in one hand and folded one behind the other with a flick of his thumb and a bend in the wrist. The tattoo on his thumb winked at her. The piles of junk began to bend and sway under the weight of his unravelling and everything sank to the floor where they both sat staring at the shape of the dark that folded along the cracks in the ceiling. He wouldn't talk, but his eyes talked plenty. They had a distance in them. They were the startled and hopeless and accepting eyes of a man hanging from a bridge.

She held his hand that rested on his thigh and she lifted his arm across her shoulder and she sank deep into his chest and brought her hands to her face. She bit the nail that wasn't there and she sucked her thumb like a baby. The dark closed around them. The doll bird told them it was time for something but she didn't know what. Time to think. Time to remember. Time to grow. Time to forget. Mum was the world and the moon and the stars and the water and the dark and the noise of outside and the pipes and the falling snow and the wood and the paper dolls and the light and even though nothing was different, everything had changed.

He wrapped the black tie around his neck and she held the mirror so he could check if he was still as handsome as he had been when he was last with Mum. He wrapped it around twice and pulled it and the collar of the white shirt was drawn together underneath his neck. She picked the tight globs of dust off his shoulder. He combed his hair behind his ears with his fingers and looked at his chin and his cheeks that were sprouting with a black and white garden.

Should I shave?

Depends.

On what?

What she would like.

She always liked me whatever way I was happy to be.

Are you happy then?

I won't shave.

She was on her own bed where she had stayed in deep thought and deep sleep and a sucking misery for the past three days. He came in and gave her food and drink and sometimes he sat on the end of the bed and rolled two smokes and they smoked together in silence underneath the paper dolls. Sometimes he took her hands and painted her nails black just like his own. She asked for a mirror so she could draw red on her lips.

How old are you, Dad?

He looked at her. Why do you want to know?

Just, I don't know, for the sake of talking.

Thirty-eight, I think.

When's your birthday?

May time.

When's my birthday?

June time. Seventeen years ago. It was raining.

How old is? I think. How old was Mum?

Thirty-six.

Is that old?

No. Not really.

So.

So.

She stood on the bed and combed the loose hairs down to the back of his neck and she tidied his front and straightened his buttons and he drank down to the end of a bottle and looked into the neck for more. There was none. He held her hand and looked at her. She was taller than him when she was standing on her bed and she was as tall as his ears when she was on the floor. He kissed her fingers one by one and told her that he would be back soon.

Funerals are. They're not nice. Coffins are unkind to those who don't understand. The body in the wood goes into the ground before the ghost can crawl back in. People cry. They drink. They talk about before with hearts as heavy as bags of sand. There's religion. It means nothing. Funerals are for the guilty and the hungry and that's not a place for you. That's no place for you. I don't want you to see her pale and stiff and dressed in something she wouldn't like.

Oh Dad.

He walked away and went into the kitchen to find another bottle and she followed him and he turned back but he didn't see her. He looked beyond her to the frame of the door above her head or the dark hallway filled with those broken plugs and sweeping piles of junk or to the TV that would not work or to the wallpaper that was ripped and shredded and stuck out like the scales of a long dead fish. The black roses bloomed on the ceiling. He walked from one side of the room to the other and took up his keys and his jangling purse and kissed her on the forehead and went out of the door and he didn't come back for three long days.

She watched the light change in the fish tank. It came through the slatted boards on the left in lines that pierced the glass and angled green in the middle of the room. She could feel it on her face. It got into her eyes and into her head. On the TV was nothing. Plastic Jesus nodded when she picked him up and he told her that Dad would not come back again. She chucked him against the wall. A chunk of the paper fell with him.

There was something that lived behind the paper that she hadn't seen before. Something blue like Dorothy's flying birds. She went to it and tugged the lip of the hole. She tore a line of blue which ran behind the Hi-Fi and the boxes that were stacked against the wall. She pulled the edges of the boxes and dragged the junk into a pile in the middle of the room. She ran her finger over the blue line and pinched the wallpaper between her fingers and pulled arcs of it away from the wall. All the dust and the dirt and the falling plaster came away and clouds of white and black circled in the air above her head. She stood on her toes and pressed her breasts against the wall and her fingers tore at the flesh and scales until all the paper was shredded into ribbons that dropped around her feet.

She stood back and looked. The blue line was more than a thin stream of forgotten paint. It was a picture of the sea. Large. Empty. The sea had lived for years behind the paper without her knowing it. There were black and white waves that crashed into the corners of cliffs and small silver fish that circled in the dark blue and a line between the sea and the sky that swirled with colour and let out its breath on a yellow boat that sat in the middle of the picture. She stared at the wall without blinking and from long ago she remembered the smell of the salt and the rabbit holes cut deep in the hot sand and the smell of vinegar and hot sugar and the feel of the air on.

Much later Dad came through the door and locked the museum up behind him. He moved slowly over the junk piles in the hallway and then he came into the room. She couldn't see him where she stood with her eyes fixed on that yellow boat but she could feel the change in the room. His presence had an altering effect. The air moved to accommodate his breath and the light changed to match his height and the floor braced itself under his weight and his thoughts drew the shadows from the edges of the room.

Do you remember it?

No, Dad.

I did it when you were six because you were having trouble sleeping. I thought it was because of your claustrophobia and I painted the wall to try and make the world a bit bigger for you. You hated Mum so much then. I wanted you to remember that day on the beach. You had these little fat hands that spent the whole day in her pocket. We built castles. Ate too much. Complained. Laughed. We were happy but we didn't know it then. You never do. Not while you're worried about the stupid bullshit things. Not until you're far away, almost at the end. Then you know. There's not enough life left ahead of you to look forward so you start to look back. It's like looking back down a long black road with pictures of your life drawn on the pavement. That's when you realize how lucky you were. That's when you realize how meaningful the meaningless days were.

Dad.

Anyway.

Was the funeral nice?

Not with those faces. Not with the well it had to happen one day, and the nodding and the now we can all move on. And the pale old woman who was so skinny, as small and delicate as fag ash. She chewed on the book of hymns. I could see her heart beating in her cheeks.

He sat on the edge of the settee and he looked at the wall and traced the waves with his fingers. She was hungry but she didn't tell him. He had forgotten the food and forgotten that the cupboards were empty and he would just have started crying again. He told her about the flowers and about the box in the ground and about the stone marker that stays until the letters are worn away by the weather and the hands of people who come to cry before it starts to rain and he told her that the TV would come back on again soon and everything would be back the way it was before.

Now I just need to sleep.

Okay, Dad.

He pulled the carrier bag that he'd dragged in with him to the edge of the settee and he killed the itches on his ankle and head and on the inside of his arm. He heated a little pearl of gutter black forget-me-not on the end of the spoon. He looked at her and she looked at him and they didn't talk. She watched him fall deep into the chase and she could hear the sound of the waves crashing against the wall and she could feel the black roses growing on the ceiling and everything that would one day come falling down.

Are you still here, Dad?

Even she wanted to sleep, he said.

Who, Dad?

Judy Garland. All she wanted was a little sleep.

I'm tired too, Dad. I'm so tired and I've forgotten how to fall asleep.

Well then. My angel. Why don't you fall awake?

Who Is Judy Garland?

OUTSIDE THERE WAS banging. She went into the kitchen and poured the last of the cereal into a bowl and filled it with water that she'd boiled in the kettle and left to cool down overnight. She ate it thinking about hot food. Dad shifted on the settee behind her and opened his mouth and closed it again like a fish. There was that banging again. She washed the cereal bowl out and dried it with a towel and drank three-day-old coffee from a cup with no handle. She went to Dad and stepped on the settee quiet and careful so she didn't wake him up and she pressed her face against the boards and listened. There was traffic. A woman shouted for her children. A man shouted for war. A dog barked. The wind scattered seeds or confetti. The banging came again and she stepped backwards off the settee and turned around and looked past the crooked doorframe and into the dark hallway. The banging was close. It came again. She brought her hands to her face and chewed her twisted finger and she turned to Dad who was still asleep on the settee.

Dad.

Yes.

Can you hear me?

No.

There's someone knocking on the front door.

Is there?

What should I do?

Answer it, Girlie. That's what you do.

He turned around on the settee and threw his arms over his face and sank half his head into the tongues of foam that spilled out of the holes in the cushions. She waited but he didn't turn back. His breathing grew deep. He had become old and frail. The sky shifted behind the boards. Dad moaned. She loosened the tie from around his neck and pulled it through the little knot and hung it on the broken arm of the light above his head. The doll-headed bird bashed its face against the inside of its house and knocked itself to the floor. She picked up Plastic Jesus and shook him.

There's a noise, she said.

Yes.

What is it?

Something.

She carried him in her arms like a doll and stepped into Dad's boots and tied the laces around her ankles and went into the hallway and looked at the front door. On the other side of the wood was a stranger. A man. Woman. Dog. Thing. Creature. Wizard. Witch. Mum. There was a stranger banging on the other side of the door. The noise came again and it was so loud and so hard that it shook the wood and the frame and all the chains and locks chimed like the bells in the bottom of the music box. A beetle and a woodlouse came out from the letterbox and fell to the carpet and disappeared underneath a cold dinner plate. Her mind played to all the fears of her girlhood. Behind the door there were monsters, demons, bad men who carried knives and forks in their pockets, politicians, grandmothers, pale ghosts, maniacs, rapists, bin men with wide arms and the fat silver moon. Laughing. The door banged and rocked again and the banging got inside her head and that's when the voice came. The stranger on the other side of the door spoke with the voice of a man.

Open up. Open up if you're there. It's me.

She listened to his voice and the raw half cough at the edge of his words. She closed her eyes and tried to think on who the stranger was and how tall and the colour of his eyes and the shape of his teeth but all she could see was a blank space shaped just like Dad leaning against the other side of the wood. He coughed again and cleared his throat and she heard the sound of his boots on the ground and his hard voice that called again and asked if there was anyone inside.

She went into the living room and turned over boxes and piles of clothes that belonged to nobody and the old grandmother looked down from her place inside the frame. She followed her as she searched the room for the keys. She went into the kitchen and stood on the worktop and kicked over jars of vinegar and dismantled the clockwork train he'd been working on and she looked back into the living room as the banging grew faint and far apart and she saw the keys that were small and brass and sticking out of the trouser pocket of Dad's funeral suit. He moved. She waited.

She stood above him and watched his face and worked the silver ring around and around the loop in his belt and then she slid them out of his pocket so fast and so quiet and made sure that it didn't worry him. He kept his eyes closed and his breath light and he said the word sober. Sober. And it was faint.

She took the keys to the front door and unlocked the big bolt next to the handle and then she unlocked the one closest to the floor where there was a metal latch for pulling and then she unlocked the two that were loose already and she reached up for the one that bolted the wood to the frame and left a groove in the wallpaper where there should've been horses. The banging grew quiet. The coughing went dry and silent. She pressed her hand against the door and she could feel the weight of the stranger there as he leaned against the other side of the wood. The smell of cigarettes drifted in from below the door and spread in the air around her feet and came up to her face. The stranger spoke slow and quiet as though he was talking to someone in his own pocket.

Are you in there?

Yes.

Who is that?

Me.

I'm looking for someone.

Are you looking for me?

No. I'm looking for.

I don't know anyone by that name.

Not even.

No.

Can I come in?

No.

Why not?

I don't know you.

Please.

She laid her hand on the handle and slowed her heart and breath that had grown quicker since she spoke to him. Behind her Plastic Jesus nodded his head like a lunatic and Dorothy ran up and down the crooked staircase and sang about scarecrows. The sea swept along the wall in the living room. She felt the light in the hallway change. She looked behind her and saw Dad who had crept from his sleep to stand at the end of the hall. She watched him and he watched her and the silence crushed her into powder.

I'm opening the door. I want to see who else is out there.

Do what you need to.

I will. I'll open it.

Then do it. Don't stay for me. I'm rotten inside.

You're not, Dad.

Look at my hands.

I'm looking.

She looked at his hands and the veins that ran through like the inside of a grape held up to the light. His fingernails were long and dirty and the hairs that used to be thick and black were now white and soft and shaped by the wind that he blew out from his chest.

Are you really sick, Dad?

Yes, Doll. I'm so sick.

He was slouching. He stood crooked in the shadows to give his eyes a rest from the light and the wind. He wouldn't look at her face while she stood there with the handle burning against her hand and he wouldn't say another thing while she cried. She said the word Mum, too softly. He picked a piece of plaster from the wall and looked at it between his fingers and told nobody that it needed fixing. This needs work too. Can't just fix the outside. Gotta fix the inside before the hangman knows we're in here all scared and dirty. He rubbed the plaster between his fingers until it was dust and then he went into the living room and back into the green glow.

She let go of the handle and stood away from the door and twisted the ugly little finger until her finger bones ached. The door didn't bang and rattle but the voice kept on talking until it knew it talked only to itself. Time passed and the weight against the wood was lifted and the smell of cigarette smoke was all ate up by the hot dusty air of the museum again. The stranger pushed a thing through the letterbox and she stepped back and watched it flutter onto the carpet. She picked it up. It was a little piece of card with long ripped edges and she held it to the shaft of light and saw the numbers scrawled in black ink on one side.

If you ever need anything, the man said.

Okay.

I honestly can't keep doing it.

Fine.

I'll see you.

Hope you do, Mister.

Her voice was small and weak and she wondered if he'd heard anything from her at all. Hope you do, Mister. She wiped her eyes and locked the locks and she watched the shadow move away beneath the frame of the door and she held the card to the light and she looked at it for a long time. White card. Long numbers. On the back of the card was a torn picture and she looked at it and thought on what it could've been when it was whole. It was blue and there were rocks and sand and the edge of a wave and the end of a. Two big eyes like. She slipped the card into her back pocket and thought on what it could've been when it was put back together again.

She went into the living room and he smiled at her from the settee and opened his arms fat and wide and she trod over the holes in the carpet and went past the green glow and the old woman who looked down at them both. She stood on the settee and turned the picture around so it faced the wall and she tucked herself into Dad and let him hold her there and cover her head with kisses.

See Sick

SHE SLEPT FOR a long.

The twisted veins that were tucked in the wells and hollows of the museum burst sometime in the night and she remembered it as a shock of pink that fell across her eyelids and drove her deeper into his coat. The lights were working again and so was the TV. It glowed and snapped with changing scenes and played a song so loud she heard it in her sleep. She heard it all the way past the toss and turn of shallow rest and down into her dreaming where usually nothing could get but the moths and Mum and some memory of happiness folded back on itself across the sharp knife-edge of time.

She woke up on the settee with the coat around her and the TV fuzzing in the corner and the lights off and the picture of the old woman still turned around on the middle wall above her. Dad was gone. There were carrier bags of food tins on the worktop in the kitchen and three bottles of pop in front of her and the piles of junk had been re-stacked against the walls and against the sea that still raged between the rocks and sky and crooked sun in the living room. The bird bashed its head against the walls of its house. She didn't know. She pushed the coat off and put in a video and played something black and white and blurred on one side. She ran the water in the kitchen and drank from a washed glass that had been left for her next to a packet of red sweets. She ate. Drank. She coloured in a leaflet that had been pushed through the letterbox and then she lay down on the worktop and watched the black roses blooming on the ceiling. She didn't think on Mum. Not then. Because.

Wasn't she a good daughter? Mad, like him. Wasn't she such a good?

In the night he came home coughing and talking to nobody while she was in bed. He moved with heavy feet and slipped past boxes and he called himself bastard and she rolled in her blankets and turned to face the door but he didn't come in. She slipped her hand underneath her pillow and touched the card that the strange man had slid through the letterbox. The rain was beating down on the other side of the ceiling and on the walls and on the glass. She turned to face the sound and closed her eyes and when she opened them again it was light.

She called him once and he didn't answer. The museum was quiet and the air was heavy and it had the smell of something that had been sat for months in the same place with the world turning sour around it. She tucked her nightie into a pair of jeans and did up the zip and the button and smelled the card with the long number and folded it up and stuffed it into her back pocket. On the handle of the door was Dad's black tie that he had put back on and done up tight whenever he wanted to talk about the burial. She took it off and went through the door and into the hall where she found his black jacket folded on top of a box of swaying junk. Then she found the smart shoes chucked next to the front door and she went into his bedroom where he was not and she called him again but he didn't answer and she couldn't feel the weight of him anywhere inside the flat. She dropped his clothes and went into the living room and stopped when she saw the armchair that had been pulled in front of the fuzzing TV.

The light changed in the room from dark to grey and then back to bright yellow and burning orange as something threaded in front of the sun and back again to the start. Clouds. Weathermen. Satellites. Stars. Moon. Drifting things that lived in the freshly dug graves in her mind.

She stopped there for a while looking at the back of the chair. His arms hung over the sides with the clean white shirt rolled to his elbows. The tattoos near his elbows and wrist bone had gone sour and blended into his skin. There was a bottle of vodka turned on its side underneath his left hand and the last bit of a cigarette burnt out and half gone in his right. Another wedding ring was wedged on his finger to join the one that had always been there.

The TV looked into the room with its wintery blinking eye and Dad's chair was turned towards it but his face was turned to the wall and the patch of sea he painted for her once. She walked around his chair, stood in front of him and looked at him for a long while. She threw her hands on the top of her head and balled them into fists at the back of her neck. Her eyes ran. Her throat grated her voice into chokes and coughs. The doll-headed bird was silent for the first time in all its lunatic years. Plastic Jesus was still and quiet in his new place lain sideways on his chest like a sleeping child. She looked at him but he didn't look at her. She looked at him but he was not there.

He wasn't moving or breathing and his eyes were open but he couldn't see the TV and he couldn't see the waves of the painted sea and couldn't see her. She called him. He wouldn't answer. She leaned against the chair with one hand on top of the other and she pressed his chest and opened his mouth and stuck her fingers inside deep. Nothing came up. He didn't speak or move and his tongue didn't fight against the taste of her fingers. She tried again and again with her throat burning and the room turning watery. She called him again and again but he wasn't there. She kneeled in front of him and threw down Plastic Jesus and wiped her eyes on the knees of his jeans and pushed her fists into his chest and took hold of his shirt and pulled his body and dropped him down and shook him. His head rolled and his mouth opened but he was not.

She rested her head on his lap and watched the light between the boards.

Where did you go, Dad? she said. I bet it's somewhere nice. I bet it's where Mum went when the hangman caught up to her. I bet it's a place with rabbits and blue smoke. I think it's good and clean there. I can't see it, Dad, but I know it's there. It's like sometimes when I catch the outside and draw it in and look at it when the sleeping doesn't come. I look at it with my head and sometimes I look with my stomach and that's the way I'll see you too, Dad, unless you want to take me with you. Why don't you do that? Why don't you take me too? I'll lay down so nice and quiet and I'll fall asleep and you can hook me with a fishing rod and lift me up. I'll try to sleep. No I won't. I'll fall asleep.

The mad bird came out of its house. Plastic Jesus nodded

on the floor and she reached down and picked him up and he nodded in her arms.

What do you want to say?

Fall awake. Fall awake. Fall awake.

She sat shaking and she cradled Plastic Jesus like a baby. She let the crying come. It rushed from her heart and straight into her head and out through her mouth. She held his hand and watched it change in the shifting light that rose up and fell down again behind the boards. He was so much older in the light. His ageing was complete. She saw the pain that had fallen from his thin cheeks and she saw the softness of the muscles that hung loose behind his skin and she held up the limbs that were like empty paper bags.

I think you went and died, Dad. You died good and quick because you were so sick and I think you were sick for a long time. Your heart was broken and I know you can't ask for another one because the hangman doesn't carry spare change. One side was for me and one side was for Mum and a heart only works with two good sides, Dad. Hearts break right down the middle when one side pulls away. I think that's how you died. I think you're beyond the rain and stars now, Dad. Happy. Lovely. Handsome like before. I can't see you anymore, Dad.

She whispered to him all night and then she fell asleep when the sun came back to the room and lit the dust into specks of fire. Outside there were heavy ships that sailed through the streets. There were men who stood calling from the decks. They raised their hands up. She closed his eyes with her fingers like the dead in the films and she took out the needle and took off the belt and folded his arms over his middle. He was no man. He was not Dad. Dad had gone away sometime in the middle of the night with his eyes fixed on the wall and his arm wrapped around a Plastic Jesus and thoughts of rabbits in his head and.

She looked at the wall. The sea raged and was still and soundless. The boat chucked and the sun pulsed and the sand burned underneath the painted light. She lay her hand there and wiped her eyes with the hem of her nightie. She smelled the salt but she couldn't feel the water.

Pay No Attention to the Man Behind the Curtain

SHE HAD LAID three coats over him and returned Plastic Jesus to the Hi-Fi and pushed Dad's chair to the corner next to the settee. She burned his mother's picture in the fish tank and then she took the blackened pieces out of the tank and threw them down the toilet and let them turn the water grey. Dorothy walked with her and held her hand.

She turned the TV up loud so that she could hear the music over the silence that had grown every day since he had gone. The music grew over the sound of the outside. Sometimes she danced. Dorothy stood in front of her and held out her hands and she took them and spun around.

There was no food left in the cupboards except cereal and old beans and water from the tap that had turned a rusted yellow. She stood in the middle of the room with a bowl of dried cereal and yellow water and ate mouthfuls until her stomach twisted and then she didn't eat for hours and hours and stood alone in the living room looking at the black roses. She was sweating and she didn't know why. Her breath was gone. She ran past the stacks and into the bathroom and she was sick in the toilet where the black picture had sunk but had not washed away.

The light stopped coming into the room. Everything was always dark and slow and she had shadows stuck in her eyes and ghosts stuck in her head and even when the bird bashed or Plastic Jesus nodded they did it slow and soundless. She wiped the wet hair out of her face and rewound the tape and played it again. The Tin Man needed oil and Dad needed something too that would loosen his stiff joints and fatten out his papery skin and there was plenty of one in that world but not enough of the other in hers.

She whispered to him with her face on her knees while Dorothy took handfuls of her hair and smoothed it over her back again and again like any mother would.

Dad. I don't think you're coming back. I think when someone dies that's the end and when you died that was the end for us both. You're not here. You're not here you're not here you're not here. How can you go away just like that, Dad? You're gone. Everything is carrying on without you like you were never here in the first place, Dad. How do you like that? I have to go now, Dad. I can't stay here and die too because nobody will know it. I have to go now.

She wiped her eyes and lit a smoke and went into the hallway and stepped over the fallen boxes of junk and climbed bits of scrap that were sticking out of the top and she went into his bedroom. It was darker in his room than any other because not even the light liked to see what he did in there. Next to the bed was a chip of black coal mostly burned into that brown gel that took him into the garden where the rabbits were digging. At the foot of his bed was a purple pipe and next to that was an empty bottle and two empty cans that smelled stale and sour when she picked them up. Underneath his pillow was a magazine of women with large breasts and long choppy hair and fat lips and. She went into his wardrobe and took out one of his band tee shirts and she held it up to the no light and she smelled it and she took off her nightie and put it on over her dirty bra and she tucked it into her jeans. She found a pair of socks rolled into a ball next to the cupboard and a box of action videos and a book of band photographs from nineteen ninety-seven and she unrolled them and put them on. She put on his boots and tied the laces around her ankles and she put on his leather bracelet that was wrapped around his bedpost and the smell of it reminded her of.

She went into her bedroom and turned over her pillow and found the card that had been shoved through the letterbox and she looked at the long number with the single word above that she couldn't read. The phone that hung on the wall in the hallway had been ripped away from the wall while he had tried to build up his museum. She climbed the pile of shifting junk and stood balancing on a stack of table legs and an old stuffed dog. She held the phone to her face and pushed the box back to the wall and heard the crackle of crumpled paper down the line and felt the heat of the sparks behind the box. She looked at the card and pushed the buttons in the order they had been written down and then she waited.

It rang.

It rang. It rang. It rang. It. And there was nobody on the other side. She balanced on the junk pile and she pressed the phone to her mouth and she twisted her hair in her hands and pushed the heel of her hand into her eye socket. There was no voice. There was only a chiming of bells. It rang. It.

Hello.

She was silent.

Hello. Is that you?

She opened her mouth but.

Hello. Is that?

It's me.

She pressed the phone hard into her cheek. The stranger was breathing on the other side.

It's me, she said. It's me.

Then the stranger began to talk but she couldn't make out the words. She pressed the buttons and tugged at the wire and said please, please, but at last the only voice she could hear was her own and there was no reason to keep talking.

She put the phone down and sat on the pile of junk with her arms over her legs looking down at the carpet below her. She smoked and flipped the stranger's card around in her hand and held it to the light that spat through the place above the front door and she held her cigarette underneath the card and watched it catch. It burned up yellow and bright and rolled back like a hungry black lip. She held the cigarette to the other end and watched that burn too. Then the number was gone. The paper was ash. That was the end of the voice, and the stranger too.

She wouldn't go back into the living room. The smell of him was too much. She stayed instead on the top of the pile where the air was stale but it was not soaked through with death or the little smells of his life that were so much worse than decay. Aftershave. Poppies. Leather. Sweat. Soap.

Smoke. Apples. She could even smell the toast he burned a few weeks before he died. That was worse. She could still smell his life even though the living was done. She held her head in her hand and wiped her eyes and smoked another cigarette that she had taken from the table next to his bed. Outside the world was chiming and rattling and there were far away noises and close noises that were not as bad as the noise in her head.

I don't want to hear it, Dorothy. I don't want it. I'm done and gone and buried in a pile like all this junk. I think I'll never die though. Dad died after he was done living but I never started so I can't go ahead and stop because there was no starting. I think I'm a ghost. I'm tired. Look at my hands.

Dorothy stood in front of her with her little dog in her arms and she looked down the hall at the piles of junk and she looked back and she opened her mouth to sing but nothing came out.

She fell asleep and when she awoke she was so hungry she couldn't think and. Slow down. Stop thinking. Listen to that lovely ugly sound. Don't. Listen to the sound of the sea rising in the living room and listen to the other sounds. So pretty, like you. She listened and then she heard it. Fast little clicks. It sounded like the inside of a clock or the hidden sound of the mechanics that twisted the dancer in the music box and it came from the other side of the door that had disappeared when she fell half asleep and half awake. The hallway began to lean to the left. She rubbed her eyes with a piece of cloth that had once been wrapped around a doll and she looked again at the front door. The moths in her head were quiet and she sweated even though the hallway was cold. Everything was cold. She twisted her arms around her body and stood up on the junk pile and watched the door.

Nothing happened.

She let herself slide down the side of the junk mountain with one hand on her head to soften the storm behind her eyes and the other on her stomach to stop her guts from playing tunes. Dorothy sank into the air like the poppy smoke.

Is someone there? she said. It's me. I can't.

The door knocked and the knocking made her knees drop. She fell for days and days and. Caught a slice of the door opening and the fresh air pouring in and so many thousands of boots and apple cider smells. The ground came up to smack her hard on the face and somewhere in the back of her mind Dad told her that Judy Gee used to get slapped all the time. Judy Gee got slapped when she was off camera. She was trying to act and the acting wasn't working so she got slapped and the slapping was. In front of her the door opened wide and the air rushed in. She saw the knees of a man pressed into the carpet. He said oh my God and his hands smelled like rain and petrol.

There's no off camera, she said. There's no.

It was raining inside. She raised her hand and waved her fingers and felt the little drops falling on her skin and felt them on her tongue too when she opened her mouth. Her mouth tasted sour but she couldn't remember throwing up. She looked into the face of the weather that was round and fat and connected to a long silver neck that came even longer when she rubbed the sweat out of her eyes. There was a little red light and hard ceramic sides and a curtain weighed down with water and grown over by a black garden.

The weather came from the shower that had been turned on and fixed so that it pointed at her where she lay fully clothed underneath it. She wiped the water out of her face and dragged the black fat hair out of her eyes and sat in the middle of the bath with the water going over her head. The curtain was drawn to the end of the bath so that she couldn't see behind it. All she could see was the shape of him sitting on the lid of the toilet, smoking a firefly that he brought to his lips and took away again.

She watched him. His head was bowed and his back was bent and he brought his hand to his head once or twice and then opened his legs and rested his elbows on his knees. His shadow was tired. Worn into blurred edges. Her stomach swelled into her heart and her lungs shrank to the size of tangerines. He brushed the hair out of his face and sighed so long and gentle. Watching him. Whoever he was. She realised. Whoever he was. She knew then that she was furiously in love with him.

Emerald Green

SHE HEARD THE sizzle of burning tobacco and the sound of the lips and throat that contracted to pull the smoke deep. She saw the glow of the little nicotine fly and watched the grey clouds come over the curtain only to get machine-gunned into nothing by the spitting shower. She wrapped her fingers around the curtain and pulled it back. Gentle. Slow. He was sitting on the very edge of the toilet seat with his elbows on his knees and his long legs wide and his rusted blond hair falling into his face and he was picking something off the inside of his hand. Around his neck and falling into his shirt was a silver chain with a cross hanging off the end. She went closer and concentrated. Sprawled on the cross and looking out in amazement was a small polished man, a richer kind of Jesus.

She watched him over the top of the bath. He spoke to the floor.

Are you all right, Girl? he said.

I'm okay.

You fell.

I wasn't feeling well.

You're all right now?

I think so. My Dad is dead.

He is.

Will it change?

No, it won't ever change.

Oh.

What's done is done and that's just life.

Okay.

Okay.

Are you here for me?

I was here for him. I didn't know about you.

Did you hear me on the phone?

The line was bad. I couldn't tell who it was.

Are you the hangman?

He took another puff of the fly and brushed his hair from his face and he looked at her where she sat with her feet curled underneath her and her arms hung over the sides. There was not a twitch about him. He was calm and his movements were small and gentle and soft and even the smoke above his head didn't swirl with the kind of dust that usually flowed about the ceiling when Dad was in the room. He was still and he commanded the room to be still also. He moved his hands between his knees and twisted his fingers together and she saw a flash of white on the inside of his wrists, a little slice of moon. She thought on a silver fish that warped its body in the agony of the waterless air and she looked again and saw it clear when he left the amber fly glowing in his fingers. On the back of his wrist was a silver scar cut straight across, just above the heel of his hands, like the still wave on the wall in the living room. He watched her watching him and he turned in his wrists so that the slice of moon was gone.

I'm not anybody, he said.

She looked at his face. He had crooked teeth and unshaven cheeks and he looked nothing like Dad as she used to think every man would. He had a lovely ugly face and lovely ugly hands and lovely ugly hair and he was lovely ugly all. She looked at his eyes and pressed gentle on the button of her jeans. His eyes were bright. Milky. Wide open. Emerald green.

He stood and flushed the end of his smoke away in the toilet and he looked at her and then he turned away and went out of the bathroom. She stood up and turned the shower off and then she was left standing in the after-soak and the air chilled the water that clung to her clothes. She wiped her face. Outside the gulls chanted like drunken men. Inside Dorothy told her to follow the man with the yellow hair. Get up. Go out. Look at him. Follow. Follow. Follow the.

She pulled herself out of the bath and steadied herself on the sink. Her legs were strong and weak at the same time and on the floor next to the bath there were ribbons of toilet roll and an empty cardboard tube and underneath the paper was a damp patch that smelled like eggs and vinegar and sour fruit. She held the hem of her nightie to her nose and went out of the door and into the hallway where he was standing with his hand on the handle of the front door and all the broken locks pushed in a pile next to his boots. He turned around and looked at her.

Don't go. Please. Don't leave me alone.

Someone will come.

Nobody will come.

I'll phone somebody.

I don't know them.

You don't know me.

I know you better than I know anyone else.

She stepped towards him and felt the moths come up through her legs. He cracked the door open a little more and the fresh air came in and the walls and floorboards shook and the roses began spreading into veins that ran down the sides of the wall further and further as they talked. She could hear the noises of the outside howling and chiming and she could feel the heat of the lights as they lay down and stood up again and shone blue and green and grew frantic in the burning night. The man combed the straw hair out of his eyes with his fingers and looked into the other room where Dad lay even deader than he had been before. He wiped his eyes even though he had not been crying.

That's my Dad.

I know.

Did you know him?

I only met him once or twice. I tried to help him.

Nobody could help him. What's your name?

My name is Lucky.

Why are you called Lucky?

You ask a lot of questions.

And never get any answers.

She picked the wallpaper off the walls and Lucky stood next to the door and he began to close it a little and open it again as though he was trying to work the stale air out. He was so much different to Dad. He thought with his hands that came up and went down and flicked out in front of him and pulled the sadness from the room. His eyes were. It would be no bad thing to never see the face of another man. He picked his lovely ugly hands and looked at his boots and looked at the dead man and back at her again.

I think I'll die if you leave, she said. I think I'm dead soon anyway. I can't do much. I can't read and I can't remember a lot of things because my mind is full of. I can't do much. I've never been out there. I think I need that. I think I need to go out and smell the air and look at something different and see all the new things that happen without me knowing. I want that before I die. I don't want all these old things and I don't want to look at these old stacks of nothing, those magazines from nineteen ninety whenever. I'm dying and now I want what I've never had. I just want to be alive at the same time as everyone else.

Do you know what food poisoning is?

No.

You're not dying.

In my mind I died already.

You don't have to die just because your Dad is gone.

I will though.

Do you have any other family?

No. Can't you see how alone I really am?

Mercy.

He came inside and closed the door and brought both hands to the top of his head and the silver wave on his wrists flashed in the light that spat through the half-tangerine glass above his head. He lit another cigarette and rolled his hand into the air and gestured with his finger. When she didn't move he spoke.

That means go on. Get dressed. Get some things together. You're coming with me and that means you're not coming back. Be quick now.

She flung herself over the piles and shoved the door to her bedroom open with her shoulder. She took some clothes off her floor and changed into new jeans that she'd picked holes in and new socks and another one of Dad's band tee shirts that came low to her thighs. She opened the door to check he was still waiting. He was standing by the frame of the living room door where the door had gone missing when she had slept too long and Dad had been bored. Lucky had his hand on the frame and he was watching the still body smothered in coats and jackets and a blanket she had soaked in washing up liquid to hide the smell. He held his hand to his mouth. Trying to stop the noises that came small and crooked and too quiet through the cracks in his fingers. He wiped his eyes and didn't look at her when he told her to hurry up.

She went into the kitchen and took a black bag from underneath the sink and filled it full of clothes she found in the washing basket and food and her toothbrush and toothpaste and a couple of paper dolls and anything she could think of. She went into the living room and held her hand over her nose and she took Plastic Jesus off the Hi-Fi and then she took the mad bird from the mantel and then she rewound her video and closed Dorothy in the box and she shoved it all into the bag. She stood next to Lucky who was watching Dad like TV. He took the black bag away from her and threw it over his left shoulder and then he spun her gently back into the room.

You'll want to say goodbye, he said.

I want to go now.

You'll want to say goodbye, Sweetheart.

I just want to go.

She looked at the lump in the corner and the sun came in through the boards and the slatted light fell onto the figure and chopped him into eight or nine parts. Dad stayed still and comfortable. He was gone. She took Lucky's hand and held it tight. He was a full head taller than her but she could still hear the sound of him swallowing away his grief. She went to Dad and put her hand on the first coat and smelled the bitter death and lemons from the washing up liquid. She bent down and closed her eyes and kissed him where his knees pushed the coat out. Her stomach twisted and the moths rose up to flutter against the back of her eyes and there was nothing to say and nothing more to do. Sometimes men die because they're too tired to do anything different and sometimes they die because the hangman has already set them a place for dinner and sometimes they die to set down stones for their daughters. She was in grief and lonely in that grief and grateful and ashamed that the little death was the thing that sent her on. She kissed him where his face should've been. Sometimes men die because they think too much on what will be and wear away the edges of what is. Sometimes wizards are just old men who hide behind big curtains. Sometimes. And that's all there is.

She bent down and whispered close to the coats. You'll only ever be mine, Dad. Think on that. Even when I go out there and find out who I am without you you'll still only ever have one daughter and that's me. I'll only ever have you. There's no one else. Bad. Good. You just were. You were. You were. You were.

She didn't cry. Lucky wiped his eyes and held out his hand for her to take and she took it and held onto it as tightly as she could. He was a little silver fish and. His fingers were steady and the little pulse in his wrist quickened when she looked at him and said.

Did you know my Dad?

He looked at her strange. His whole body seemed to step back to comprehend her while his feet had not moved an inch. His lip twitched and his head tilted to the side and his eyes locked on hers. It made her feel like. She scratched

the inside of her arm and looked at her feet and then up
again. It made her feel like a bad little dog. He gave her the
doglook once more.

I told you no.

I know you did.

Now in Technicolor

SHE WAS ALWAYS in the last hour before her father's death.

The smell and the shape of him and the thought of the needle and the black cobwebs that filled up his head kept her with him and thinking on those minutes before and minutes after. Pain was with him. Always. Misery. Upset. Numb thoughts ripened by the bitter fix. Trembling. Sorrow. His boyhood bloomed in the roses on his arms and so did thoughts of the hangman who came at last while he was dressed in his funeral suit. She wondered if he saw it coming. She thought on him gasping his last for light and life and breath and then realizing that there was no more for him. Old men always shout for their mothers before they die and she knew that he was no different. She spat her grief into a bucket at the edge of her bed. He would always be dead and she would always be the one who was left. There was no changing him now, and going through the door was the only way to cut the line that ran like liquorice between father and daughter and then to grandmother and so on, tying her up in beautiful promises that burned as soon as she exited the bloody and slick throat of birthing. Leaving was the only way to kick time on, as only she and Dad and the mad bird knew.

He opened the door.

It was easy.

She stepped over the lip of wood with her eyes closed and her hand holding his and he was standing so close that their hips touched and she was breathing so hard she felt like she wasn't walking at all but falling a long way down. She opened her eyes. They were standing at the end of a long white hallway with long lights pinned to the ceiling flickering between dark and light like the world was deciding whether or not to wake. At first she couldn't see anything else. The lights were too bright. The flickering got behind her eyes and scratched at the cords that sent pictures into her head where everything was white and she felt as though she was drowning in a glass of milk. She was dizzy. Her nose itched with all the different smells. Chemicals. Petrol. Sugar. Grass. Dog fur. Piss. She held onto him and he held onto her and she could hear the noises she had heard all her life echoing in waves from the tiles underneath her boots. A little broken window on the far end of the hallway blazed with lights and noises and burning specks of orange set in rows on the high black shoulders of the world. He said everything is fine. Everything is okay. Everything is. She rubbed the cutting lights out of her eyes and let the grassy steaming air fill her chest.

We have to go.

Where are we going?

Further.

Is there more?

There's outside.

I'm more outside than I've ever been.

He held her hand and he walked with her underneath the tubular lights. Somewhere outside a dog howled and it was so much closer than before. The cold air soothed the itches on her skin. The lights swelled and then settled enough for her to focus. She looked at the other brass numbered doors set two by two down the length of the hall.

Nobody lives there, Lucky said. You and your Dad were the only people living in this whole tower. Everyone else moved away. It's too damn old and the rooms are too damn small and the stairways are too narrow and the walls have to work to hold it all up. It's a miracle that something didn't hit you on the head while you were in there. I saw the cracks in the ceiling.

There were cracks everywhere.

Her eyes became accustomed to the light and she could see better the hallway and the inky scratches and rude pictures drawn in reds and greens and purples and blacks all over the paint. The lovely rude art followed them as they walked. She reached out through the window and touched the cold on the other side that was threaded with all the tangled light of those other lives. They turned the corner and went into another hallway where lying on the ground halfway along was a face she recognized from years she couldn't take back.

She looked at the face. It was part of a stack of plastic headless dolls and yellowed newspapers and broken lamps with tilted shades and she dug through and pulled at the little ear and brought up the black velvet nose and dusty chewed face and missing right eye. It was the brown stuffed dog that Dad had brought home one day to fatten up and sew and take back out into the world again. She named it Gravy. The ears smelled of old potato peels and damp wood and the fur came out in her hands when she let it down again on the top of the pile.

What a mess, Dorothy.

What did you say?

Nothing.

There were mountains and leaning towers of junk piled high and wide along the corridors of the many halls that wound around her little haunted museum. They were made up of things that she and Dad had worked to fix and change. There were cabinet doors in dark oak with painted flowers and bird boxes that hung on chains and rocking horses and satellite dishes and mirrors with rusted frames and filthy backs and planted among everything in rows that leaned crooked towards the walls and windows were street signs set like headstones.

She pointed but she couldn't read them. Down the next corridor the wind was cold and fierce and it drove her hair back wild and whipping in tufts that flicked behind her. She held his hand. Paper balls and cigarette packets rolled around her feet and plastic bags went floating up like jellyfish. Electricity fizzed and cracked in the tubular lights and the walls creaked and she picked up the mended pieces of her past and looked at them awhile before letting them drop out of her hands again. She closed her eyes and listened and turned around the next corridor and went through two heavy doors and into the next hall where she saw the source of all that lovely chiming.

Beer bottles. Cans. She walked through and watched the bottles and cans rolling around in the wind that whipped through the last door at the end of the last hall where the storm was heavy and the rain got in between the two handles that were held together by electric tape. The smell of yeast and sour fruit gave way to the smell of the petrol and stone and dirt and weather. The bottles hit the walls and chimed over and over and.

I want to go, she said.

Then we'll go.

She slipped her hand into his pocket and he touched her on the shoulder and drew her to him and moved through the hall with his hand out and the wind blowing them both back. Next to her, she realized, was a large hole in the wall that smelled of.

What's wrong?

That.

The chute?

I hate it.

It's just a place to throw rubbish.

I hate it all the same.

He led her to the door on the other side of the hall and the smell followed them even though they were far along. It was bad. It smelled of fish and eggs and everything rotted into glue and it reminded her of those lovely dead fish and lovely dead Dad and how the two were the same now. Her mother got into her head and. He took her to the door and slipped the electric tape from one side and pushed against the long metal arm and went through. They went down a staircase that went on and on and her ankles ached and her muscles burned. The final door had another thick bar across it and a blurred window and a big red sign with a word that was lit and burning above them.

What does it say? she said.

Can't you read it?

I can't read anything. What does it say?

Exit.

She felt the cold air on her forehead. She stepped on a concrete path and the texture was strange underneath her boots. It was harder than wood. Flat. It didn't rot like wood and it didn't tear like carpet and it gave way to patches of grass. She could smell the sea in the air along with dirt and vinegar and cooked meat and petrol and chemicals. She could see life and she could hear it too. Her eyes were open. They were wide. Ablaze with everything that there had never been before.

Outside the door there was a path and beside the path was a wall and behind the wall were flowers that had closed themselves to the cold and dark and down in the grass were the voices of insects. The path led to the pavement that cut across the top. Behind that was a large paved space and in the middle of the space was a car that stood alone between two white lines that had been painted there.

The car was yellow.

Beyond the immediate everything was the rest of the world and it was made of high buildings and black hills. There were concrete walls, fences, stone steps, rubbish bins, bags, signs with fat red writing, blue and red flashing lights, grey pillars, red bricks, rainbow writing painted on the walls, swearing children playing behind crumpled cars, neon shop signs like magic spells. Children. Children. There were windows and behind the glass were people. Everywhere. She held his hand tight. Tried to think. Tried not to. The cold air didn't rest. Somewhere behind her was a dead father and in front of her was everything else. All the world. Painted. They walked down the path and over a steep banking still slippery from yesterday's rain and she looked so hard and fast that the world washed into a fizz of spinning electricity. She lifted her head up.

He stopped next to her. What are you looking at?

I've never seen it before.

What?

The sky.

It was everywhere. It wasn't like the background in films or the edges of the pages in children's books. It was something else. It was fluid. Organic. Clouds towered over the tops of buildings and leaned but never toppled. The stars flashed soundless and unafraid. The black night was alive with shapes and colours she didn't recognize. The moon looked through a gap between two towers. He pulled her along while she looked. There were sirens and fat whistles behind them. He pulled her quicker.

Come on, he said.

I need to smoke.

Do you?

Yes.

So do I.

They walked across the hard grey space with the white painted lines and when they got to the yellow car he took out a pack of cigarettes and lit one for her and lit one for him. They smoked. He opened the car door with a key that he kept in his back pocket and it blipped and flashed its lights and he opened the driver door and got in and closed the door again. He leaned over and pushed the door open on her side and she got in and sat down and looked through the window. Inside the car the air was petrol fumes and leather and the salt in his skin and the cherry scented piece of card that dangled from the mirror.

He threw the black bag on the seat behind where there were sweet wrappers and cigarette packets and papery junk and he looked at her and she looked at him. He leaned over and she could smell the smoke in his hair. He took the seatbelt and pulled it around her and clipped it into place.

He turned the car on and it rumbled and chugged and she grabbed hold of the seat with both her hands and looked at Lucky as he shifted his legs and pulled the stick that sat between them and worked his feet and turned the wheel in front of him and looked at the mirror. The strap was tight. She loosened it.

They drove slowly around and around in a big circle for no reason. She laughed. A smile caught the corner of his mouth. He sped up and then drove off and stopped the car as the wide concrete space narrowed into a small path that became a thick black road. Above them was a streetlight and she could feel it hot inside her eyes and she squinted and raised her hands to her face. She looked at him. He leaned over again and threw his hand into a drawer that was next to her knees and pulled out a pair of glasses with round green lenses set in silver frames. He gave them to her.

Put them on.

Why?

They'll help with the sharp edges.

Are they yours?

My gift to you.

She put the glasses on. She looked through the window

at flickering streetlights and the glow from the shop signs and the aches from the bulbs in the window. Everything was numbed into green. The lights on the hills didn't make her eyes ache anymore. The world was tinted. She looked at the end of the smoke and waved it in the air and she smoked and blew the smoke in green streams that circled their faces and kissed the air between them.

He looked at her with those eyes and she felt that lovely ugly love.

Cool, he said.

They drove. The yellow car drove on down the black road and the world rushed past on waves of hot green light. The smoke from their mouths whipped through the gaps at the top of the windows. She saw men and women standing underneath lights. She saw the rabbits in the eyes of the sweetly insane. She saw children crossing the road in front of them wearing nothing but their jeans and socks, holding bottles of booze that they supped from as they flashed into existence and disappeared again into the naked arse of the world.

Cool, she said.

He went faster.

An old woman with witch-grey hair crossed the road

in front of them thinking on sleep and her own two feet and holding a carrier bag behind her that swung against the backs of her legs and drove her staggering to the other side of the road. Children pretended to be frightened as she came and they screamed away with their hands raised over their heads. The car stopped at the red light. Women shook their breasts to the music that poured from the windows and doorways of blacked-out houses. A man came to stand and smoke beneath a red sign and another came to ask for a light. A woman laughed like an engine. There were so many people. Everywhere. They walked in front of the car and into streets to the side and into the town and into the gutters and up the road and on and on to the ends of their lives.

The light changed to green and they drove on. On a street corner there was a dog. The dog barked hatred through the legs of its master, snapping at nothing, and lay down again to bend its body to the hot concrete where one day its bones would rest. She took off her glasses to wipe her eyes and she put them back on again. She wiped the sweat off her window and watched the world rise to meet the glass. She sank into her chair and looked at Lucky and she pulled the hair out of her face and pretended to be beautiful. He drove on laughing and talking and calling her Sweetheart.

Sweetheart, are you hungry?

Oh yes.

He pulled through a side street. Two rows of houses were stacked shoulder to shoulder on each side. They turned a corner and came to another road much wider than the other with street lights and neon signs and cigarette smoke and a building with arches and long windows and a garden with old stones stacked in rows over patches of dirt with flowers alive and dead and names she couldn't read.

She was junked on people, mad on living, driving, light, dogs, buildings, children, the sky and the long tall spaces, the road, the on and on and on of it. The all. Everything. They went through the acid green lights and wide concrete corridors that were slicked with oil and water and they were laughing manically at something Lucky had said. Joy and anger was gutted out of the houses and tossed against the walls. Green. Green everywhere. She was mad with all the green and the new town baring its bones to her lovely bright eyes. A drunk man whistled at her from a bench and tossed his bottle into the air and it went spinning and spitting high and then down into the gutters where rats came to drink and to sniff the broken glass. She laughed. Lucky reached into the drawer in front of her and pulled out a plastic case and he peeled the clear packaging away with his teeth and popped it open with his thumb and pulled out a disc with one hand and slotted it into a box that whirred and lit up above the gear stick. Music played. He asked her if she liked music and she nodded. She listened. The music was new. Different. A sad man sang about his mama and papa. She listened and watched the world. A piano chimed and a guitar hummed and drums came cutting through all of it like a storm in an empty room. Another man sang miserably and said oh Hell, oh Hell, oh Hell over and over. He said a well-lived life is full of regrets and a well-timed death is what he needs and on and on and on and.

This is my favourite band, he said. This song is new.

It's good.

Are you upset?

Why are you asking?

You're crying.

I don't think I am.

She dried her eyes with the little piece of cloth that had fallen out with the glasses and rolled her sleeves up past the elbow as they turned a sharp corner and another and took it slow and heavy through an empty street. They rolled into an open space almost the same size as the patch of concrete that lay flat outside her old home. They stopped. Stranded in his headlights was a row of shops that stood vacant, dark, boarded and abandoned and spilling envelopes from beneath their doors. One shop stood lit and alone with a fat sign burning white and suspended in the dark above an oblong window through which she could see tables and chairs and pictures on the walls of cartoon food that looked bad enough to eat.

This place is open twenty-four hours, he said.

That leaves ten or twelve hours for sleep.

He doglooked her and turned the car engine off and leaned over and she pushed her lips out for a kiss but it didn't come. He unclipped the belt and pulled it from around her and opened the door and she got out and stood beside the car blowing tusks of smoke while Lucky locked up.

Oh Dad.

He took her hand and they walked and she stopped to look at a tall box that stood next to one of the abandoned shops and Lucky told her it was a phone box. He said it doesn't work anymore. Someone ripped the phone cable from the phone and put the handset back and I don't know why anyone would do that but that's just life. I suppose. Nobody knows why anyone does anything.

The box had plastic sides that were blistered and black as though suspended in a state of burning. Lucky looked at the box while they walked. They threw their smokes to the ground and kicked the fire out with their heels. The air smelled like fat and vinegar. A rat on a box looked at her and she looked at it. A bell rang and the doors to the shop opened and a man with ripped clothes and swollen fingers and dirty wrists came out and stood muttering and swearing on the step. He banged his fist on the door handle and walked towards them and Lucky pulled her by the hand to the other side of him and didn't look up. The man came and killed the itches on his face and stood in front of them and muttered.

Lend us a quid, Mate. Lend us something. I ain't got money for chips or nothing and I ain't got money to get home or nothing. I'm hungry and that twat in there won't give me nothing the Indian prick what's he doing running a chip shop anyway shouldn't it be a curry house or a Tikka masala? Lend us something, mate, I ain't got one thing.

He went on and on trying to stagger when he was standing still and he smelled like museum poppies and looked like bloody Hell. He had fallen deep into the chase and she looked into his red veined eyes and his arms and the black roses that grew there too. Lucky went into his pocket and pulled out a coin that worried the man and stopped the words in his mouth. He looked at the coin.

Mercy, the man said. Mercy. Mercy.

He killed the itches on his ears and held his hands in front of him and said God bless you and Lucky went into his front pocket and pulled out more change and the man said God bless you, God bless you again and again as his hands were filled up. Lucky went into his pockets and turned them out and poured whatever he found into the hands of the man who sank lower and lower with the kindness that weighed him down. Lucky went into his coat pocket and pulled out his wallet and slipped a tenner from the inside and gave that to the man who sobbed and said mercy, mercy, mercy over and over. Lucky held his hand on top of the man's head and left it there for a while before the man looked up. Stood up. Silent. Calm. He looked at his shoes and then raised his head and breathed hard and calm as though he had come out of the other end of some great labour. He smiled toothless and joyful and staggered forward with his hands in front of him as though he was carrying a cup of milk that he didn't want to spill. He said God bless you once more to the houses on the other side of the road and he sang a song about Jesus before staggering away into the dark.

They turned back to the shop and she tried to understand God. Wondered what he was as they walked through the luminous door of the chip shop. She thought he lived in the hearts and heads of black veined men and women who muttered his name into the bowls of toilets and asked to feel better. Saying please, please, please and then sinking comfortable and strange into that good old ache, right into the yellow womb of that pretty Oh Dee. She thought of Dad who told her once that he was going out to look for God. When he came back he brought a bottle of vodka and a packet of crisps and a dirty photograph and scratched the roses that had begun to bloom on his skin.

I couldn't remember what I went out for, he said.

It wasn't that important, Dad.

Toto the Dark Skinned Man

THE SHOP WAS as white as milk.

She drank up the smells when she went inside and looked at the light that buzzed above her and in front of her in white sheets fast and slow. Most of the light came from long tubular bulbs set in rows on the ceiling. She wiped the steam from her glasses and the lights pulsed and fizzed just like the TV screen when the video was unplugged at the back. She rubbed her tongue on the roof of her mouth and the lights sank back to the ceiling again. Inside the shop everything was metal. White. The light reflected off the shiny surfaces and Coke cans turned on their sides on the floor near the window where there were two rows of plastic tables and chairs. The plastic was dirty and scratched with pen marks and holes gouged and plugged with chewing gum that had dried to extra limb and bone. At the back of the shop was a long worktop and behind that was a metal station with deep vats of oil filled with chips and fish and battered meat long past its time of slaughter.

A dark faced man stood behind the counter. He lifted the silver cages high above the oil and shook the meat and the chips and sighed and shook them again and dropped them back into the amber fizz. He spat into a cloth that rested on his hip and used it to wipe the oil that had hissed onto the worktop. His jaw chewed on insults she was too far away to hear. Above his head was a sign, burning white like the rest of the shop, and written on it was a long list of names and numbers edged with symbols and signs and beneath that were pictures of potatoes and meat and badly drawn fish swimming joyfully towards sharp little hooks.

Lucky looked at her. Do you know what you want?

I'll just have what you have.

They never have fish in stock here so I'll get you a small bag of chips and a sausage and a can of Coke or something. He told her to sit down wherever she liked and he slipped the last note from his wallet and went to the counter. As he walked she could hear the slap of his boots as they stuck to the floor and she could feel her boots sticking too when she went to take a seat that was near the misted window.

She sat close to the wall and wiped the window with the back of her hand and searched outside for the man with mercy in his mouth and God in his head but she could only see her own pale face reflected back at her. She turned back to the room and watched Lucky as he stood next to the counter and addressed the man with the cloth. She repeated everything he said in her head. When he said Mo, my friend, and opened his arms she said it too in whispers that the two men couldn't hear.

Mo, my friend, how've you been?

The dark man turned around and looked at Lucky.

Oh no, he said. You go away.

I thought you were open.

I am. To anyone else I'm open, but not to you.

A spider came from a crack in the wall to sit on the back of her wrist. The man behind the counter waved his hands and lifted the cages and shook them again and sank the food back into the oil once more. He turned to Lucky and told him he wasn't welcome. You're not allowed. I'm fed up with you and I'm fed up with your boy. She flicked the spider off her wrist.

What's he done?

What has he done? What has he done, he asks. That boy is a terror. I tell you he is. He haunts me. Every time I see him I want to cry. I'm always watching for him. Always wondering what he's up to next. I'm miserable, man. Depressed. Shoot me up with morphine. I want to die.

Look, he's a good boy. He just.

You think so?

I know it.

You don't know as much as you think you do, Lucky. I was here yesterday morning getting the shop ready for the day and in comes your son when all the other boys and girls are in school. He walks to my counter and asks for some pop and some chips and I serve him even though we all had that letter telling us to turn him away if he comes around when he should be in school. I say to him that he doesn't have enough money for chips and a drink. He asks me if I would let him pay for the drink later. I say I'm running a business and I tell him he can't just come in here and have things for free. The world doesn't work like that I say. What happens if everyone comes in and wants one thing for free, man? What happens then? I say this to him and I tell him to go away and come back when he has the right money and you know what he does?

Lucky turned his hand in the air. Keep going.

I'll tell you what he does. He goes to the fridge and helps himself to a can of whatever he wants. I come around and try to take it from him and he snatches it back and he pushes me right here. He pushes me this far back. He stands there and I can see what he thinks, man. I can see the nasty little cogs turning in his head. I try to stop him before he does it but there's no stopping him. He shakes the can and throws it hard into the counter and the thing explodes like a bloody grenade. He gets another and another and shakes them all and throws them at me like boom boom boom. I'm on the floor with my hands over my face and these Coke cans are spinning and gushing and I'm trying to stand up and falling right back down and everything is chaos. I stay down until he's done and when I get up again my shop is a mess and there's shit dripping from the walls and shit on the floor and the pies are soggy and your son walks away leaving me to clean everything up. He threw them, man, one grenade after another, boom. Boom. I don't need that, my friend. I'm tired of everyone always trying to kill me. How do you think I know to keep my head down? I moved to this country to get away from grenades.

He went on cleaning and when he thought of something else to say he turned back again. In my country they'd punish both of you. In my country children don't have time to go around throwing cans at people because they're too busy making jeans for three pence a day. You know what happens last night? Your son comes back, man. A demon. Your son comes back last night and he looks at me through that window over there and before I know what he's doing he walks across the way and he lights my bloody phone box on fire.

Lucky scratched his face. He had been listening while the dark man spoke and slowly his head began to sink until he was staring with sad wide eyes at his own boots that were gently kicking the edge of the counter. He didn't say anything. He worked his fingers on the counter. Drummed them. The man stood back and folded his arms over his chest and looked at Lucky as though another grenade was about to be launched at him. Lucky looked up and brushed the blond out of his eyes and spoke. She leaned forward to listen.

How's your Mum?

The man stepped back again and protected his back from the heat of the fizzing vats and looked at Lucky. His eyes were wide and he rubbed the back of his neck. It was as though another bursting can had been thrown his way. Lucky kept on throwing.

She been to the doctor's yet? She told me she wanted to go when I picked her up from the shop and took her to see her sister. I hope she did. She looked like she needed it with the way her legs are. That's why I had to help her up the stairs the last time. She couldn't make it with the broken lifts. I practically had to carry her. Actually, you know, I did carry her.

The man looked at the counter and began to wipe the nothing that was spilled there. He chewed on his lip and stroked the back of his head again and spoke quietly to the surface and his own open hand.

She's fine. She's well, man. Healthy.

Good.

She wants to know if you can pick her up again Thursday morning.

I will.

It'll help. I've been meaning to go over there more but.

I know.

It's hard.

The man didn't look at him while he spoke but instead spoke to the back of his hand and then his palm as his hand twisted around and disappeared back underneath the counter and he wiped a spot of fat again. You're good, he said. You're a good guy. I'm glad to know you, but your goodness isn't an umbrella for your boy to walk under. You know it. It only stretches so far.

He wiped the counter once more and twisted the rag in his hand and wiped his own face that was wet with the steam. Lucky kicked his boot off and then slipped it on again. He looked at the man and then he looked at the food listed on the sign above the counter. He told the man what he wanted and it was fetched for him and chucked on top of large pieces of paper and salted heavily. The man wrapped the chips up and went into the fridge and got two cans of Coke and came back to the counter. He gave everything to Lucky and then he put his hand on Lucky's shoulder and they looked at each other. Lucky placed his hand on the top of his. He said I know, I know. Don't worry. Then he turned from the counter and the man went back to shaking the baskets.

Outside the sun was coming up. There were large white birds that came low and landed on the concrete next to an open chip packet and they stabbed at the paper with their sharp beaks and tore it up and then stabbed at each other until they all flew back to the rising day.

What birds were they? he said. I didn't see them.

White ones.

Gulls then.

Sounds about right.

He gave her one of the paper parcels that was already beginning to darken and she opened it out on the table and smelled the salt that rose up with the heat. He unrolled his own. They ate with their fingers even though there were wooden forks in a box in the middle of the table.

Slow down, he said. You'll burn your tongue.

She fanned air into her mouth and chewed fast and sucked the salt from her fingers and she drank from the Coke can that he opened and put down in front of her. The

Coke popped with sweet electricity. She drank half the can at once and filled up her stomach with the slush and fizz and then she ate again. Lucky ate slowly. He bit a chip in half and looked at it before throwing the last of it into his mouth and then he sat back to think.

When Lucky was done he slid the packet to her and told her she could have the rest and he sat back in his chair and wiped his eyes with a clean sleeve. She ate. When she was done she folded the packets together and shoved them into the middle of the table and rested against the wall and looked at him.

You must've been hungry, he said.

I was. I'm tired now.

Let's rest here now. It's a nice place.

They both leaned back and said nothing. Outside a dog barked and tired people began to come out of their houses to look at the rising sun or lean down low and pull something out of the garden or to shoo away a cat or to get inside their cars and drive away with coffee cups in their hands. She watched them and waited for some kind of murder. Chaos. Mad rush. Blunt edges. Something that told her she wasn't safe outside because Dad always told her that the world was the worst place she could ever be. She waited but there was nothing. The night burned away and all the shadows began to draw themselves back from the streets. Birds came and went. Dorothy sang somewhere among the black bagged pavements. In her head her father swung from a hanging rope that had been fixed to a post long before she was born and. She watched it all and listened to the sound of the moths in her head.

She turned to Lucky who was looking at his thumbs.

Lucky looked at her. What is it?

Why did he let you have the food?

Who?

That man. He was angry before.

Lucky sank back into his seat and scratched the inside of his wrist where the little moon winked. He picked up a chip and looked at it in his hand, turning it one way and then the other. He brought it to his mouth and twisted his face and dropped it back down again to the paper where the rest of his food was losing its steam and growing cold. He looked at her and leaned forward.

You know, he said. You should never use guilt as a weapon. It's such a terrible thing to do to someone else, don't you think? Don't ever do that, okay? Don't ever use guilt as a weapon. Even if you think you'll end up getting something good out of it. It's not worth it. It destroys people. It gets in their head and doesn't come back out again. It's like planting a seed inside them that grows and spreads and blocks out all the light. It's worse than shooting somebody. It's worse than killing them.

He looked at her and she looked at him. Both leaned across the table with their hands barely touching. They didn't talk. His eyes were greener when she wore the glasses. Clear. Burning. Amphibious. The lenses seemed to cut him from the rest of the world, drawing him closer than anything else in the hot white room. He leaned back again in his chair and rubbed his eyelids with his fingers.

She looked out of the window. She watched the gulls gathering around a paper packet that they tore into shreds and dragged away and she looked at the people who drove and walked and came and went on the outside. An old dog passed. It was gentle. Alone. Its muscles were shrunken by time and ownership and memories of wildness that still ebbed in his blood. When people saw each other they stopped and talked. When they left their homes they locked them up and checked the locks once or twice by tugging the handles down. She looked at Lucky again. He had fallen asleep with his head in his hands. She kissed him on the back of the neck and went into his pockets and smelled the petrol and exhaust fumes in his hair and took out the lighter and the pack of smokes and she put one into her mouth and lit it and she sat back and smoked.

The dark faced man looked at her and raised the cloth over his head and shouted something in another language and came from behind the counter and shouted again and waved his dirty cloth and stamped his foot. He came and stood in front of her. He waved his hands. She stood up in her chair and held her hands up like they did in those black and white films with the gangsters and the violence and all that hoochy talk.

You can't smoke in here, the man said. Are you crazy? You can't do that here. Put it out. Put it out right now.

She rested the cigarette on her bottom lip. Why?

It's against the law. You stupid. Put it out. It's against the law to smoke in here and you shouldn't be smoking anyway. It's bad for you. How old are you? You're a kid, aren't you? Didn't your mother ever tell you that smoking is bad?

I'm just smoking. I'm not a kid. I don't know the laws. It's only smoking. I didn't know. It calms me down. You can have one if you want.

I don't want one. Disgusting. Filthy.

He spat on the floor and then looked at the spot and cleaned it up with his cloth and Lucky woke up and looked at her and looked at the man. He saw the cigarette that was now resting between her fingers. He wiped his eyes and stood up and raised his hands to his head and then. He laughed. He laughed hard with his hand on his face. The man opened his mouth but nothing came out. Lucky held his hand out for her to take. I think it's time to go, he said.

Emerald City

HOME WAS IN the sky.

They had not been driving long on the road when they reached the end of it and the end of all things was waiting there. The day had ignited. The sun heated everything into blue and grey haze with swirling patterns and small far away spots. The houses came less often in that part of the estate and the only buildings standing were the ones that were boarded up and empty and labelled with fat signs and bold red letters. Grass grew through concrete slabs. Brick walls stood slantways and sideways and spilled themselves onto patches of white dust and broken glass and black bags weighed down by weeks and weeks of rainwater. There were fewer people. The ones who walked did so quickly and with their heads down and the ones who remained in one place were sleeping on blue padded coats and sodden blankets and they were brave enough to be drunk and clever enough to be mad.

Where are we going?

Home.

Where's home?

Home is up.

He pointed towards a black mass that rose out of the ground as they travelled towards it. It grew high, unfolding above them like black paper. The towers here were miles wide and layered one behind the other, linked together by bridges that were stacked like ribs between concrete walls. There were wire fences topped with razors, corrugated tin roofs and stone steps that led to nothing. There were a hundred thousand windows gleaming, white sheets that swung on black lines above plastic chairs and buckets and baskets and chunks of bread not thrown far enough for the birds. There was life. There was living and there was a wall that went around it all. As they arrived children came to stare at them and to spit and stick out their belly buttons and kick the muck up with their unlaced shoes. They drove under a bridge. The sun and sky were covered in concrete.

This is where I live, he said.

I'm in a dream.

Lucky turned the mirror. His eyes were reflected there.

We call them the streets in the sky, he said. They're around sixty years old and they go from over there to over there and it's like a little world above everything. If you don't want to come down to the town you don't have to. There are shops here. Some of them are halfway up. I know a man who has been up there for fifteen years and he only came down once for his sister's funeral. He pays kids to do his shopping and he pays other people to walk down the road and back again and tell him what's happening at the other side of the world. You can live happy and high up and away from the rest of the world. There's even a church on the third floor. It's like God's estate.

Plastic Jesus nodded in the back.

They came to an opening between two long towers. There were other cars. White lines. Overturned bins. There was a lamppost that buzzed and crackled and around everything was another wall made of thin wood held up by beams that had been leaned against it. The wooden wall was painted with words and pictures just like the hallway and it leaned in the wind and came back again. The beams creaked. Lucky stopped the car close to the lamppost on the far side. She took off her seatbelt and opened the door and stood outside and closed the door again.

Lucky got out of the car and wrestled the black bag from the back and swung it over her shoulder and Plastic Jesus swore furiously at him but he didn't hear it and didn't talk back. On the other side of the wall she could hear the sound of running water. She asked him what was on the other side and he told her it was a river and there were houses beyond that and a factory and a field and new developments for well-off families who dreamed of driveways and blue front doors.

They walked. He kept her close. Above her the gulls sang and circled a patch of grey sky and she followed them with her eyes until she was dizzy.

Be careful, Sweetheart.

Everywhere was a place she had never been. She was tired. She was thirsty from the salt and heavy from the fat and Dorothy was singing somewhere on the other side of the wall. Her stomach worked on the chips. She thought that if she fell asleep she would disappear or wake up dead just like Dad who hadn't been done with life when life was done with him. Plastic Jesus nodded in the bag. She held onto Lucky's hand.

They walked down a path and followed the wall of wooden panels standing taller than Lucky and topped with metal that was twisted into cutthroat roses. She followed him down the path and through a heavy door set into the base of the block. She kept her hand inside his coat pocket. Before they went into the tower she saw there was nothing at all on the other side of it. The tower was the end of the world. It was the edge of everything and she didn't stop to think on that.

Through the door was a corridor covered in more words. When she asked him to read the words out loud he laughed and said Fuck, fuck, fuck. In the middle of the corridor was a set of wide concrete steps. On the stairs were crushed cans and bits of smashed glass and carrier bags of discarded waste and a lonely little crack that went all the way up and came all the way back down again.

She wasn't used to walking so much. She fell behind him on the stairs when the backs of her legs began to throb. Her body was not built for more than a few rooms of walking. One set of stairs. A small space to fall down if the standing gets too hard. A bed and a hard floor and time spent in front of the TV watching the world go by. She sat down and Lucky came back and put his hand on the top of her head and she got up and went on again. The stairs fell away behind her. All the moths gathered inside like drifts of leaves.

Are you crying?

No.

They went on.

She held his hand and he opened a steel door with a bar

across it and the wind sucked all the air out of her body and she walked out onto a stone corridor suspended above the world. In front of her was a wall that came as high as her waist and beyond that was the tower on the other side and beyond that was the town and the hills and the black road that cut through everything on the ground. She could see the whole of it. The wind whipped her hair around her head. A dog barked but she couldn't see it. A man called. She thought on everything. She was too tired for words and drunk and sick on memories that wouldn't stay still. Lucky picked a crisp packet and an empty cigarette box from the ground and then he rubbed the dust off the corner of a window. He turned to her and smiled big and fat and asked if she was ready to go in. She looked at the low ground and the road below that was no bigger than her wrist and she thought of Dad and the hangman and Mum and. She nodded.

His door was at the end of the street where the bad words were scratched out with black pen and there was a smell like paint and bleach and he told her there was a factory down the way that pumped chemicals into the sky. A potted plant grew crooked on a painted wooden chair. He turned a key in the door. She watched smoke rolling and she watched the sky draw it all up. She thought that Dad was in the smoke. Mum too.

What's the matter?

Nothing.

Are you coming in?

I think I just.

It's okay, Sweetheart.

Is it?

Yes. Let's go watch TV.

Inside the door was a short hallway with no carpet and one pair of flat red shoes that had begun to curl up on the toes. At the back of the hall was a room with a closed door and to the right of the hall were two rooms and to the left was another and there were no pictures on the walls. A red bag was chucked on the floor next to the shoes with words scratched into it that all began with F and inside the bag was a stack of books. The shadows receded when he flicked a switch and the light above them flashed and drowned the whole hall in pale green.

You can take the glasses off now if you want.

I want to keep them on.

He closed the door and it rang with all the chains and locks that were on the inside and he checked the frame with his finger and spent a long time locking it all up. She picked the red shoes up. They were too small for her feet. She put them down again. He touched her on the shoulder and walked down the hall and she looked at the doors and empty walls and cast into her mind for piles of junk and stacks of magazines from nineteen ninety whenever through to the just-before-now. She looked at Lucky.

This place is like my home, she said. Everything is the shape and size of Dad's place except it's all on the left and not on the right and I feel like I've walked into a mirror or something. Look, this room was my room. This room was Dad's room. This room is the living room and at the back is the kitchen and there are no windows there. There aren't windows in the kitchen only cupboards and shelves and a mess under the sink. It's my house and it's not my house. My house. Not my house. Everything is facing the wrong way but it's exactly the same. It's home. It's just like home but different. Look at all that light.

She picked her nail. A thought clotted in her head. For a moment Dad almost walked out of the back room before she remembered to stop him. Her head hurt. Her eyes had been open far too wide for far too long and when she closed them all she could see was. She couldn't think. Everything was facing the wrong way and she was so tired she could die and be happy about it. I feel funny, she said. Sick. I think I need the toilet.

She went to the end of the hall and reached for the door handle and twisted it once and the door popped open and inside the room it was stuffy and dark and she stood for a while without stepping in. It wasn't the bathroom. She hung onto the door but didn't go inside and Lucky came behind her fast and pulled it shut. That's not the bathroom, he said.

What is it?

Nothing. The toilet is in here.

I don't have to go anymore.

Lucky doglooked her. He picked up the black bag that he had dragged up from the car and he twisted it and swung it over his shoulder. He opened another door that was next to the bathroom on the left side and he went in and she followed him. It was a bedroom. It was where her bedroom would be if this was her home. There was an unmade bed beneath the window at the back of the room and above it was a wall that had posters of beautiful women standing and crouching next to cars or motorbikes and they were dressed only in knickers and small see-through tops stretched around large breasts. There was a desk next to the bed with papers and books chucked all over the top and good clean pages torn from their staples and thrown about. She couldn't read the writing on the side of the books and she couldn't read what was scratched into the wall in crooked letters above the desk. The wardrobe in the corner had no doors and there were holes in the carpet and grooves and scars that were bashed into the legs of the desk and bedpost and hinges and screws chucked on the carpet next to an old plate with crumbs and an old cup turned over. Inside the wardrobe were black tee shirts and jeans chucked into a pile and socks rolled into balls and it matched her own mess in the museum. The room knew she was coming. It was made for her. This is my room, she said, and she sat on the bed and looked at him.

This is my son's room, Lucky said. He's been missing for a few days. You can have it until he decides to come back. I'll leave you here to get settled and I'll make us both some tea. There aren't any more sheets so you'll have to use the ones already on the bed. They're okay though. Clean. I don't think they've been slept in.

He picked up the sheets and held them to his nose and then he held them closer and he was quiet and his eyes were closed. The lines beneath his eyes were hardened in the sunlight that came through the window and she watched him sink back into old age as Dad did so often in those long silences between them. He opened his eyes and flung the sheets onto the bed and straightened them and said nothing and he walked out of the room and closed the door and she was alone and thinking on that.

She picked her nail and looked out of the window at the towers on the other side of the world and she began to tidy everything into neat piles that had no order and no meaning. She stacked the papers on the desk with the rolled up socks and looked at the books with drawings of boys and dogs on the front and she opened the pages and looked at the letters and she made up stories in her head. She closed them again and stacked them in piles of three and on top of the largest pile she stood the Plastic Jesus and shook him to see if he was happy. He nodded at her.

Are we alone? she said to him.

Very.

Am I going to disappear?

One day.

Should I change my clothes?

It's all you can do.

She took off her jeans and knickers. Folded them and stuffed them in the back of the wardrobe where her own baby shoes would've been if this had been hers. She covered them with a heap of the boy's dirty clothes and fetched a fresh pair of jeans and knickers and a clean tee shirt from the black bag and put them on. She got the cuckoo and put him on the windowsill and turned him to face the rain that had started out there while she had been getting dressed. She set the time on the clock to whatever time she thought it could be and fitted the bird back onto the spring and spoke softly to him so he would sleep. She looked out of the window. The weather bounced right up from the concrete. It was. She had never seen the rain.

She watched a black tree with black branches on a hill past the next tower along. The rain made the potted plants shiver. She cried because she felt like it but she didn't make a sound. The glass was cold on her cheek and her breath couldn't warm it and Dad was a fish and Walter was a poet and her mother was alive in a deep pit on the moon and everything was different and nothing mattered as much as she thought.

When she was done with crying she smoked. She tied her hair up and put on her lipstick and looked at herself in a mirror that was buried underneath some towels and a book on space. She watched the smoke rising and straightened the pillow that Lucky had put on the bed and she took the video out of the bag and looked at the picture on the front. The picture was torn underneath the plastic sheet that held it in place. She slid her fingers down and flicked back the corners and she straightened out Dorothy's face that had a crease running along the middle just above the nose. They were ugly like her. Lovely like her. The yellow brick road was green in the lenses of her glasses. She hid the video underneath the pile of papers on the desk. She tipped the black bag up and put all her clothes onto the wire hangers that were unused along the metal bar in the wardrobe. She took down the pictures of the women on the wall and she rolled them up and shoved them down the back of the headboard so that the wall was clean and empty and the women couldn't stare at her. She sat on the bed and crossed her legs and lay back on her elbows and looked at the wall and thought of the sea and the roving, jumping tide. Then she thought of the fish and.

The hands of the clock on the windowsill had moved five or seven or nine minutes while she had slept accidentally above the covers. Moths had gathered again. She thought on something that she had kept since girlhood and tried to flush away with that little silver fish. She stopped the thought before it. She always. When. Dad died without knowing it and she cried on that for hours and. Let me in, Love, someone said from long ago.

Let me in.

It all went down with the fish.

~~Witch~~
Tin Woman

SHE WAS DONE with thinking.

Outside the rain ran down the side of the block that stood on the other side of the black road. She left the room and went along the hall and found the kitchen that was in the same place as her own and she went through the living room door and looked at Lucky. He was standing and looking at the wall with a spoon raised in his hand and three cups steaming on the counter. He had taken his jacket off and it was slung past the worktop behind him and into the living room on top of a chair with a crooked back. She went into the kitchen and leaned against the wall and looked at his face and the ugly love burned in her throat.

You and Dad, she said. Were you friends?

He didn't look at her.

How did you know him?

I didn't know him, he said. Not even a little bit and I'm sorry about that. I was just trying to help him. I saw him out there one day. Wandering. He didn't belong anywhere and he didn't like himself. I could tell. I saw him wandering and I looked at him and I said to myself there's a man who needs help and love. I wanted to help him. I talked to him and I bought him a meal. We talked. We were alike in a lot of ways except one or two and I can't remember what they were. I gave him money. I gave him a little time. I gave him a card with my number and later on I found it jammed into a wire fence so I followed him home and I posted my number through the letterbox. I tried to help but in the end I couldn't and that's just life. For a lot of us life is hard until it gets harder.

I phoned you.

I know. I heard. I'm glad. You could be dead.

And we wouldn't be here now.

Mm.

He moved his hands in front of him as though he wanted to take hold of something that she couldn't see. He talked slow and calm without stopping and he didn't look away from the wall. She covered his hand with her own and brought it back to the counter and he looked at her hand which was pale and thin and then he turned to her and smiled and wiped his eyes that had been open all this time. He finished making the tea and she thought on the way he stirred slow and one-sided. The tea was brown and thick. He stopped stirring for no reason. He was like a bad clock that thought too much on the minutes and on the seconds and not enough on the days. Sometimes he watched people with his hand on his face and his little finger pointed at his lip and sometimes he stared with open eyes and an open mouth as though he was falling into all the minutes and the seconds, into all the time that he should never have stopped to consider.

How dark do you like it? he said.

Dad does it milky white.

He raised the tea bag on the end of the spoon and threads of brown sweat spindled into the water. Damn, he said. He took the bag and chucked it into a green carrier bag that was open on the worktop, fat with old food. He got milk from the fridge and poured it into her mug. They drank their tea and she looked at a third cup that was left on the counter with a tea bag still floating upright inside it. She looked at him and he looked at her.

She likes it dark, he said. Bitter. Near undrinkable.

He scooped the bag out of the cup and chucked it with the others and spooned four sugars into the tea and he counted out one and two and three and four and he stirred it and asked her if she would help him carry it in.

Carry it where?

I think she's awake now.

She picked the cup off the counter and held it gentle and careful in front of her without spilling anything from what was too full inside. He cut the crust off the sandwiches and sucked the jam off his thumb and wiped his thumb on his jeans and stacked the bread on a small plate and walked ahead of her and she followed him into the hall.

Lucky stood before the closed door at the dark end of the hall and he looked at her and she showed him the unspilled cup. He twisted the handle and opened the door. He went into the room and she followed him. Lucky bustled open some curtains and light shocked all the dust into the air. There was a bed next to the window. Lying in the bed and wrapped in loose sheets was a woman. Pale. Thin. She was beautiful and long-limbed and naked as the light that came to rest on the tops of her ears.

Lucky sat on the edge of the bed and touched the woman's forehead. The woman opened her eyes and looked at him and turned her head and she smiled and he smiled back. In the dust and the half-green light the woman let the sheets fall below her left breast and she took Lucky's hand and placed it there.

Feel my heart, she said. It was so fast just now. He looked at her and he spoke so gently she couldn't hear him and as they talked the age that had come upon him was taken inch by inch from his face. She watched them with the cup in her hands.

Caring was all over their faces and set in the photographs and furniture that were placed all around the room. The woman didn't see her there standing upon the edge of the scene looking in and steadying the cup. The woman in the bed said she dreamed it was snowing. Lucky said it hasn't snowed for years. The woman sat up and pulled the sheets and then she let them fall like white roses in her arms and uncovered her body down to the stomach that protruded a little just below the tracks of her ribs. He kissed her on her shoulder where there was a tattoo of a blue heart and the dust swam around them and she was both in the room and far away.

She steadied the tea and wiped her eyes. Oh damn.

The woman in the bed looked at her. They looked at each other. She stretched her thin neck from the bed and she touched Lucky's hair and moved it behind his ears and she whispered something to him so quiet it was as though she hadn't spoken at all. He turned around and gestured to the doorway.

She was lost. She's seventeen I think. She's the daughter of a friend who died not long ago. You don't know her. She's full of trauma. I'm helping her because her father is dead. That's just life, Sweetheart, like I always say. That's just life.

He kissed the woman's hands and pushed the hair out of her eyes and the woman leaned in without taking her eyes from the doorway where she stood with the tea and she whispered something else and Lucky nodded. The tea was hot and unbalanced and she didn't spill any of it.

Anna, this is my wife, he said.

The cup fell.

The woman in the bed turned over and Lucky mopped up the steaming stain on the carpet with a black tee shirt that had been hanging clean in the wardrobe. She said I'm sorry and looked at her hands, just like Dad used to, as though they had betrayed her.

I'm sorry I didn't mean to. I'll help you.

Don't. It's okay, Anna, you didn't mean it.

She looked at her hands again and then at the woman in the bed who was looking at her. She felt cold. Tired. Transparent. She wanted to be taken away. She wanted to jump into the water that was hidden behind the wallpaper.

I didn't mean it, she said again and she looked at the woman and they watched each other while Lucky sweated over the mess.

I didn't.

Don't worry, Sweetheart.

I really didn't.

It's okay.

The woman doglooked her. Lucky picked up the handle that had broken off when the cup fell and she rested her hand on his shoulder while he cleaned. Then he took his hand away and chucked the cup into a bin that had been tipped over next to a chest of drawers with pearl necklaces and tangerine scarves and pretty red and black knickers draping out. He went to the woman and sat on the bed while she stood in the corner. They whispered and she strained to hear.

You want another cup?

Not now.

You want anything else?

I'll tell you. I want you, the woman said. I want to feel something good.

The woman took his hand in hers. The brown tea stain spread out and then stopped beneath her feet. It wasn't her fault. It was all her fault. It wasn't her fault. She wanted to be bad. Lucky turned and looked at her and she stepped out of the room before he could ask her to leave.

The lock clicked on the other side of the door. She went into the bathroom and closed the door and sat on the edge of the bath and looked at the pile of clothes spilling out of a basket and the toothbrushes that were clean and white and had straight bristles that were not frayed and yellow as hers and Dad's had been. There was a new bar of soap in the sink, medicine in pots and packets inside the cupboard and a mirror on the outside that she didn't want to look at. There was a flannel that smelled of old water. There was a bottle of aftershave that she sprayed into her pocket. The tiles had no fish and no flowers and no garden that grew there in black lines towards the ceiling. They were blank and white and cracked here and there and inside the cracks was white gunk newly spread. She went to her knees next to the toilet stained between the seat and the rim with piss and black hair and she pulled her hair back and tried to throw up but nothing would come. She was empty. She didn't cry and she didn't speak and she sank into the quiet of the bare white room.

She took off her glasses and washed her face with the soap and a small clean towel that was draped over the bath and water that was burning hot straight out of the tap. She took off her tee shirt and soaped the hair underneath her arms and watered it and dried herself in the towel and put the glasses back on and cleaned the dirt from underneath her fingernails. She brushed her teeth with one of the toothbrushes that had old lipstick on the neck and when she put it back again she didn't rinse it. Dad moaned in her head but she wasn't listening.

143

She brought the mirror out from its zigzag frame and pulled it close to her face and looked at herself and poked her tongue through the gap in her teeth and wondered if she had a good face. Not as good as. When she brushed her teeth and spat into the sink the white foam had a flick of blood running through. She didn't look good and she didn't look bad. She was something more than and less than beautiful. She was herself. Her chin was like Dad's. Her lips were like Mum's. Her nose was her own. She took the lipstick out of her pocket and unscrewed it and drew it on her lips and pressed them together and arched her shoulders and pulled her head back. She stayed in the room and sat on the closed lid of the toilet and didn't look at herself again.

After a while he knocked on the door.

Are you all right?

Yeah. I was washing but I'm finished now.

She opened the door and he was standing outside with a cigarette in his mouth and the smoke swam to the ceiling. His shirt was buttoned wrong and his hair was messed and his eyes burned boyish. He looked away.

They sat in the kitchen and drank milk like children. He talked. He talked with his hands and with energy about the kindness of the world and how everyone must be kind to one another because God said so. She listened and didn't listen. He asked her if she knew who Jesus was and she told him he was made of plastic and he lived on top of the Hi-Fi and she said she once buried him in a pot of dirt. He talked about Jesus and black books and holy houses and she picked her nail and killed an itch on her thigh. She asked him what was the matter with his wife.

He sipped his milk and filled his glass again.

Nothing. There's nothing wrong with her. I don't. Nobody knows. She didn't get up one morning and she didn't get up the next morning and that was a long time ago. I don't know why. I don't think she knows why. Sometimes I pray. I ask her every morning if she wants to get out of bed and put clothes on and she always says no. I don't feel like it, she tells me. I have too much to think about.

Perhaps she's not happy.

Perhaps.

I'm happy.

That surprises me.

She had slept for hours. She dreamed of Dad and Mum and Lucky and the woman who wouldn't move and chip-shop nights under the glow of hot vinegar lamps. When she woke up it was early and she watched the sun rising through the window in the boy's room. She thought on death because she was alone. Then she thought on her own living that hadn't begun until she was coming close to eighteen. She thought on a lot of things and a lot of things seemed to look back at her. White rooms. Hot lights. Food. Drink. Cigarettes. Towers. Green clouds. Dad. Rot. She thought of Plastic Jesus who nodded in his dark corner. She reached over and bobbed his head with a pen and asked if she had disappeared in the middle of the night.

Yes, you did.

Is Dad really dead?

Long gone, Girl.

Long gone and so sad.

She looked out of the window where there would never be boards and far below there were people walking and muttering and children scattering and there were cars on a road far away. Threading. She followed the line back down where one car came upon the black road and turned around and went off again. Below there were black bridges and red doors and patches of grass. Above the estate the clouds were stacking into towers. She had not realized that the sky was different every day.

Her belly and mind were still full from all the fat of the day before and she got out of bed and drew the sheets back to the pillow and fitted them around the mattress exactly like she never did at home. She kissed her fingers and stamped the kiss onto the pillow and took off the clothes she had slept in and dressed in those she had hung in the wardrobe that was hers now and she went out of the room.

She had a headache she was trying to ignore.

Lucky, are you there?

He wasn't.

She went into the kitchen and the bathroom and the living room and looked for him but he was gone. She pressed her back against the wall in the hallway and looked through the gap in the room that belonged to the woman and saw the turning of a head and the raising of a shoulder that was not his. He had gone. He was gone off to get junk or magazines or music just like Dad. She went into the kitchen again. There were two cups set out with sugar and a clean tea bag and beneath one of the cups was a pen and next to that was a note that she couldn't read. She looked at the two cups and boiled the kettle and poured water in one and then the other and poured a lot of milk in the cup she chose for herself and she looked at the other cup and at the note. She tried to force the scratches into something she could understand but they were lawless and drifted when she looked at them for too long. She splashed milk into the other cup and folded the note and slipped it into the pocket of her knee-cut shorts and took the two cups into her hands and walked as carefully with them as though Lucky was standing just behind her.

The woman's room was lit weakly by the day that pressed its face against the window. The dust rose silver. The stain from yesterday was still sopped into the fibres of the carpet beneath her feet. The room smelled different but she didn't know why. It was hot. Musty. She swore in her head because Dorothy told her to.

The woman was sitting up in bed with the dirty sheets wrapped around her waist and she was scratching the white paint off the wooden windowsill. She couldn't see her face because she was turned wholly towards her work but she could see her back that was bare and long and pale down to the place that was covered by the sheets. She balanced the hot cup between her hands as she had done the day before. She stood in the doorway and looked at the woman and the woman kept on scratching and she collected snowflakes beneath her nails and drew crooked lines in the wood. The sheet fell to her hips. Between her shoulder blades was the most beautiful place she had ever seen.

I know you're there, the woman said.

I'm sorry, I didn't mean.

I'm writing my name. Can you see that?

I can't read your name.

Why not?

I just can't.

Are you stupid?

I don't think so.

You probably are.

I made you some tea.

The woman turned around and the sheet rolled around her waist and she rested her back against the wall and uncovered her breasts.

Where's Lucky? the woman said. Tell him to come to bed.

She balanced the cup on the woman's palm and went into her pocket for the note and she pulled it out and held it up for the woman to see and then slipped it into her pocket again. The woman blew the steam from the cup and said it looks like he's abandoned us both. He's gone out to do Dog's work. That's my name for God. It's just God spelled backwards, don't you know? Everyone knows that. Everyone thinks it too. Dog. Dog. Holy Dog. Lucky's off helping poor people feel even more guilty and ashamed than usual. Do you think that's a cruel thing to say?

I don't think anything about anything.

You do. I can tell from looking at you. You think a lot of things.

He'll be back.

One day he won't.

I think you're wrong.

Think what you like.

She drank her tea and blew the paint from beneath her nails and she looked at her from the bed and churned her up in her eyes. She looked all the way down to her legs and she lifted the hem of her shorts to her thighs and lifted her arms and she drank more of her tea.

You're supposed to shave your legs. Didn't you know that? You're supposed to shave your legs and under your arms. You're supposed to shave your pussy too but that's up to the man who strips you every night. That's what a woman is supposed to do. Shave there and there and play dumb and moody or no boys will want to touch you. Your nose is too big. Did you know that? Your breasts are too small. I could twist them and squeeze them right off like little grapes. How old are you?

Seventeen.

You look twelve.

I know.

The woman gave her the cup and she took it and lowered it on a table and looked down at her own legs and thought on Lucky and his lovely ugly love. The woman pulled a green packet from beneath her pillow and she untwisted the top and pulled out a stack of tiny white papers and a red plastic lighter and a pinch of loose tobacco. She took one of the papers and more tobacco that she bunched on top and she rolled the paper around and around in her pretty fingers. She licked the end of the paper and rolled it together until it was a cigarette and then she put it into her mouth and lit the end and smoked it. She scratched the blue heart on her shoulder. She propped her elbow on a pillow and looked at her and held the made-up smoke high and threw her head back to blow all the smoke into the air.

I used to be an artist, she said. Can you tell?

I can't tell much about anyone.

You'll learn. It's all in the eyes and fingers. What are you supposed to be?

I didn't know I had to be anything.

That's a shame.

Why?

You have to be something. That's just life. You have to be someone and you have to do something. You have to follow the living path. Make plans. Fuck about. Make regrets. Who wants to just exist? Who wants to live and die and be forgotten? That's why people have goals and dreams. People spend their whole lives trying to be something else. If you're not something you're nothing.

You have to go to sleep to dream and I don't sleep that much.

I don't understand you.

They were silent again, both of them looking at the window, at the sky turning cloudier and darker and the rain picking and the concrete blocks getting drenched and all the wetness darkening the concrete and all the lights that were beginning to come on and show up all the faces that lived over there. Between the sky and the dirt.

Don't you just hate artificial light? the woman said. I hate the way it looks and the way it makes me feel when I see it. It makes me feel sick. It turns everything to oranges and lemons. I hate the way everyone tries to replace what's already outside. It's ugly. It's like giving birth to a limbless doll. A stillborn. Out there there's nothing but stillborn lights in stillborn houses with stillborn wallpaper and stillborn shoes with clean rubber soles. You want to smoke?

She nodded and the woman made another rolled smoke in her lap and handed it over and lit it in her mouth and they both smoked together. Dog bless you, she said, and laughed. She lay back in the bed with her breasts peeping out and then she covered herself with the sheet.

Are you another of his broken birds?

I don't know what that means.

You must be. I can tell just by looking at you. You're broken up about something and you need fixing and that's what he's going to try to do with you. He'll give you all the love and care and attention you can take for a few seconds of your life and it will be wonderful and you won't want it to end but it will. Sooner than you know. He'll take himself away again. Better to stay broken I say.

Why do people need help?

Watch the news. Take a walk. Open your eyes.

Do you and him. I think. Do you love each other?

The woman looked at her. Her skin smelled like ash. She didn't speak. She looked deeply at her without moving. The smell from a breakfast she would never eat seeped through the window that was jammed open with a folded piece of cardboard. The woman doglooked her and then she brought her hand to her face and began to laugh quietly. Then she closed her mouth and stared at her own knees that had become unmasked beneath the sheets and drawn up to her chest.

She waited in the room but there was nothing more to say and nothing more to laugh on. She pulled the sheet over the woman to the shoulders and tucked it around her as Dad used to when the house was too cold to sleep in. The woman didn't take her eyes from the plain wall on the other end of the room. Before she had moved to the bedroom door and wrapped her ugly fingers around the handle and opened and closed the door behind her the woman spoke once more.

Has he told you why people call him Lucky?

She turned around and the woman was looking at her. She took another puff of the cigarette she held in her fingers and there was this little glow that lit her face for the smallest of moments before she shrank into the clouds and dust and the ugly artificial light once again.

She shook her head.

The woman turned her face back to the wall and said nothing more. She was gone into the writing there that she couldn't read or see. She waited for an answer or a nod or a movement of the body that didn't come and then she left the room and closed the door and shut the woman away from the rest of the world. Only Lucky and Dorothy and that Dog in heaven would be able to bring her back from wherever she had gone.

Hey Dee Dee

SHE DIDN'T LIKE herself when she was alone.

She liked who she was with him. Pretty. Good. Funny. Kind. Kinder. Honest. Lipsticked. Green glassed. Worthy of. Different. So different that he looked deeply at her when he thought she wasn't watching and talked to her for hours and hours until there was nothing but eating or sleeping or listening to the sounds of living through the open windows of parked cars. It had been hours and he hadn't come back. Not yet.

The woman in bed was singing rude songs and demanding company in the other room but she had closed the door and she didn't want to go back there again. She went into the living room to smoke and not think.

She looked out of the window at the tower on the other

side of the world that was full up with faces and lives all lined side by side and praying to the barking God. Dog. She wanted to see them better so she turned on the kitchen light but when she looked into the glass again all she saw was her own face looking back into the room. That's all she ever saw. She was hungry. It was dark.

I think we should watch a video, she said to Plastic Jesus.

He looked at her and bobbed his head.

She went into the bedroom that she decided was hers and she fetched her video from the pile of books that she had shaped into stacks and she looked at it in the light that hung in rows in the hall. Dorothy stared up from the front of the video box.

She brought the film and Plastic Jesus into the living room that was clean and empty as though it had only been lived in for a few hours or days and no longer than that. She couldn't tell what colour the walls were. They were a shade before colour. A shade to which normally colour is applied. Clay or that grey-brown shade made by rolling too many bright strips of Plasticine together. Like Dorothy's world before she steps out into that other place all done up like a rabbit dream.

There were no carpets or mats in the room. There was only a hard wooden floor with black stains and tea rings and it collected all the cold and it creaked and moaned when she walked across it. Beneath the window was a settee and it was broken the same way Dad's had been. Next to the settee there was a small table with one leg missing.

She closed the door and pulled the TV away from the wall as much as she could without dragging the cables too far and she looked at the little video player on the shelf beneath it. The TV was skinny and the player was flat and there was no room for people in one and no room for videos in the other. She looked at it for a long time. Looked at Dorothy who grinned from the front cover so happy and daft, looking at something she couldn't see. She poked a button and then another and a lip came slowly out of the middle. It was thin. Small. It had space only for something round and flat. She felt it with her fingers and looked at her video again. It wasn't the right shape or size for her film. She pushed the lip back in. Dorothy shouted curses from the yellow side of the room.

She couldn't play her video. This was not her home. She cried for herself and cried for Dorothy and cried for Dad who had been shoved into a box by the new front door. The woman in the bed shouted shut the fuck up and she wiped her eyes and looked at the blank TV and didn't make another sound. She smoked. Next to the small player there was a stack of films but the boxes were too small to hold videos and when she opened them up she saw only CDs with shiny silver faces and writing that she couldn't read. She took a CD out of the box and looked at it and went back to the video player that wasn't a video player and she pressed the button for the lip to come out and when it did she lay the disc down and pressed the button and sent the lip back again. The TV flashed and turned on. The screen was green and bright. The film from the box played on the screen and she watched it and blew smoke and waited for Lucky to find her there.

The film was good. Funny. Different. She hated it.

She turned the TV off. Outside of the window in the living room was a concrete balcony with a column and a rusted metal pole and a little light that came on whenever something walked past it or the wind caught it wrong. There was a man. It flashed on. There was a bird. It flashed on. There was a black cat and it sprang onto the wall opposite the window and watched the light and bent its unblinking face and flicked its tail and then looked through the window where she was sitting looking out. She looked at the cat. It couldn't see her in the room. She came to the window and rested her hands on the cold glass and watched the little thing while it played and rested. It looked at the window and then it looked at the ground and balanced on its paws and raised its back. She came back into the room and watched another film and the mad clock in the other room banged its head and told her that the hour was fifteen.

Cats are things that hunt, Dad said in her head.

What do they hunt?

Whatever they want to eat.

Can we have a cat?

No.

Why?

Remember the fish.

She was thinking of Lucky when she saw the shadow moving on the balcony outside and heard the sound of someone coughing. The TV faded between two scenes and a cartoon mouse preached about family underneath a falling heavy boot. That's just life. She went into her pocket and twisted the lipstick up and used the green glow from the TV and her reflection in the black window to draw the red fat lines on her mouth. She closed her eyes and listened to the sound of the key clicking in the door and she pressed her lips together and waited for the ugly love to spread into the room.

She opened her eyes. A boy stood by the frame of the door. He wasn't Lucky. He was a boy. Not a dark visitor with a noose in his fist and dogs snapping around his ankles but a short boy with blond hair stuck into a knife-edge above his head. He wore baggy jeans turned up above his ankles held up by red braces and boots that spilled their tongues and twisted their laces around and around. Dark eyebrows. Bitten lips. A boy. He had a picture of Plastic Jesus on his tee shirt with big fat red lines running through and writing she couldn't read just above that. He twisted the keys in his hand and looked at her with little eyes that shone bright in the TV glow. His mouth was open. She could see the shine of something silver that covered his teeth in lines and she could feel his eyes wandering down and then up and she brought her hand to her mouth and wiped the lipstick away.

You're not Lucky, she said.

The boy slipped the keys into his jacket and stood still with rainwater dripping off his cheeks and off the end of his freckled nose. He made little noises and twitched the corners of his mouth and jerked his chin and head this way and then the other way and his body twitched too, strange and uncontrolled in the glowing hall.

Are you making fun of me? she said.

No. I can't help it.

I don't believe you.

It's true. I can't help doing it.

If you wanted to stop doing something you could.

Not this.

Who are you?

I live here. I'm Tick.

Tick is a funny name.

My real name is.

That's worse.

I know.

The boy looked at her. He brought the keys back out of his pocket and played with them in his hands and jerked his chin again. He wiped his face with the sleeves of his jacket and clenched his jaw and relaxed it again. She couldn't hear anything on the outside of the front door. The little noises and movements the boy made kept her in the living room and out of her own head. She watched him like TV. When he talked his teeth shone like treasure.

What school do you go to? he said.

I don't go to any school.

Cool. I wish I didn't have to go.

I think I'm too old.

How old are you?

Seventeen.

You look my age.

How old are you?

Thirteen.

He stepped into the room and she stepped back to the corner and didn't take her eye from him. She had never seen a boy before. His eyes pulsed big and black like the eyes of her father and his hair was the same shade of wheat as

161

Lucky's and his mouth was just like the woman in the bed, slim and curved upwards. The blue-green-orange-yellow neon light had come on again on the outside and it shone through the little slit in the letterbox. In another room the cuckoo barked like a dog. It was the hour fifteen. Again. She looked at the stolen shoes on her feet. It was the hour fifteen. Time had not moved an inch.

He stood and looked at her where she had brought herself to stand closer with her arms folded over her chest. She looked at him and he looked at her and his mouth was open and she could see the shine of the silver cable that lined his funny little teeth. He didn't doglook her. Not even once.

Who are you then? he said.

Anna. I came from. I live here.

I live here too.

Lucky said you hadn't come home in ages.

He tried to stop me from going out last time so I decided to punish him. I do whatever I want when I want to do it. I'm in charge of myself. When someone tells me not to do something I deliberately do it. They can't stop me.

She thought on this. The boy rubbed the tracks on his teeth with his tongue.

Lucky brought me here, she said.

He jerked his head to the left and flicked his jaw and thumped himself in the leg and made a whooping noise.

He took something from his pocket that was flat as a cigarette paper and wrapped in foil and he opened the foil and took out whatever was inside and threw the foil on the floor and shoved the thing in his mouth and chewed it. The boy didn't speak. He looked at her for a while and when he was done with that he walked towards her and then went past her and as he passed he laid one of the foil sweeties into her hand and went off into the kitchen without saying anything else.

She opened the packet and smelled the sweet. It smelled like toothpaste. Sugar. Lemon. She folded it into her mouth and rolled the foil into a ball and flicked it onto the floor next to Plastic Jesus who was still bobbing with the affirmations of before. In the kitchen the boy was singing and clattering and he made so much noise she couldn't think on her mother or father or the moths or the black bags or the creaking face of Plastic Jesus or the bad mood bird or anything else that was clinging to the roots inside her head. She thought of nothing. She was empty.

Finally.

She leaned on the wall in the kitchen exactly as she had done the day before when Lucky made milky white tea and talked of Dad and love and miserable lives that couldn't be changed. She looked at the boy but didn't want him to know it so every time he looked at her she looked away or pretended to fall asleep. He laughed. His voice was broken up like a scratched record. He looked like Lucky, and didn't.

What are you doing? she said.

Making a sandwich. Do you want one?

Do you know where Lucky is?

Don't know. Don't care.

I'm hungry.

Okay then.

He opened a jar that he had got from the fridge and he stuck in a knife and scooped out white cream from the inside and chucked it on top of a slice of bread and spread it around. He went back into the jar and scooped out more white stuff and spread it over a second slice and stuck the two slices together on a plate with the stuff in the middle. She could smell eggs. Salt. She was hungry. He cut the crust off the edge of the bread and cut the slices into triangles and he slid the plate to her. She watched him working on his own sandwich. The light from the bulb that he had turned on in the living room sat upon his shoulder and the cat from before came to the wall on the outside to watch them eat.

He bit into his sandwich and looked at her as he chewed.

She drew her own plate close. What is it?

Mayonnaise.

I've never had it before.

Try it.

It smelled like eggs and chemicals and vinegar and sweets and looked like something Dad would've used to stick the wallpaper back to the walls or reattach the bathroom tiles to the place above the bathroom sink. It was different. She picked it up and bit the bread and tasted the bitterness that ran along the edges of her tongue and rolled beneath all sour and creamy and. She finished it all and so did the boy and the cat jumped away from the wall outside.

Are they Lucky's glasses? he said.

He gave them to me.

They look better on you.

I don't believe you.

I normally don't lie.

The boy was strange, wonderful. The taste of the sandwich was still in her mouth and she pushed her tongue around and mopped all the flavours that had sunk into her gums. His face twitched and he made those little noises again and he swore for no reason fuck, fuck, fuck and wiped his mouth with the back of his hand.

I don't have to swear, he said. I like doing it. I can get away with it easy because people just think it's one of my tics. It's not. I just enjoy doing it. Like smoking.

I like smoking.

Smoking is an act of bravery.

I've been smoking since I was eight.

You must have a cool Dad.

Do you know why Lucky is called Lucky?

He didn't speak.

What does it say on your top? she said.

He pulled the shirt out and pointed to each word. This is a picture of Jesus and above it the words say I hate Jesus. I hate Jesus. There. It's funny because it's true. Also, Jesus isn't real but some people think he is and I want them to know I don't like him and I don't like them and everything is a big joke. Couldn't you read what it said? Don't you think everything is a big joke?

He talked so fast it was like hearing ten different voices all at once fast and slow and back and forth and she listened but she couldn't understand everything he said. The silver track in his mouth reflected the light from the bulb and he laughed and when he did he laughed silver and when he talked he talked silver and when he smiled he smiled with more silver than she had ever seen in one place before. Every part of him jumped and ticked and laughed and jerked. He was a carnival. He was many fish.

My Hey Dee Dee medicine gave me Tourette's, he said. I don't have Hey Dee Dee though and I never did. I don't listen to boring people and I don't like rules and I like to do whatever I want and I like to draw mad things and because of that they told me I had to take medicine. Tablets. I could write and draw and paint and everything before but I don't do that now. Some prick of a teacher told Lucky I didn't listen and some prick of a doctor told Lucky the same and they gave me some tablets and told me to sit still and now I can't sit still even if I really wanted to. I told my teacher that school is a big fucking joke. Don't you think school is a big fucking joke?

I don't know, I've never been.

Don't bother; it's a big fucking.

What if I wanted to go?

You're too old now.

Well. I.

One teacher accused me of cheating on a test because my mark was so good and he didn't think I could do that. I told him I was just trying to make my Mum proud. Another teacher accused me of plagiarism when I wrote a short story for school and it was the best thing she'd ever read and that's why she said the work wasn't mine. I said I didn't know what plagiarism meant and she didn't believe me. After that I decided not to be good at anything anymore. I decided to be thick and mad and mean and to swear and smoke and piss in the kitchen sink and drink whatever I want. I don't go to school much. I don't listen. It's all so funny. It's such a big game. I'm not a good boy anymore. I'm a little shit.

He laughed.

Do you like being a little shit?

I try to be worse.

He smiled and laughed and said fuck and hit his thigh with his fist and jerked his neck so much he had to rub on his collarbone. She said sometimes I feel like being bad. I think about bad things and then I do them.

I do bad things when Lucky tells me not to.

Where is Lucky?

Don't know. I told you.

Will he come back?

Don't care. I saw him outside earlier. He was walking back from one of the flats carrying a box of food and he told me to go home. He told me about you.

What did he say?

He told me he was helping you. Saving you was what he said. I had to come back so I could see you. He doesn't normally bring his work home with him. He usually goes outside to fix and mend everything and then he leaves it all there and comes back and goes straight to sleep. I had to see you.

Why did you have to see me?

I thought maybe I could ruin you.

Plastic Jesus nodded from another part of the house and the noise returned in small waves that came gently against the window. She looked at the boy and the boy looked at her. In his eye that was brighter than Lucky's was a little speck of shining glass that she thought she could see her reflection in.

You're different to the others, he said. Better. I thought that maybe I could ruin you. But I think you're already ruined and that's a good thing. I bet Lucky knows it. You don't have to wait around for anyone else to come and fix you. You're not really broken and you're not fixed either but being fixed is like something that stays in a plastic case and never comes out and never gets chipped or damaged or seen. Being ruined is like being free. Don't you want to be seen? Don't you think you're good as you are? I know I am. I'm fucking perfect in every way and wherever I go I make another perfect mess. You're perfect too. Perfectly broken. Lucky told me I should try to keep you in but I'm not going to do that. I'm going to take you outside. What do you think of that?

I don't know. I don't think anything.

That's good. Don't think. Get out of your head.

I'm out, and I feel tired.

That'll pass. Pretty soon you'll be electric.

He sat on top of the counter and looked at her hands and then looked out of the window. She felt her heart sliding down to the soles of her feet and felt the moths dancing inside a cage inside another cage inside her head. She poked her tongue through the gap in her teeth. I think you should ignore everyone, the boy said. I think you should do whatever you want any time you want to do it. Don't let anyone trap you. You should be able to cause as much chaos as you want because you're not dead. When you're dead and you don't have a choice, that's when you'll regret that you ever listened to anyone.

She looked at her shoes all red and clean apart from a little white spot of mayonnaise that had spilled from her bread when she had eaten too fast. She wiped it in the carpet and went to the settee and got onto the cushion and held the wall and jumped up and down like she used to when Dad had been chasing rabbit too long to care. She did the drums like Tick. She did them better. Shook the bugs from the nooks inside her head and thought of nothing but the beating heart in her toes.

The boy laughed and the silver in his mouth shone and Dad was knocked back into that part of her mind that forgets to brush her teeth. Mum was gone too like a passing flash she never really believed she'd seen. Everything was everywhere. Burning. Gathering. Smoking. It was all over the rainbow. Chucked in the left eye of the green witch and down into the toilet bowl. And the boy was a fish. The boy was alive and jerking his fins and spinning through all the weather that he caused. Real.

Dog on the Wall

THE BOY'S NAME was Matthew. Or something.

Lucky was still gone and Tick was making faces in the mirror and she was standing behind him watching his ear that twitched slightly when her breath blew there. He turned around and looked at her and the shining glass in his eye flashed green and then yellow. They went into the living room and turned the TV off and went into the hallway and he took his key into his hand and she was standing behind him thinking about. He twisted the key in the lock and then he stopped and turned around and he was silent and still. He looked at her.

Did you hear something?

No, she said.

Listen.

The woman in the bed called from the other room and Tick looked at his shoes and became as still as Plastic Jesus in a dark empty room. He drew his eyebrows together and rubbed his cheek and spat the chunk of gum he was chewing into the skirting where it landed and stuck and attracted an ant that got stuck there too. They listened to the sound of his name being called louder and louder and haunting the dusty room at the end of the hall. She said you don't have to listen and she took two steps towards the door and twisted the key again but he stopped her and walked back down the hallway half covered in green light.

He went into the room.

She followed. The boy changed his face to smiles and winks and she watched him in the crack of the door that he left open behind him. She looked at the woman wrapped in the blanket with one loose breast peeping out and watched Tick step into the middle of the room and hardly look at anything at all. He stood there and the woman watched him and neither of them spoke until.

I just wanted to look at you, the woman said.

Tick played with his fingers and rubbed the edge of his shoes together. The dust fell. The curtains drifted out and then they were sucked back to the window again. The woman looked at Tick and then she turned around and faced the wall and pulled the blanket around her shoulders again. Tick said something in the room that she couldn't hear from where she stood. He whispered it so gentle and calm that it didn't even disturb the dust. He muttered the same thing over and over. He turned around and came out of the room. She leaned in to hear. She walked with him down the hall and she watched his mouth working on the quiet words.

I am me. I am me. I am me.

What did you say?

Nothing.

The light that had come through the little window above the front door had become stronger as the sun sank and the sky changed to orange. It would soon sink below the hills and then the buildings and the men and women would sit in their living rooms and eat from their laps and their children would watch TV and laugh for a long lovely while with little dogs warming their ankles. She took the key in her hand and twisted it inside the lock and the door clicked and opened.

Outside.

The boy locked the door and went across the balcony and climbed the wall and stood on it high above the rest of the world to show her that he was afraid of nothing. She got up there too and looked out at the dark and all the lights that spread out behind the tower and the reds and yellows and greens that trailed behind cars as they sped up and slowed down along that long black road.

Never look down, he said. Balance. Don't look there. Look straight ahead. You're not up high, you're down low. This is all a game.

I've a feeling we're not in. It was all a game.

He got down and held her hand and she walked upon the wall and felt the wind rushing around her legs and through the sleeves of her tee shirt and under her arms that were wet from all the fun and all the fear. She went to the end of the wall and jumped onto the path and walked beside the boy down the concrete corridor and listened to the people that lived inside the houses all the way along. Tick watched her. Sometimes she watched him. He showed her a brick and a potted plant and a child's bike left to rust outside a broken front door and a word written over and over again in red paint on a wall. He took her onto the bridges that webbed the towers. They went through thick doors that took them inside and then outside and inside again and he showed her how to take the stairs two by two and slide down railings and he showed her how to spit at cats. He talked about his Mum but she didn't listen. He didn't talk about Lucky and she wished he had.

They walked on a dark path between the towers and followed a fence that was topped with razor wire down to an open space that smelled of smoke and meat. A man

walked out from the dark and another came out after him
both with long beards and red sores on their foreheads and
brown stains on their clothes and teeth. The first man held
up a sign and the other stamped out fires that were not
there. She turned to Tick and asked him what was written
there and he kept walking and didn't speak and didn't look
at the men and didn't look at her.

In the town that was lined up along both sides of the
black road there were boarded shopfronts with cracked
lights. Cars came and went speeding up and slowing down
carrying people who looked at her as she looked at them.
The lights shone in endless greens and yellows and the boy
pushed her and she jostled him. Men and women with signs
and without came and talked nonsense into their ears. Spare
change please? How many times do I have to tell you? There
was a baby and now she's gone. I can't find my Mum. You
kids. They told me I did it but she was strung up before I
got there. The best day of my life is not today. On and on
chattering and spewing their thoughts drunk and smart as
machines that worked in ways she couldn't understand. She
threw her hands over her face and laughed into her hands
but didn't know why. Tick smiled at her with that little speck
of glass spinning forever in the reaches of his fat open eyes.
The streets were beautiful. Ugly. Just like her, him, Lucky,
Dad, Dorothy and everything else.

A shop was open and Tick went inside. She followed him through the aisles that were lined with sweets and toys and dust and food with dirty packaging and a man who stood behind a counter and watched them. Bars of light radiated pink and hot above each aisle. The floor was sticky and spotted with gum that had been walked flat and indented with the patterns of small shoes. She had only seen the inside of a shop on TV and she stopped to look and touch the things that lined the floor in rows and boxes that spewed out multicoloured packets of crisps and cereal and coffee and small rat shaped holes. Tick went onwards to the corner of the shop and looked back at the counter that had disappeared from view behind one of the shelves and he took a packet of sweets and a bottle of pop and a magazine from a stand and asked her if she was playing.

What?

Are. You. Playing?

She nodded and watched him and did what he showed her. She picked a necklace made of hard sweets from a plastic box and a packet of crisps and she stuffed them up her tee shirt like Tick and held them there. They heard the pop of a chair and the quick feet of the brown-eyed man as he came down one of the aisles. Her heart was wild in her chest and she looked at Tick and Tick looked at her and they both started and then they were both running. They left the shop and ran through the streets and hit the shoulders and arms of strangers so hard that the sweets burst through the bags and exploded in a rattle on the pavement. They laughed. Her heart was bigger than it had ever been. The voice of the man that had shouted after them grew quiet as they went over a black hill and onto a path and over the green and found a bench to sit on awhile. They calmed their chests and watched rough men and children who gathered under a bridge to start little fires and go to sleep with their clothes on.

You see that? Did you see me not giving a shit? he said.

Oh damn yes.

I don't listen to anyone.

I'm glad.

You shouldn't either.

I won't.

Not even if Lucky tells you to do something.

I feel so. I'm too far gone now.

They ate the sweets they had saved and drank the pop and sat beneath the streetlights whose faces were shattered on the grass below. The air was cold and it filled her all the way to her feet when she breathed in. They ate and then they smoked and when they were done with that they walked upon the path that cut across a large garden that led back to the estate. The air was grey. Thick. The ends of her fingers were cold and she warmed them on a patch of grass that was blackened by a fire that hadn't long died down.

She was awake. Bright. More awake than ever. And her heart was. They walked beneath a thick concrete bridge with silver fencing along the top and bins turned over and brick towers loaded up towards the sky where the moon was swollen big and fat and beating between the flashes of light and cloud and smoke. Tick ran ahead and she chased him and they knocked on a door and ran away. When they were on the black road again she looked at him.

Why is Lucky named Lucky?

He stopped and went into his pocket and brought out a silver lighter and crouched on a patch of dry grass and tried to ignite a flower. He's called Lucky because he can't die, he said. He's invincible. Didn't I tell you that already? He's called Lucky because he tried to kill himself four times and it's never worked. He survived all of it. He tried hanging himself with a tie and it snapped in four places. He tried cutting his wrists but a retired doctor found him while he'd been out walking his dog. He tried swallowing pills but his body just kept throwing them back up again. He first tried killing himself when he was a few years older than you, what do you think of that?

I don't know.

Tick burned the petals of the flower and then he held the

lighter against the dry grass until the flames took and began to whip. He stood up again and walked along the path and she followed.

He tried to do it, he said, but he failed each time so he decided not to try anymore. He woke up one morning and decided that Jesus or someone was telling him he had to live because he had to help someone. He's been going through people ever since, trying to find that one person he has to help before he's allowed to die. He's helped a lot of people. He does everything for them. He's selfish like that.

Why do they need help?

Everyone needs help. Watch the news. Take a walk. People are poor and nuts. They're sad. Look at those people with signs over there and you can see for yourself why they need help. Look at what they say. Too hungry to beg for food. Been made redundant. Need a job. Kids to feed. Benefits stopped. Kids starving. Can only eat what my kids don't finish. Need to work. Need anything. Any spare change? Will accept any job. I don't have to read them all to know what they say. People are poor. Unhappy. Downtrodden. Too hardworking. Not the right work. Abandoned. It's not their fault. It's not anyone's fault. It's their own fault. It's just the way things are. I don't know. Watch the news. Nobody cares about them. Not even me. See it all for yourself. Or don't. Watch cartoons instead. Watch cartoons and you'll be happy just like me. Watch TV just like anyone. It's good.

She watched Tick while he talked and she looked at his shoulder and then at his hand that jerked at his side. She reached slowly and opened her fingers and slipped her hand inside his. He stopped and looked at her. He was still. They looked at each other. He tucked his chin to his chest and smiled. His cheeks grew roses. They walked on. They held hands and kicked the beer cans that were chucked along the path and she tried to climb the fences that were still wet from the rain that had fallen sometime in the twenty-ninth hour while she was asleep. Somewhere along the black road a dog barked and a woman screamed and a pack of drunks went running into the dark and she didn't care about being happy or being bad or feeling sad for others. She only cared about being alive. Being outside. Smoking cigarettes. Eating sweets. Playing games. Fast cars. Ugly love. That's all. And that's just life.

She was outside longer than she had ever been before. She shivered. Tick talked and the talking sped up and she listened and tried to force his sentences together in her head but she couldn't. She didn't feel well. His words went from his mouth into the air and sailed colourful and fast on the smoke waves that rose up from the tower block. Between the wooden wall and the estate she took off her glasses and closed her eyes to give them a rest from all those green fizzing shapes. There were black boxes shoved underneath a concrete balcony alongside the path and they were marked with white numbers four and six and eight and inside there were black bags stuffed too fat that rose up out of those thick plastic mouths like food that had not been swallowed. Some were tied and others were open and she could smell all the junk that was going bad on the inside. She didn't think of her mother and didn't think of Dad. Chasing rabbits and. She didn't think of any of it. Not even once. Not even when it was. She was hungry.

I want to see what your eyes look like, the boy said. He tried to take her hands off her face but she wouldn't let him. What colour are they? What do they look like? I bet your eyes are nice.

She was stronger and taller than him and he struggled and then he returned his hands to his pockets and jerked his chin.

Ugly, she said, and put the glasses on again.

You shouldn't say that about yourself.

Ugly isn't bad. Ugly is ugly.

They walked. There was a long concrete staircase with a blue rail that led to another patch of concrete separate from everything else. Beyond that was a path and beyond that was another tower and above everything were stairs and bridges and more wire and railings in blue and green and red paint chipped and peeling and squeaking with all the noise of disuse. On the path there was an abandoned wet coat and a deflated orange ball and a doll that cried when she stepped on it with her broken red shoes. The path split into two and went around a wide patch of wet grass and through towers that broke apart at either side. The patch of grass led to a park that Tick wanted her to see.

The park was set in a wide hollow in the ground where the concrete was laid flat but had been churned along the edges into mounds of dust and broken stone that raised up underneath their feet as they walked. In the middle of the hollow were tall metal frames that stood holding hands like iron skeletons. They were bolted together and he said they used to be red but were then peeling and flaking like burnt skin into orange and grey. Beneath one of the frames was a rubber seat that had two chains on either end hung long and low, connecting it to the frame again. The seat swung when the wind blew and she steadied it and looked at all the other frames with turning swinging parts and she looked at it all as it stood there shining in the concrete.

She thought that she had seen it before. Something like it, years ago. When the sky was dark and there were no people around and her mother pressed her hands against her back and pushed her so high and so fast that she lost the ground and the sky and everything became the same. One colour. Dizzy. Wild. She closed her eyes and thought hard. Her thoughts were fragments in which she recognized only the closed doors and windows of the rooms in which she stood. It was. And no. The past would not stay still. She looked through the green glass once more and though she didn't see anything she heard something in the back of her mind and far away. It was some kind of music, clicking, a driving rain and then.

She heard it all from the long ago and it was. She heard the word fuck over and over. There was a breeze kicking dust into the air. There were children talking fast and loud and running with unlaced shoes and there was a knock and the smell of burning. There was a fast suck and then came the slow quiet. It sounded like. They were all the sounds that ever were and they were jumbled and slipping inside her head. It sounded like something she had been waiting to hear for years. It sounded like her mother. Stupid. Gone.

This is our park, Tick said. I used to come here all the time when I was a kid with Mum and now I just use it as a place to smoke or whatever. I watch the little kids sometimes. When they go home I tie the swing to the frame so they can't reach it and I have a good laugh about that. I sometimes hide under the slide when I'm supposed to be in school and sometimes I pick up those rocks and throw them against that wall there. People chuck all their rubbish down here, like that old fridge with the door off. I once pissed in that.

They walked through the park and she touched the junk that was thrown along the edge like the junk that swayed and creaked along the edges of her museum. There was a kettle with the plug broken off and the cord broken into three pieces and twisted back through the spout and into the bowels again. There was a rusted fridge that smelled like piss and a microwave with a smashed face and a broken mirror with bulbs all down the sides that she looked into and pretended to be beautiful.

How come you look *into* a mirror and look *at* everything else?

Beats the shit out of me, the boy said.

Tick picked up a stone and so did she. He chucked his so hard it cracked into pieces and coughed up dust when it landed against the hard broken back of an old TV. She raised the stone high. The wall that went all the way around was higher inside the park than outside of it because the path level was raised against the towers and the park seemed to have been dug up out of the ground. A child's bicycle lay discarded and rusted on a pile of stones. A scooter was planted in the dirt. A toy man lay headless and alone. A dog barked. She dropped the stone next to her feet and wiped the dust off her clothes. She looked at the wall.

What's that? she said.

That's the bit of the wall they were going to knock down to get the machines in to start work on the new park. It's partly knocked down now and there's a gap over there with rubble all about and it's pretty dangerous but most kids can climb it. It's a bit of a building site. There's some tiff going on about something so the men stopped working on it. It's kind of like a building site with an old swing set and slide in the middle and we're not supposed to play here but there's fuck all else to do so whatever. He lit a cigarette and gave it to her and lit one for himself and they sat on the swing and smoked.

She didn't understand him. He looked at her when he thought she couldn't see and then he looked away and smiled into his pack of smokes. Although he had Lucky's eyes he was not Lucky. He was boyish and rude and quick and loud and the estate was an audience that turned back and sat down to watch him. He talked too fast and drew looks from birds and dogs and naked children with their faces pressed against windows. He was young and yet so much older than her.

She got inside the rusted shell of an abandoned car with no seat and pretended to drive it and said sit next to me

I'll take you someplace. He got into the passenger side and pretended to press the buttons for the radio and started whistling songs through his front teeth. He sang. She took his mind to the films she'd seen growing up and spoke the words from famous scenes and talked about endings that weren't always happy but always mattered. He listened. He told her they could do whatever they wanted because there were no walls or old men to stop them and when they were outside they didn't have to follow rules and they didn't have to listen. She got out of the car and so did he and he picked up a stone and so did she and they threw the stones far into the sky and beyond the edges of the estate. She pointed. What's that? she said.

That's the dog on the wall.

The dog was painted on the inside of the wall and it was big and black and it watched her as she watched it. She lowered the other stone she had picked up and tossed it into a bucket that was half filled with water and floating bits of leaf and dirt. The dog had a mane of black fur that stuck out star shaped and wild and a shiny black nose and grey patches and pointed ears and feet ready to run and a tail ready to whip and a wide laughing mouth and big yellow eyes.

He's laughing at me, she said.

No he isn't.

I don't like him.

Why?

I don't like his eyes.

Why?

I've seen them somewhere before.

The junk dog would not turn away and she picked up another stone and threw it as hard as she could and it smashed against the wall into specks and stars. Her legs were sinking into the ground like the lopsided swing or the burnt out car that had no tyres on one side. Inside the tower a child ran around a table in a room behind glass and its mother caught up and slowed down and sent it off running wild again. In another room a baby was held up to that cold artificial light glowing green in a million different rooms that were all the same. A man scratched his bare chest and smoked and leaned over the side of one of the concrete balconies. There was nothing left of Dad but that one big eye beating grey and cold above the tower. She could see too much of everything on the outside and too much of what was inside and she could see everything that was and everything that hadn't happened yet. She could see nothing at all and she wanted to disappear.

Tick held her hand and said fuck really loud.

She laughed.

Do you want to see something?

She looked at him and he looked at her. He had a serious

face and his body didn't jerk once while he spoke. The freckles on his face blended into pale skin and the Plastic Jesus on his top seemed to sit on his chest and nod yes, yes, yes, so happy to be surrounded by all the colours of hate. His eyes were big and she saw her own face twice over in the shine there. She was hungry.

Something you're not supposed to see, he said.

Yes.

That's good.

I want to see all the things I'm not supposed to see.

Good.

I want to do the things I'm not supposed to do.

He squeezed her hand and she squeezed back. The dog on the wall looked at them and tossed his tail about and began to bark and the Dog in heaven stayed quiet and let the world chase its own hairless tail. They stood up and left the swinging seats and walked back along the slant of rubble and broken junk. They went beyond the wall and through heavy doors and shouted and called and swore to the empty corners of empty stairways. She didn't turn again to look into the eye of the dog as she went and didn't turn to think of her father or her mother who both died over and over again somewhere far behind, in wide colourless rooms, a long, long time ago.

Please Knock

I'M HUNGRY. I'M hungry. I'm hungry. I'm hungry. I'm hungry. I'm hungry. I'm hungry. I'm hungry. I'm hungry. I'm hungry. I'm hungry. I'm hungry. I'm hungry. I'm hungry. I'm hungry. I'm hungry. I'm.

You talk too much.

The boy walked and she followed. Chip-shop and take-away smells bellowed on the back of the smoke and steam that washed over the black road and then down the paths where good people did terrible things for no good reason. Four people smoked out of the back of a building that could've been a Chinese or Indian or anything and they looked at her as she passed. A cat chewed a piece of plastic. Its little tooth bright and sharp in the green light. A tribe of people ran. Somewhere someone cried but it wasn't her. It was nobody.

Where are we going?

Not too far. Round here. Up a bit. There.

He slid his arm around her waist and she didn't stop him and they walked like that beneath the sky and she thought about everything and her thoughts were misshapen and strange. Round the wooden wall slashed with curses and long letters and up a concrete staircase with an iron rail painted blue was a row of flats too short to be another tower block. There were gardens outside and crumbling walls and crooked paths that were narrow and raised towards red front doors and the grass was not cut and the windows were not cleaned and everything was slanted under a thirty year press that would take another thirty years to fall. There was a road outside. There was the rain washed pavement and a wall and a half-paved half-grassed field with concrete blocks and big red metal doors that Tick said were garages.

A place to put cars, he said. Metalwork. Hobbies. Boxing bags. Old stuff you don't want anymore. Somewhere to stash what you don't want anyone else to find.

They sat on one of the half-fallen walls that went around the garages and they tried to kick each other's shoes off. They were watching one of the flats in the middle of the street when the light came on and a man in dark clothes stood looking out through the window. It was Lucky. The boy watched his father with one hand in his jacket pocket and the other holding the end of a cigarette that he brought to his mouth and supped in sharp bursts. He kept the smoke behind his teeth. His mouth was twisted. His chin jerked. He blew two jets of white smoke through his nose. His eyes were slanted against the lifting smoke and she thought that he watched Lucky like she sometimes watched Dad. With monstrous love and anger and fear and care and pity all spilled from a loose cage. Contempt. Fear. Irritation. Need. And such longing.

All the lights on that side of the street were smashed or wounded and the dark closed around them where they sat. They held hands. A habit. She watched the lovely ugly man who stood straightening the curtains in the window and felt the moths in her stomach wake in dust. Lucky turned in the window and went into another room and sat down and talked to a small man and laid his hand on his shoulder and then on his head. He stood up and went into his pocket and took out his wallet and counted out the bills and handed them to the man who cried into the money like it was his own mind or his own heart broken into pieces and falling through his fingers. Lucky rested his hands on his shoulder again and took off his jacket and wrapped it around the crying man and then he went off and came back and handed him a steaming cup. He said something that she couldn't hear. The man rested the cup on his knee and held the money to his forehead. He looked up again as Lucky left the room and she saw his eyes that were dazed and lost and searching the room as though he was looking for a TV or a remote or his own Plastic Jesus that was not nodding in the corner. Lucky opened the front door and lit a cigarette and smoked it and it shone ginger in his eyes and he closed the door and walked the garden path and went through a gate that was hanging off its hinges. He stood for a moment in the middle of the road. He smoked in the dark and scratched his face and looked at them standing on the other side of the street but didn't see them near the garage door. He was older than she remembered. Hunched over. A crow. In the bad wind. He rubbed his eyes and crossed his arms against the cold and walked away and went down the road looking at his own two feet that were as slow and soundless as the smoke he blew into the sky.

When the little light from the end of Lucky's cigarette disappeared around a corner the boy went into the middle of the road and stood watching the window. She followed. They stood there while the man inside finished his hot mug and rubbed his face and when he was done with that he stood up and pulled his arms through Lucky's jacket and went to the front door and opened it. He came into the road and didn't speak. The boy went into his pocket and took out a clear plastic packet with a round white sweet inside. She got closer. On one side of the sweet was a little rabbit with long, long ears. Tick gave it to the man and the man handed the boy all the money that had come out of Lucky's wallet. He held the little white sweet in his hand and then held it to his head and he said bless you, bless you, bless you over and over and walked backwards stumbling into his own front door again. The boy stuck his cigarette back into his mouth, turned to the girl in the dark street steaming with green smoke, and smiled.

That's how it is, he said. That's me, winning.

The boy bought a pack of biscuits from a shop that didn't close except to eat and piss for five minutes at a time. Afterwards they sat in the park and looked at the dog on the wall and ate the biscuits one by one until the whole pack was empty. On the other side of the world Lucky went into a door and came out of another one and so on and so on all through the cold night while they watched. Tick said that he was a man and Lucky didn't know it. He said he was king. He was master and head teacher and he was Jesus and all the heroes from all the films she'd ever seen. She looked at him and he looked at her. He looked at his feet that scraped the floor when she pushed him on the swing.

I'm saving up for a car and when I get it I'm going to load

my stuff in the boot and I'm going to just drive off forever. I'm not coming back either. No fucking way. I hate this fucking place. If you stay here for long enough it gets into your blood and you can't leave. You stay here and so do your kids and so do their kids and nobody ever does anything and nobody sees anything and nobody ever leaves. You start thinking that there's nothing over that wall. I've seen it happen. I've seen parents begging their kids to be different in the same place that their parents took them aside in nineteen seventy whenever and said the same thing. It's the place that makes them useless. The sameness. That's why I have to leave. I have to. I have to. There's plenty more fish in the sea and Mum can do better.

Better than Lucky?

Better than me.

They smoked. She was tired and so was he. They took turns swinging and pushing and they swung higher and faster to wake their bodies up so that they could stay awake longer than Tick had ever stayed awake before. She told him that she could stay awake easy because a long childhood of fake living room lights and loud TV had cursed her with insomnia and it meant she couldn't sleep much and it meant she was tired all the time. A moth came out of the dark and floated between the smoke and returned back into the dark again.

She could smell Lucky on her clothes and she thought of him then and thought of the woman with the long beautiful back. The boy got down from the swing and pretended to be tall. He looked at his little phone that he kept in his pocket and he lit it up and pressed the face and pressed it over and over and then he put it back into his pocket and threw a stone at the dog.

Mum wants me, he said. She says she wants me to come home so she can take a look at me. I don't know why she does that. It makes me feel weird. Like she thinks she's going to forget who I am. I don't want to go home. Let's walk around the estate a few times and you can talk and that'll keep me from falling asleep. Don't worry about Mum. She'll have to watch me in her head is all. If we walk this way I can show you all the ways to take if you're ever running from something. I can show you where to hide if you're ever feeling scared. I can show you all the places you shouldn't walk if you're ever walking on your own.

The Good Kiss

THE BOY BARKED like a dog in his sleep.

They were home. Tick wanted to go to bed and she didn't mind helping him along. He started off sleeping quiet and gentle and then he began to whimper like a lost little pup. She had been lying next to him in the same bed because he said he hated being on his own. They talked and looked at the ceiling and then the boy curled up on her chest and sucked on his knuckles that were raw from punching garage doors and he fell asleep while she sang Dorothy's songs. She listened to him when he made those little noises. He whimpered. Then he growled. Then he barked. The barks twisted into howls that went on and on while he moved his paws and chased after rabbits in his sleep.

She got out of bed and watched him. She was still in

her clothes, her tee shirt had begun to smell and so did her jeans and underwear and even Plastic Jesus who had been ignoring her these past few hours. Everything smelled like cider and burning junk and sweat and that lovely chemical spray in the black can that the boy used to make him feel good. Older. Better than himself.

Doesn't it?

I don't know, Dorothy.

Why don't you know?

What is better supposed to smell like?

Hey-Dee-Dee.

I'm hungry.

Hey-Dee-Dum.

In another room a door opened and closed and a key twisted in a lock and then it was released again and she knew that Lucky had come home. She stood in the frame of the door and opened it and watched Lucky wipe his face with Tick's school shirt that had been slung in the hall. He held it to his face and breathed deeply with his eyes half closed. Then he dropped it and stood there looking at his own hands in the green light. He had the hands of a woman. So she thought. She had noticed this about him the first time they met. They were softer than Dad's Slender. Hairless. Pretty. The fingers were long and the nails were picked clean and there were no blooming roses or black branches. He had the hands of a. All the better to touch.

He turned the light on in the hallway and went to the bathroom to piss and to think and when he came out again she was standing there under the swinging light waiting for him to look at her. She twisted her tee shirt in her hands and forced her hair behind her ears and didn't scratch or pick at her finger while he was watching.

I don't sleep well, she said.

I don't either, Sweetheart.

We're the same.

Maybe. Yes, I think.

He went into the kitchen and she followed him and he set aside two mugs and told her he was sorry for not staying with her when she needed him. She tried a smile and told him it was all right. She was all right. He made the tea and took the mugs into the living room and gestured for her to sit before he gave her the tea in her hands. She sat on one end of the settee and he sat on the other. He blew on his mug and she did the same though her tea was lukewarm and pale. He looked at her.

I would've come home sooner but I knew you were doing okay.

How did you know?

I saw you.

Where did you see me?

I saw you both. You were playing in the street. You were near the garages and Tick was sitting on the wall. I didn't say anything because I know he likes to think I don't see him, that I can't find him there in the dark, that I don't know the sound his shoes make when he's walking, or the way he sucks his braces when he's thinking about being naughty. I pretend not to notice him. It's just one of the games we play. I'll tell you something though, Sweetheart. I always have this secret hope that if I stand there long enough with my head down one day he'll come up to me or call out. I think to myself that he's going to call me today, tomorrow, two weeks from now, I'm going to stand there with my head down for long enough and I'm going to hear Dad, Dad, Dad in my son's voice. He's going to say that and sound just like he used to when he was five and he had a million questions in his head and he thought I was the only one with answers. Yeah, it'll be something, Sweetheart. Right now Dad would really be something.

He laid his head back and balanced his cup on his jeans.

I haven't heard that word in years, he said. It's funny, I didn't realize it until I was out last week trying to save somebody and a little boy in the park called out Dad to one of the men who was coming up the road after finishing a shift in the factory. The kid called out Dad and I dropped the box I was carrying and turned around and opened my arms. Strange right? I mean, I just turned around without even thinking. The kid ran right past me and down the street to his tired old man and I, I don't know, I stood there and then I picked up the box and went back to what I was doing. I felt so stupid. Then I realized how long it's been since I heard someone calling for Dad, and how long it's been since Dad was me.

He blew his tea and then sipped the rim.

Anyway, he said. I stand there and I wait but he always stays where he is. I don't know what he gets up to anymore and I'm done with trying to build walls around him. I told him he's not to go out after eight or nine and he goes out anyway. I told him not to drink and he drinks so much he has to get his stomach pumped. I tell him all the time not to start fires and he starts them anyway. He burns everything down. He's a good boy though. I know that makes me sound daft, like a blind fool, but I'm really not. He's good. He's not just good but honestly good. He has a good soul. I've seen it myself, but good people can make bad choices and that's just life. Life pushes us down streets that we don't want to walk through. Then we panic. Then we run. We run for our lives. We think we're getting away but we're just going faster in the same direction and we don't know how to stop. The boy is like me. I don't know what he gets up to when I'm not around. I haven't spent enough time with him lately. I'm glad he has someone else to spend time with though, a friend to keep him out of trouble. You, I mean. He's good. I'm terrible. I'm a lot worse than him, a lot worse, just the same as anyone.

They drank tea and sat and there was no noise except the noises the boy made from the other room fast asleep and running for his life. Lucky lay back and rested his head on the cushion and let all the air out of his chest slowly until he was empty and then he was still and breathless for a while. He looked up and finished off his tea and sat up again and rolled a smoke for himself and rolled her one too and lit them both.

Have you thought about what you want to do with your life? he said.

I didn't know I had to do something with it.

Everyone has to do something.

Do they? I just thought it was mine so it didn't matter.

It is yours, but nothing is free so you have to do something if you want money.

I don't want money.

Nothing is free and everything costs something and that's just life.

You say that a lot. Why can't life change?

Well, because everything goes in one direction really fast.

Like on the black road.

Like on any road there ever was.

He sat in silence and lay back again and looked at the ceiling. She was tired. She half listened to him as she closed her eyes and opened them again and looked at a spider that was climbing up the TV cable that stuck out to the side behind the Dee Vee Dee box. In the corner was an old table that was good for nothing because it leaned too much to the left and everything rolled from the top. Lucky was talking. She wasn't sure what he was saying anymore. She looked at the small wrinkles next to his eyes and at the yellow stains on his slim fingers. The smoke caught a draught of air and swam into the hallway where the green light burned it into nothing.

I don't want to be anything, she said. Is that so bad?

What do you mean?

I want to be nothing. I want to make no difference at all.

They smoked the hour away and he fell asleep. She looked at her red shoes and listened to the sound of his steady breathing and she cried into her hands because she had not done that for weeks or hours or. When she was done with crying the moths were gentle and faint and didn't bother her again.

She looked at Lucky. His mouth was open slightly and she could see the shine of his crooked front teeth and the grey hairs buried in the blond on his chin and she heard the sound of his tongue gently clicking against his gums and smelled the ash and dirt and petrol on his clothes. She slid towards him and he moved his head from the back of the seat to his shoulder and she placed her hand on his chest. Her heart drummed in her ears and her stomach twisted and tugged. She pushed her lips together, moved her hand to the back of his head, and pulled him gently closer. She didn't breathe and didn't talk and she stopped her heart for a little while. Everything was dark and silent and still. His breath was warm and smoky. She leaned in and closed her eyes and kissed him. She kissed him on the mouth. He didn't wake. She kissed him again. Softly. In the hallway there was a little creak and then the sound of a door closing. She could see herself in the TV screen. A beautiful shadow.

The Passenger

LUCKY WAS GONE from the settee and there was a note stuck to the TV screen that didn't say a thing in big red letters. She looked at the note and around it the TV fizzed with a black and white cancer that had come sometime during the seventeenth hour when the rain grew fat and noisy on the outside. She pressed the buttons on the remote control and changed the channel with the note still stuck to the screen and the news came on and a man talked about thieves and riots. She changed the channel and put on cartoons and left the cartoons running for the whole morning. She laughed. A mouse got hit on the head and refused to die and a cat laughed big and fat in his belly and she decided that there was more truth in that than in the news or in the writing she couldn't read.

She made jam and toast and ate it standing up in the kitchen. The boy was still asleep but he had stopped barking and his knuckle had come out of his mouth and when she checked on him she saw that his jaw was clenched and his eyes were half open. He wasn't awake. She listened at the door to the woman's bedroom and heard a faint whistling that became a song that didn't end while her face was pressed against the cold wood. She made another piece of toast and stood alone in the kitchen chewing on the crust and she wasn't hungry anymore.

When she went back into the hall she found the boy standing in the living room doorway looking at his feet. He squeezed the frame of the door and stood there without talking. She sat on the settee and he came and sat there too.

I need to take care of something, he said.

All right.

You should come with me.

Okay.

Her mind was on Lucky and the note he left that she gave to Tick to read out loud and it said be back later with two crosses that meant kiss kiss.

Love. Love.

Do you like Lucky? the boy said when they were standing in the middle of the black road looking down at all the cars that didn't drive that way. He was looking at his shoe that had a piece of chewing gum stuck to the end and he scraped it against a rock until the minted rubber rolled away.

Yes, she said. I like him.

He jerked his head. Fuck. Fuck. Why do you like him?

I don't know. He's different. I just do.

Do you like me?

Yeah.

How much?

I don't know.

Do you like me as much as you like him?

I'm hungry again.

You're always hungry.

The boy jerked and twitched and looked her in the eye and scratched the back of his head and flashed his silver mouth when the words called him to it. She had watched the sun set and rise behind the tower block every day and night since she first came beyond the wood of her own front door and she had seen the people and heard them talk and saw them work and play and mend and fetch and do all the things that they did because their lives and the lives of others and love and money and hunger called them to it. The moon and sun were in the sky at the same time.

What are we waiting for?

We're waiting for him.

A silver car came down the long black road. It came

slowly. Soundless and shimmering in the far away and trailing smoke that split into two tails behind it. They got off the road and stood on the pavement and waited for the car and the boy kept telling her to be quiet and say nothing even though she had not said a word since he talked about Lucky. He pulled a handful of notes out of his pocket and counted them out in his hand and it was more than the man had given him the night before when they stood outside the garages selling rabbits. She held the boy's hand because she was afraid but she didn't know why. The boy's wrist pulsed quicker and quicker as the car came and slowed and stopped when the blacked out windows were just in front of them. Nothing happened for the longest time.

She couldn't see into the car and she held the boy's hand and he held hers and he stood taller on the very edge of the pavement and closed his mouth that had been hanging open since the car stopped. The thumping music grew as the window was wound down with an electric switch that the passenger kept his finger on until it disappeared all the way into the door. The music pumped from the window and then it muted as the man in the front seat turned it all the way down and looked at them both.

You got something for me, Lad? he said.

The man in the front seat looked at her and she looked at him. He was as young and old as Lucky with eyes that were wide and mean and blue and the blue seeped into the white and made everything seem uneven. Blurred. She had not seen eyes as large as his that were not looking out from the face of a child or a cartoon mouse, and the skin around them was thin. His face was open like a wound. The mouth parted and contained her where she stood like the walls of her long lost room. She couldn't look away.

What are you looking at? he said.

I know you, she said.

The boy stood on her foot on purpose and she looked at the muddy smudge that was now on the front of her shoe. The boy's jaw twitched madly and his fingers shook and he sucked on his cheek. He didn't say anything and she couldn't tell what he was thinking. She wiped her muddy shoe on the tyre of the car but it would not come clean.

You don't know me, the man said.

I do. I've seen you somewhere before.

You don't know me, he said.

The rough man who was driving looked at her and two other faces came forward from the back seat and they looked at her too. Everyone was watching her. She stepped back onto the pavement and she played with her fingers and she didn't say anything and somewhere in the car was a frantic whispering and somewhere else a dog barked on a wall.

I don't know, she said. I don't know.

The man reached out of the car and took the boy by the shoulder and Tick yelped like a dog and squeezed the man's fingers and pulled but he couldn't move and couldn't break away. He cried. He said ow, ow, ow and then he hissed through his teeth. She lunged for the boy and she pulled him by the arm but she couldn't get him away from the car or from the man whose face had become dark and opened even more like a fleshy trap.

You haven't seen me before, the man said.

She pulled.

You haven't seen me before.

I haven't seen you, she said.

You haven't seen me before and you haven't seen me today.

Let. Him. Please. No. I haven't.

He let go of the boy and took her by the arm instead and held her close. She wanted to bite or scratch or punch him but she couldn't. His eyes made chains for her feet. The boy pulled her by the waist and he told the man to stop.

Stop it, please.

Who is she?

She's nobody.

Who is she?

She's. She's retarded.

He looked at Tick.

Yeah she's retarded. She's my cousin. She's staying with us and I have to look after her. If I don't get her back in one piece or. Or. Or if I mess her up or get her hurt she'll be sent off to one of those nut houses or something. She's retarded. Honestly. She doesn't know what she's saying.

The man looked at her. He let go. He looked at her feet and then he looked at her legs and her crotch and her stomach and her breasts and he looked at her neck and her face and then he looked at her arm where there were four little nail marks in bloody moons deep and stinging in the cold that whipped between them. She rubbed her arm and stood back onto the pavement and out of reach of the passenger. He didn't say anything and he didn't look at her again. He held his hand out through the car window and hooked his finger and told the boy to come. She stepped back again and the boy stepped forward and put a stack of money into his hand.

Is that everything? the man said.

Yeah. I did well last night.

I didn't ask how you did. I asked if this was everything.

Yeah, it's everything.

Good. I need you to do the evening shift later on.

Yeah.

And I need you down on Sweet Street tomorrow.

I got school but I don't care.

Good.

The passenger opened the glove box and stuck the money inside and closed it again and then looked at the boy and smiled. Tick smiled back. Wiped his nose in his sleeve. The faces had disappeared from the back of the car and there was only darkness then and a plume of smoke where they had puffed on cigarettes while they looked out. The man who sat in the driver's seat didn't look at her and didn't look at the boy but looked in the mirror that faced backwards down the long black road. The passenger looked at her once more and then looked at the boy.

How old is she? the man said.

Seventeen.

She looks your age.

She knows.

He rolled a smoke on his knee and licked the paper flat and smoked it deep and long and held it behind his teeth. He let his arm hang on the outside of the car door and then breathed out through his nose and the smoke spiralled up towards the green air that rose loveless into the ever-changing sky. He pointed at the boy.

What do I always tell you? he said. You have nothing to learn from your parents. They have no souls. They have no art. They're faulted and they're afraid and the sooner you learn that the better it'll be for you.

He pointed to each of the towers and he pointed to the people on the streets and the people standing on their balconies and smoking alone in their bedrooms and he said they're all scared. Look at them. Terrified, the lot. Their children know it. I know it. They're cowards. Everyone's afraid and everyone is ashamed and everyone is guilty but they don't fucking know it. Look at them. I said look. Little rabbits inside little towers. Cowering. Hiding. Guilty. You don't know. You're young, boy. Sometimes I think you're too young.

I'm not.

Well.

I'm not too young.

Childhood only ends when you can see the faults of your parents.

I have seen them. My Dad is such a.

Your Mum too.

Yeah. I just. I don't know.

Your. Mum. Too.

He slipped the smoke into his mouth again and he gestured for the boy to come and she tried to hold him back but he wouldn't let her. He went to the car and she stayed back and the passenger took hold of Tick's shirt and drew him close and he pointed at the boy's chest and he said don't. Use. That. Word.

What word?

Retard. Don't say it. Don't use it. Don't even think it.

Okay.

I'm serious, boy.

What should I say then?

She has a name. Why don't you start with that?

Curtains

THE STRANGER TURNED the radio up again and raised the window and the silver car took off and followed the black road around the estate and out of sight. The cold wind came and whipped at the little scratches on their shoulders and she sat down and doused her cuts with water that had collected in a hole in the pavement. Tick kicked a stone and didn't talk. He rubbed his arm but he wouldn't show her the bruise. He turned around to wipe his eyes and when he turned back his face was dry and he was smiling.

He was pleased with me, he said. Don't you think? He was pleased with the money and he was pleased with how hard I've been working. It's all a game with us. That's all. Everything. I'm not a kid and he knows it. Didn't I say that? I said I've already seen the faults of my father. I have. I have.

I have. I've seen the faults of my father and my mother and I'm not scared like they are. I take care of things. I can take care of me and I can take care of you too if you want me to. I'm going to make a lot of money and I'm going to have respect and nothing Dad does can make up for all the bad shit I do.

They walked.

Lucky came out of a door near the park and saw them and stopped and the boy looked at him and then he turned away and walked down an alley that went alongside the left of the estate. She looked at Lucky and he looked at her. He went into his car and took out a black bag and slung it over his shoulder and went back into the tower and up the stairs and into an open door. She turned away and followed the boy and there was no sound from anything and all the people that had stood on their balconies had all turned around and gone back inside. The whole world had turned its head and the day fell into the ground.

Tick looked at his phone and lit it up and read the words written on the screen out loud and it said come home and he said it's only my Mum and rubbed his forehead and turned it off and put it back into his pocket.

Want to hear a joke? she said after a while.

He nodded.

A man once went into a pub and sat down and the moon

came in and he saw his wife kissing someone else and he went over to him and punched him and the barman threw him out and then he forgot where he lived.

That's not a joke.

It was funny when my Dad told it.

On the other side of the world and on the other side of the black road was the last tower. It stood gigantic and empty and so wide that she couldn't see beyond it. Each brick and stone and column and window was like the one before it and the ones surrounding it and it stretched on and on wide and tall and covered the sky in concrete. She looked at it as they walked past. It mirrored the towers opposite in size and shape but it was empty and the rooms were black and solemn in their dead rows. The grass in the gardens had grown long and yellow and the black washing lines that stretched from one wall to another horizontally against the back door were unfilled and broken and they hung limp on wire fences and walls and little stone posts. The windows were closed and covered in a film of dirt and dust and inside there were empty childless rooms and walls without photographs and there were spilled paint tins and pieces of filth and cans of lager and sheets of newspaper turned over or spread out in the middle of the floor. Outside the lights from the lampposts had turned from green to grey and she and the boy had turned to black and white and she couldn't see another living thing. There were no dogs and no men and no birds in the sky and nothing crawling on any stone. She had never heard her footsteps so loud and she had never felt so lonely while she was standing next to someone else. Dorothy was gone. Dad's voice was quiet.

I have to do one more thing, the boy said. Then we can go home and watch cartoons or something. You have to come with me even if you don't want to. You have to stay with me now because he saw you and if he has seen you you're not safe on your own anymore.

I could go with Lucky.

You're only safe with me.

I could go with Lucky.

Please. Just come on.

The last of the light that clung to the lower lid of the sky sank into the ground to be with all those who had already gone from the world and everything became as black as the road. Two minutes in the eyes of Plastic Jesus and four hours in the eyes of the mad bird went by. She faced her own shadow stretched out on the floor in front of her. It was tall and it was thin and it led her on. Dad watched TV in her head and Mum looked through the letterbox and said fuck and it was so loud and.

Have you really seen him before, the man from the car?

Yes. What's his name?

I can't say.

My father had a little box that he kept upstairs. Inside the box was a tape cassette that I was never allowed to listen to and a picture cut from a newspaper. The picture was of a man sitting on the side of the road with his hand drawn up to his temple and his jeans ripped and his face crooked and furious. The man in the picture was the man in the car. I don't know what that means.

Me either. He's done some pretty bad shit.

He was young in the picture.

Why would they take a picture of him unless he did something bad? The worst people end up in newspapers. Maybe that's where it all started.

Do you really think that?

If you're bad once you're always bad.

The boy looked at her and held her hand. The clouds fell down around their ankles and the street lights lit it all up. The tower curved and ended and at its end she saw that it was burned and broken. The walls were blackened and twisted and the whole front face of the building had been torn off and she could see the construction of the floors and pipes and rooms that were laid bare and leaning to one side. The rooms and halls were caved in. Bits of concrete stuck to rusted pipes like the sparse leaves on the branches of a winter tree. The walls and rooms were black and open to the sky. The picture frames were still hanging on the wall though the faces of the families were all burned away. It was beyond the end of the world. It was the end of all things.

Where are you going? he said.

Her red shoes were alone in their own thoughts and they took her to the lower garden that had no grass only dirt and she went to the window and rubbed the smoke from the outside and looked in and saw nothing but that same darkness hanging fat in the air. She walked around to where the end of the building was gone and the whole side of the tower had fallen down and black bricks and toys and dolls and lamps and broken wood from chairs or cabinets were spread from it going back to another car park that was empty except for a few discarded balls and another discarded bike thrown next to two overturned bins. She looked at the rows of floors and ceilings with steel spikes sticking out in all directions and places all the way to the top until she had to step back over the loose bricks to see further up and then she started to climb.

The little slit of moon was high and it shone its silver light up there to all the rooms she couldn't see and the living that had its end and all the hard front doors still closed and for no reason at all. He came behind her and pulled her down and said you can't go up there and she scratched her hand on the first iron rail that she had reached up to hold.

She looked at her hand. It bled. She held her hand up and the cut ran down to her twisted finger and the blood was black in the light of the moon.

All the moths were alive again inside her. She took a stone in her hand and threw it and it went through a window. She was calm and quiet. She looked at her shoes and then back up at the large sky that changed fourteen times a day and Tick wiped the blood off her finger with the end of his tee shirt. She let him look at the twist and the missing nail she had got when she had decided to hurt herself and she let him kiss it.

I didn't know they came down so easily, she said.

What?

All those walls.

Tick touched her face and then he went up to the edge of the smashed concrete floor and he rubbed his hand all the way across it and as he did there was ash that fell down and dust that went up. He looked at the building and he told her that the tower block had been set on fire a few years ago.

It didn't burn for very long, he said, but something exploded and it made everything worse. The whole side of the building collapsed. Nobody died. The boy who did it was my friend and he was taken away soon after that. If the man tells you to do something you do it. It doesn't matter what it is. Some of us steal and some of us tell the police our parents or our teachers touch us. It's amazing how much power you have if everyone thinks you're innocent. Some of us stab people. We all sell rabbits at the side of the road. It's the way things go. You have to work hard to get what you want and this is the only way people like us can do it. My friend comes back to see me. Sometimes. He gets scared and sad and that's why he burns everything up. He can't help it. Everyone is scared though. Everyone here. There's a lady who lives just on the end of our block and she goes to catch the bus at quarter to ten every morning to see her sister. Gets dressed up really nice in a green hat and a shawl and everything and puts on a bunch of makeup and goes to sit in the bus stop but she never gets on the bus. She can't. She's too scared.

Scared of what?

Being too far from home I suppose. Going somewhere new.

Dorothy cried on a stone at the other side of the street. They walked the length of the tower to the side that the fire had not reached. The walls were grey again and there was a red door with a gold number. The garden grew there and it had been tended and the path was clean and the fence stood straight but it was the only one. The number on the door was seven and she traced it with her finger and said seven. Seven. Seven.

She was hungry. She had worn the same clothes for days and days and she had sweated in them and the wind caught the sweat and made her cold. She was thirsty too but there were no shops. Everything was boarded and broken and it made her feel so much like she was going home that she couldn't think and. Tick knocked the door and the number rattled on the wood like bells and someone with a small high voice shouted back through the letterbox.

Who is it?

It's me.

Say the thing.

I'm a little white rabbit and I think I'm running late.

The door opened. Inside the last tower the walls were naked and the brickwork and cement was uncovered and everything was stripped down to its bare bones and covered with spray painted words that she couldn't read. The letters were big and small and zigzagged running down the long corridor from one end to the end that had been destroyed by black fire and low smoke. Two metal doors with a split in the middle stood opposite them and inside was a silver box that had blue and white tape crossed over the front.

Don't go in there ever, the boy said.

She was hungry. Thirsty.

The red door closed behind them and she turned around. Standing behind the door was a little girl who was latching locks and spitting into a castle shaped bucket. The girl climbed onto a stool to see into a small hole in the middle of the door and after a moment she came back down again and stood in front of them. She opened her mouth and blew a pink bubble that grew and grew and then popped. She sucked it back in again and chewed loudly.

You really are fucking late this time.

I know.

Who's she?

My friend.

Is she allowed?

Yeah.

She's ugly.

So are you.

The little girl scratched her head and went to the lifts and tore a little of the tape away from a rusted nail and she took her hair in her hands and tied the yellow ribbon there. She was singing. I don't like anyone, she sang. I don't like you or anyone and if I say she can't go upstairs you have to listen to me. I don't like anyone and I don't have to let you up if I don't want to. I don't like you or them or anyone else because it's good and I feel good and so, so, so.

The little girl finished tying her hair up and went back

to the door to spit. Tick kissed the girl's cheek and she sat on the stool and looked at her toes and began to sing again. She was quiet while the boy turned away and went along the corridor to a stone staircase that led up and up and up in the dark and the green light from the town that pulsed ripe and pretty in the blurred glass. She followed the boy up the stairs and through a heavy metal door that was covered in the same blue and white tape that told them to not go on. Do not cross. Any spare change? Any?

Mercy.

I come here sometimes when I'm supposed to be in school, the boy said. I come here when I'm too mad to think and I come here when Mum is getting too much and I come here when he tells me to because he trusts me. There's only a few of us he picks for this job. We're the ones he trusts the most. I like it though. It's such a big game. Everything is.

Is it?

You should hear us.

I can hear you now.

They went through the door they shouldn't have gone through and down a corridor that was pale and narrow and covered with crooked drawings of men and rabbits and rainbows and women and hills next to houses with one window and a smoking chimney and three sets of stairs. There were trees drawn along the wall. Birds. Cars. Sunny faces that smiled with closed eyes. Further up there were schools burned down and shops with flowers and rabbit chasers with tired generous faces.

This is my one, he said.

She looked. The boy pointed to a picture of the beach and the sea and himself playing football and waving off to someone who had not yet been drawn. There was a big white house with open doors and a garden and a dog that dug and held its face to the sun. There was the sea and one silver fish that looked like Walter but may have been someone else, another poet dressed in scales with a shining silver eye. The boy pointed.

I wasn't allowed to draw my Mum, he said. There are no adults allowed on the wall. I had to draw a dog instead. I drew it barking. Look. There's a beach close to the estate. You can't see it but it's there tucked away from everything else a few miles outside of town. We used to go all the time when I was a kid and Mum was happier. I haven't been to the beach in years.

I've been once. Ages ago. I can't remember it.

I'll take you again.

I can still smell it though.

Can you?

Or maybe it's just Dad blowing air into my head.

At the end of the long corridor was a window and the

window was painted black. Next to it was another set of doors and through the doors was another short corridor and at the end of that corridor was another set of lifts. Tick pressed the button once and it lit up in red and they waited. A Plastic Jesus minute later and there was a bell and the silver doors opened. They went inside and the doors closed and then the floor rose below them and she held onto the sides of the box and looked up at the ceiling with the little light that glowed yellow and green behind a panel. There was music playing somewhere. She heard it crackle and whine playing old tunes like the kind from black and white films. She held Tick's hand in the box.

Do you hear that?

Hear what?

The music played on a loop over and over and she reached out and pushed the walls and the boy asked her if she was okay and she told him that she didn't like small spaces. The moths inside grew fat and hungry at the same time and in her ears they chewed and in her stomach they spat and everything made her sick except her shoes. She looked at them. Saw the shape of the bow and didn't think of the face of Dad whose eyes had bulged and lips had sagged and hands had snatched for anything to root him to that one painful life. She didn't think on that.

Why don't you like small spaces?

I just don't.

Why?

Be quiet.

The doors opened and the air came thick and fast and cold and light. The moths fell down and the sickness went away without being chucked up and she breathed like she hadn't been breathing the whole way up. They stepped into another hall that was stone grey and covered again with writing and curses and drawings in different coloured spray paint.

This is mine, he said. He read it out. It was the word fuck, over and over.

The long lights cast dark green shadows on the walls that followed them as they walked. They flickered on and off and the hallway turned from green to grey to black and then back to grey again and their shadows shuddered in front of them.

What's the matter?

Nothing.

We're allowed to write or draw whatever we want because the passenger says it's important to be creative and let your inner something be something else. I can never remember. He always has these cool ways of saying things. Look, I wrote that big fuck on the wall. I drew that tree there too.

They walked for a long time. Tick pointed out each of the rooms and said this is where we go to talk. This is his bar. I had a drink there once. This is where we go to think and make plans. This is where his girlfriend sleeps. This is where his other girlfriend sleeps. This is where we can sleep if we want to worry our parents. This one kid stayed up here for ten whole days. He was mad at his mother for being scared of his father. I think he went to stay with his uncle after that and his mother went off to a mad house or something. I liked that kid. I told him all the grown ups are scared at everything all of the time and all the Mums and Dads are the same. Do you know what a doll smells like when it's burning?

No.

I do.

She didn't know. She only knew what face someone makes when they die and that wasn't enough for the boy who went on about bicycles and toys and melted plastic and the faces of dolls buried in the ground that cried Mama when someone walked across the dirt.

That's sad.

That's just life.

They stopped at a numberless blue door and the boy knocked with the side of his fist and someone from inside shouted that he was coming and he told them to keep their knickers on. A tall boy opened the door and she looked at him and he looked at her and he was skeleton shaped she thought with sunken cheeks and eyes and collar bones that stuck up and other bones that made shadows where there should have been fat and flesh.

You're late, he said. Is my sister still by the door or did she wander off again? We had to be home an hour ago to take care of my Dad and all you care about is running around with your girlfriend. I cleaned him up and I took care of his nappy so you'll have to feed him and give him his medicine and read that stupid book for him. I saw your Dad earlier. He was helping my auntie take shopping in. He asked me where you were and I lied and said you were down by the river thinking about Jesus.

Did he believe you?

No.

Good.

Your Dad is a nice guy.

I thought you had to be home an hour ago.

The tall boy got out of the way of the door and Tick went into the flat and took her with him and turned around and asked the taller boy if there had been another accident. The tall boy looked at the basket he carried in his hands that was covered with a towel and he said that there had just been the one that day. Tick shut his eyes tight and rubbed his head and said fuck a couple of times loud and then he opened his eyes again and looked beneath the towel in the other boy's hands. In the dark cage she saw a small white face and behind the face was a thick long ear and behind that was blood. Bones. Teeth. Red mash. Red soaked into the white fur. Where there was no fur there was all this skin that was rolled up around small red bones and a shiny swollen muscle and everything that should've been on the inside was turned out. She closed her eyes. She could still see it on the back of her eyelids.

In her head was the little black eye that was dead and turning and around it were a million little broken veins burst up and stretched like pulled roots and she saw the clenched teeth and the mouth drawn back and she couldn't forget anything. She would always have Dad and Mum and that heavy front door and rabbits, bloody rabbits in her head.

I'll pick up another pair tomorrow, the boy said. I've bred some of them but they're too young to be turned from their Mama yet so I'll have to send in the ones I gave to my sister. She has to learn about the hangman one day and there's no better time than now. It'll prep her for Dad and his time is coming fast.

She'll hate you.

Hate is better than upset.

The two boys looked at each other and she said fuck really loud and there was nothing more to say than that. The tall boy left and closed the door and they were alone in the quiet white hallway that had no drawings and no words and smelled like new paint and Dad's poppy smoke. There was a noise from another room like the wailing of a ghost from far away. She listened and didn't listen.

Tick said that the tall boy was called Milo. He doesn't like women or music because his Mum hit him over the head with a sculpture of Elvis Presley when he was three. His Dad wanted to send him to a mental place but he needed help doing the garden. He still doesn't know how babies are made.

On the other side of the door there were these bolts and Tick slid them into place and clipped the padlocks and checked everything to see that the door was locked up tight. He said that sometimes people try to get in here thinking they'll be able to get a fix but he doesn't keep his stuff here. He keeps it all around the estate and only he knows where it is. People come hungry and he sends them all off starving. That's just life and life is their own damn fault.

The flat was larger than the one she had lived in with Dad and it was big enough to get lost in and empty enough to find something if she had been looking for it. There were rooms off rooms and a long white corridor and pale flooring made out of real wood and a big kitchen with a white table and everything was clean and pale and empty. The boy looked inside a fridge filled with bottles and picked something up and showed it to her and put it back gently exactly where it had been before. He sat on the bed looking at the ceiling and she sat there with him for a while. On the other side of the room was a stack of safes that were labelled with numbers that she couldn't read.

I know where the keys are, the boy said. He looked at her and she got off the bed and looked out of the window at the black hills and black roads and signs that advertised twenty-four hour drinks and twenty-four hour girls and twenty-four hours until the doors were closed for good. The boy came over to touch her shoulder. Do you want to know where the keys are?

They're under the floor.

How do you know?

That's where I would put them.

Cool.

The passenger had converted a whole floor of flats into one by knocking down walls and repairing doorways and building hard columns and spending a long time with the same shade of paint. It was white. Whiter. She looked at the colour and she forgot how to think and then she didn't have another thought that was her own. The boy took her by the hand and led her from room to room and showed her all the places he was allowed to go and all the places where he didn't play because playing is for children.

It was all such a great game, he said. It's fun getting the

money and a laugh selling the stuff and so funny to stand on a corner and pretend to be important. People come and people go.

Just like dying.

Better than that.

He took her through another door that needed a set of keys that Tick kept looped to his jeans that he had not changed for weeks. He smelled like grass and cigarettes and sometimes he smelled of his mother and sometimes he smelled of Lucky though he didn't like it when she said that. She slipped her hand into his pocket and he told her to keep real quiet and close the door behind her or all the rabbits would get out. You don't want to let the rabbits out do you? That's what I thought. Good.

The room inside was whiter than the white of before and she was glad of her glasses that blunted everything and turned it all green. The walls were pale and the floor was carpeted and the carpet was pale and there was no furniture except a single wooden chair that she hadn't seen at first. They stepped from the hall into the room and closed the door. There was that haunted noise again and she searched the room and saw a grey box that whined in the corner and projected a light and she followed the light to the ceiling where there was a film playing outside of its box. The film that played was an old cartoon with whistles and bells in two dimensions and no colour at all and the projector whirred and the screen changed in flashes on the ceiling. She watched the cartoon and she walked into the room and Tick pulled her back and pointed to the walls and then to the mass in the middle of the floor and then there was another haunted sound.

She saw a flash of pink and black and white faces that darted from there to there and she wiped the green lenses of her glasses with the sleeves of her jumper and saw then the little rabbits that were darting all around the room. Seven. Eight. Twelve. The room was full of white rabbits that jumped and bounded and ran and then settled to stare at the strangers in the doorway and to chew the fibres of the carpet. There was another low sound and it came from the mass in the middle of the floor. She stepped slowly towards it and Tick held her hand that was still pushed deep inside his pocket next to the newspaper cutting of an obituary he thought was himself in a past life and a stick of unchewed chewing gum that he was saving for a later that had not yet come. There was a white towel spread out on the carpet and on top of that and lying on his back and watching cartoons that were painted on the ceiling was a boy.

Simon likes the rabbits, but he can be rough with them, he said.

The boy was a few years older than Tick but he was not

like Tick. He pointed to the ceiling and made noises in the back of his throat and clapped when the cartoons were violent and wailed when the cartoons were nice. He was wearing white pyjamas. His legs were bowed inwards and his toes were curled under his feet and his hips were out of line with his back and his back was twisted and his head was heavy and rolling to the side and his ear was too close to his jaw and his face was misshapen and he was not the same as Tick. He was not the same as anyone.

Tick sat on the carpet and moved a rabbit out of the way and reached to his boots and undid the laces and slipped them off and he slipped off his black socks that were dirty and wet from all the rain that had made deep mud in the park. His big toe was bruised and his nail was turning black and Tick looked at her and said I felt like kicking something really hard and wiggled the big toe to show her it still hurt.

I kick things with my boots on, she said.

You're not wearing any boots.

She looked down at her own feet and slipped off the shoes when Tick told her that they needed to be barefoot or they'd dirty the carpet and she slipped out of her socks and kept looking back to check on the shoes where she had left them next to the door. She stood away from the door and looked at the boy who lay in the middle of the room and she watched Tick walk over to him. Tick sat next to Simon and spat into his sleeves and cleaned the boy's face and Simon made wet noises in the back of his throat and laughed.

Don't you want to see Simon? Tick said.

No.

Why not?

I don't like him.

You can't say that.

Why?

You just can't. You can't say that about him.

She was dizzy. Hungry. Thirsty. There was at one time blood in the room that had sunk somewhere into the fibres of the carpet to seep and spread and she watched the rabbits chew and pull.

Some people kill rabbits. Some people kill each other, he said. Some people buy sweets and others buy junk and some sell it and others can't stand the sight. When you say things about people you better be ready to own what you say because even if you change your mind you're still the same person who said it and there's no going back. I wish I hadn't called you retarded in front of him but there's no going back from that now. That's just life. Simon doesn't think or worry about anything I say and that's why he's my friend. My brother.

The two boys laughed as one wiped the spit off the other.

Tin Boy

SHE STOOD ABOVE the snatching wriggling boy with a glass of water that Tick had fetched from another room and she drank it so fast she made sucking noises and had to pant when she stopped. She drank it all. Reminded her of. She felt like she did when Dad was gone and she was alone and the water had been turned off. There was the rain but that was on the outside. There was a father but he was lying in a ditch singing to Dog in heaven and he was out of his muddish mind and out of his body and there was no getting him back again. There was a mother. Yes. There was one of those too.

She drank the water.

Tick took care of the boy that lay on the floor and he laughed at the mouse that caught the cat that caught the dog on the ceiling. He pulled off Simon's white pyjama bottoms and checked the nappy that had been tucked under the waistband and he told her it was clean and said that Simon was a good boy. She couldn't look away from Simon's misshapen face, all strange with those rolling searching eyes that were too far apart and as small as the backs of sinkhole beetles. His tongue sat swollen in the middle of his mouth and stuck out between teeth that were crooked and a jaw that hung too low. His lips were wet and fat and spit tracked from the corners of his mouth and down to his ears. Tick wiped it with his own sleeve and the boy gurgled and pointed to the ceiling and spat some more and Tick said that's better but it never was. It didn't matter. He wiped the boy's face but he couldn't wipe away the deformity. His head and body were still the same and the room was whiter and emptier than when she had first walked in.

That's Anna, Tick said when the boy twisted his neck to look at her where she stood against the door. She's nice but she's weird. Can you say Hello Anna? Can you tell her not to be afraid? You're different but we're all different. Can you say my name? Tell Anna how pretty she is. Tell her.

There were no sounds from the other floors and no voices from the walls because the flats were empty all around. The single window set into the wall where most of the rabbits huddled was covered with black paper and on the paper in green and yellow chalk was a picture of the sun and the hills and the sky. There was no real light. Only the light from the little flat bulbs overhead and the black and white of the projector that twisted and turned and violated the ceiling with the bop and crush of exaggerated death. The sun on the window wasn't real. Nothing was. She looked at the boy who had eyes too wide and teeth too close together and there was nothing in her head but the thought of that too perfect sun that would never set and the night that would not come.

Tick opened a pot and scooped cream out with his fingers and rubbed it between his palms and he rolled the boy over and lifted his pyjama top and there on Simon's skin was a red sore that he dabbed the cream into as gently as he could while the boy whined and jerked.

Can't we take him out?

Where?

Outside. Can't he go outside?

He never goes outside. He likes it here. Look at him.

He doesn't, she said. He doesn't like it in here.

It's huge.

It's small and nothing ever changes.

Why would he ever want to leave?

He wants to see the grass and the other kids.

No, he doesn't.

He wants to see dogs.

He wants to watch cartoons.

He wants to go out.

He has everything here.

Life isn't just watching TV.

It is. That's all it is. It's just watching TV and keeping yourself from thinking too much and you know it. Look at him. He's happy. If he wants to see grass I'll draw it for him. If he wants to see cars I'll show him a picture. If he wants his Dad his Dad comes and spends time with him. He gets food and he gets to touch something soft and warm. What's the point in spending time out there? Everyone hates everyone for no reason and they're all afraid. The world is enough to make you sick.

He wants to go and.

I'm not talking to you anymore.

He wasn't talking to her. Simon gurgled and spat and watched the sun on the paper and time passed. She looked at the rabbits that danced and fought and raped and jumped from wall to wall with fear in their eyes and rooted deep in their pumping back legs. There was no other sound than the noise of the boy and the cartoon and the sound that Dad made in her head when she was lonely for him. She needed to piss. She held it in. In another place there was a wall and on the wall was a dog painted in black and white and it was laughing. Loud. Long. It opened its big eye wider and laughed long and hard for miles and miles all the way down that long black long yellow brick road.

When Tick was done with feeding and washing and rubbing cream and scooping medicine and taking temperature he sat down next to Simon and pulled his head into his lap and told him he was a good boy. He opened a book that he had pulled from a bag and set it in front of Simon and began to read. In the story there were children that played and trees that dreamed and animals that talked and loved with joy and courage and Tick didn't say the word fuck, as he usually did. Not even once. She stepped closer and sat down beside them and learned to love the sound of him reading.

I'm your brother, Simon, isn't that right?

The boy gurgled.

Your Dad is a better Dad.

The boy spat.

The bells from the cartoon became lost in the background. Tick turned the black shapes on the page into words and the words became stories and the stories were pictures that she saw playing on the projector inside her head. Simon laughed wet and lovely in the back of his throat. Tick did all the voices and played all the characters. She killed the itches on the back of her neck and pulled her hair behind her ears and played with her fingers and moved her hands closer to Simon's that were fisted and braced tightly to his chest. Tick read on and she touched Simon's fingers with her own. The boy's soft miniature eyes rolled towards her and she looked at him. She moved her fingers into his hand and he released his arm from his chest and let it drop. They held hands. They held hands for a long time.

Tick looked at her and asked if she wanted to sit closer and she said she did and he asked if she was comfortable and she said that she was. The boy read and showed the pictures to Simon who wiggled happy and crooked on the bathroom towel with daredevil rabbits darting around his head. The story was over but before Tick closed the book she asked him if he could teach her how to say some of the words.

Can't you read them?

I can't read anything.

Why can't you read anything?

Dad never taught me.

The boy looked at her and she looked at him. Her own face was reflected deep in his eyes once more, and she looked there at his pupil that grew and shrank and she watched a little muscle twitch in his eyelid. She was close. She could smell his salt and vinegar breath and she could hear the wind that rushed up from his lungs like autumn rolling into winter. He held the hand that was resting on the floor and he pointed to the book that he lay flat between them and he said can't you even read this little word?

She looked at it. Her mouth was dry and the moths were gentle in her stomach and when she looked at Tick she thought of all the good things in the world and her skin tingled like there was sunlight on it. She was warm. The boy was the weather. He flashed his silver mouth and rubbed his fluttering eyelid and made a crooked face and she thought on him and thought on Lucky and she was then so sick and unwell that her mind was pulped like a wet newspaper. She was cold and hot. There and here. She was thirsty and hungry and full up with all the mess that she couldn't forget. Tick took a pen from the kitchen and came back and sat down shoulder to shoulder with her and wrote a word on the back of his hand and pointed there.

Can't you even read this little word?

Um.

This one here.

She looked at it and she tried to make the lines talk.

I can't think. I can't remember. I feel funny. I.

Try. You're clever.

I did try. I can't. I can't do it and I'm never going to be able to.

Tick looked at her and she looked at him, she felt the moths coming up from her stomach and trying to fly out through her eyes but she forced them back in again and swallowed them down. She asked him what the word said. Her voice broke apart and then came together again.

What does it say?

It says Anna.

Heart's Desire

ANNA. ANNA. ANNA.

Tick taught her the lines that made her name and she looked at them and copied them on a piece of paper and read them over and over and the more she said her own name the more the moths and Dad and Mum fell away down a silver track never to be heard from again. The building and the rabbits were buried and the sick spinning feeling was gone. Reading was harder than she thought. Each line made a letter and that letter looked like all the others but it was different and she had to learn why. Every letter made a sound and she had to remember the sounds and say them out loud and only then could she make words. Some letters didn't make a sound. Some made the same sounds but they were not drawn the same.

Anna. Anna. Anna.

That's enough for today, the boy said. You look tired.

I'm always tired. I just need to.

They stopped. Tick held her hand and kissed it and she told him that she would learn because she was clever and that was all she needed. Outside there was no sound and nothing happened. It was just as quiet as it had been before. Tick's phone made noises in his pocket and he ignored it. The three of them lay on the floor and looked at the ceiling and watched the cartoon projected there. They laughed. Simon clapped and mewled and blurted sounds that she tried to understand. She watched the grey turn to green.

Let's play a game with Simon, Tick said.

What kind of game?

It's such a fun game.

He got up and went out of the room and came back with a red helmet that had small pillows stuffed inside and he cleaned it with a wet towel and put it on Simon and he fastened it underneath his chin. It made Simon's ears stick out like a little cartoon monkey and she thought that he was a lovely strange cartoon boy. He looked at Tick who stood above him and he laughed and grabbed at the Jesus on Tick's tee shirt. The rabbits darted from corner to corner to huddle and twitch and leave their little brown pellets in zigzag trails behind them.

It's such a joke, Tick said. It's such a mad game. Leave the rabbit shit for the next boy or girl to clean up. That's their job and not mine. We'll play a game instead and you can see how clever Simon is.

Tick showed her the game. He stood up and clapped his hands together so that Simon would concentrate there. He looked up and whined and spat and opened his mouth and made sucking noises and stuck out his swollen tongue and rubbed it along his teeth and clapped again and again with that flash of violence in his burning right eye.

Look at me, Tick said, look at me, Simon.

The boy looked.

Simon says sit up.

The boy thought on this and then he whined and rolled his eyes back into his head and searched out thoughts that wouldn't come to him by themselves. He uncurled his hands and forced them behind him and then laid them flat against the carpet at his sides and he rolled his eyes back and thought once again. His eyes searched and his head translated what the boy had said into his own gurgling cartoon language and then his eyes rolled forward again. He looked at Tick. He pushed against the carpet and lifted his back and rose up with pain and struggle and strength that she didn't know he had. His head fell back as he lifted and the apple of his throat popped up like a fist and twitched as he mewled. He lifted himself further and his head came forward and rolled onto his neck and then he was sitting up. Someone said fuck over and over, but it wasn't Tick and it wasn't Simon.

It was her.

The broken boy's hands were in front of him. They fell heavy into his lap and he sat looking down at them and he began to rub his fingers together fast and faster as though he was trying to start a fire in the palms of his hands. He looked at her and then at Tick and he was smiling big and fat all the way back to his gums.

Watch this, Tick said, Simon says stand up.

The happy spitting boy looked at his legs for a while. He reached to his knees and took hold of the white pyjamas and he pulled. He rocked his body from side to side and struggled and fought with his legs that didn't want to move.

On the ceiling the picture changed and there were no more cartoons, only adverts for sweets and food and toys and all the fun and happiness in the world moulded into plastic and sold for ninety-nine ninety-nine ninety-nine.

The boy struggled in his body.

Come on. Simon says stand up.

Simon looked into his own head again and rubbed his fingers together so fast they made clicking sounds and turned red. Once the thought was fished out of his mind he rolled his eyes forward again and looked at his own two legs and took his hands and pushed them to the floor and got onto his knees and then onto his feet.

She stood back and pressed her hands against her mouth. She looked at him. Simon was taller than she had expected him to be. Taller than Tick even though he was crooked and his body was bent to one side and his head hung off the end of his neck like the bauble on the end of a woolly hat. She thought he was even more cartoonish the more he struggled to look like everyone else. Cartoon face. Cartoon hands. Cartoon voice that tried to talk and couldn't. Tick began to clap again and the boy laughed and clapped and grew taller still as he tried to straighten himself out.

Last one. Good boy. Simon says jump.

She moved back to the walls of the room and the boy turned to look at her. He pulled his head up and rolled his eyes back and then rolled them forward again and he stepped towards her. One foot went smoothly and the other dragged behind him and had to be set right again by Tick who was watching Simon there. He took another step and Tick set him right again. The third step was better. He held his hands out and lifted his rolling head onto his neck and laughed and rubbed his fingers together and made wet noises and bleeps louder than the adverts on the ceiling that had become all about sugar and pop.

He wants you to do it with him. He likes you.

Do you think he does?

Look at him.

She picked her nail and held her hands in the air for Simon to take and he took them and his hands were burning and his face was hysterical and he pulled her into the middle of the room and she closed her eyes and bent her knees and she jumped as high as she could. She jumped so high that she thought they had fallen deep into the TV light. They went past the adverts and past the cartoons and into those films that she had loved so much when she was with Dad. She heard herself laughing. She heard Simon's ghostly whines. She imagined that the paper dolls were hanging from the ceiling and thought that maybe she had lived there once. She imagined herself as the boy. All those yesterdays ago she had lived there and she had watched the same cartoons playing on the ceiling and she had eaten the same food and her body had lain the same way and there was a picture on the wall and it was a picture of the sea and her mother's eye and a small fish that she had named Walter. She jumped again. She was laughing, far away. She wasn't the boy; she was that little flash of violence that sat in the corner of his mind and forced his fingers to twist around small necks and pull. They both jumped again.

She looked at the boy in that suit of skin that was drawn

too tight on his bones that were always leaning to one side or another. His eyes rolled back to check for answers to questions that she had not asked and she was there with him because. She was herself and she was the boy. She had been happy and sad and clever and furious like him, sitting or lying down in an empty room with no windows, staring long and hard at a black and white TV and an outside that Dad had drawn on the walls in crayon and paint and jittery rabbit talk. Staying awake. Trying to stay sane. Looking for Mum who had disappeared down the drain. Trying not to suffocate in her father's sad moods. Wondering what was different. Looking at all the light that fell into the room, and tearing the world from the skin of white rabbits.

Twister Town

EVERYTHING WAS A GAME.

A boy came to the door and he was sad and he didn't talk and he walked past them and waved goodbye and went to see Simon and didn't say a thing and even that was a game or so Tick said. The quiet boy went into the room. He turned the sound of the TV down low and went to work on Simon's dinner and they left through a different door to the one they had come in. There was another boy working on the main door of the building downstairs and he looked exactly like the quiet boy because they had lived in the same womb at the same time. They were twins, Tick said. The other twin didn't stop talking.

Hi Tick. Haven't seen you in a while. How's your Dad? We all love your Dad in my house. He helps us all the time and he helped my uncle really well. Wish he was my Dad. You're lucky because my Dad was a cunt. I mean what I say. Your Dad is invincible. He doesn't care about himself at all. You know what he did? He went into the middle of traffic on the main road to help a dog that had been clipped by a car. Nearly got clipped himself. Mad. It's your turn to work on Sweet Street tomorrow. Did you know that? My auntie wants to know what's wrong with your Mum. She said she used to be different and everyone always asks what happened to her. Your Dad is great but everyone thinks your Mum might need to be locked up or something.

On and on.

When they were outside they lit their cigarettes and walked along the back of the estate where the wooden wall wrapped right around and they couldn't see anything on the other side. They smoked. She sang a song and taught him the words when he asked her and he taught her a few letters that were spray painted on the wall in deep greens and morbid blacks.

What's Sweet Street?

I'll show you.

When?

I'm working down there tomorrow.

Can I come?

You have to come.

Why?

He told me you did.

The cold air sank all the way into her bones and shook them up. The eye of the moon blinked at her and she held hands with the boy who knew the way better and they hit the long wall with rusted pipes as they went and watched the clouds drop to the ground and stick to the road and turn into sticky graveyard grease all eerie and black. They went through a tunnel and into the park and up the steps and over the bridges and past the other doors with the numbers that she couldn't read and all the words that began with F. He turned his key in the lock and they went into their home laughing like all the world was good and there was no death or mayhem or reason to think otherwise.

Lucky was standing in the living room. He had a book in his hands and he was reading from it out loud with his finger pressed against the page and he read so fast she couldn't understand him. She let go of Tick's hand and looked at Lucky and Tick watched his father too as he spoke a hundred words at once. He read and questioned what he'd read. He pointed to a page and then flicked the pages over and muttered to himself and paced to one side of the room and then into the kitchen where he took hold of a brown bottle and drank deep from the neck. He wiped his mouth and came into the middle of the living room again and when he saw them standing there he dropped the book to his side and looked at his feet. He was quiet.

She looked at Tick and Tick looked at Lucky who screwed the lid back onto his bottle and walked it into the kitchen and threw it into the bin. He came into the room again and wiped his mouth and swiped the hair out of his eyes.

I think I might sell the car tomorrow, he said. I think we can manage without it. Don't you think, my boy? It should give me a little extra so I can get some clothes and nappies for the woman down the way with the new baby. I might have some left over for the man who just had his benefits stopped. Did you know that people are hungry? Did you know people are failing? I don't know how many times I have to do this I'm so tired. I'm trying.

The boy looked at his father underneath the hair that had lost its spikes and fallen across his forehead. The room was almost empty. It had been emptied of books and furniture and curtains and photo frames and all the things that turned a home into a museum. Tick threw a punch at the frame of the door that cracked beneath his knuckles and he said fuck loud and he turned and she watched him go out of the room and into the corridor and into his mother's room. She followed him and tried the door but the door was locked and she stood and listened there instead. Tick was inside shouting I've had enough, I've had so much, over and over and there was banging and then things were quiet. She listened as hard as she could.

I want you to stand there so I can look at you, she heard the woman say.

No, Mum.

I'm lonely.

Don't, Mum.

Your father doesn't belong to us.

Please.

Oh mercy. Not that.

Shut up. Everyone just.

It was quiet again and she listened and tried the door but there was no way she could get inside and no way to know what was going on. She came from the door and went into the living room and she sat next to Lucky who was holding his head in his hands on the settee. She took the book from his lap and turned the pages and the book was small and so were the words and she couldn't read anything because the writing was not meant for her. She looked at Lucky.

A boy talked about you, she said. A boy we saw said that you were kind and you helped his uncle and you helped a dog and he said that everyone loves you because you're crazy and invincible.

Lucky took his hands from his face and looked at her. His eyes were sore and red and the green had turned greener through the lenses that she hadn't taken off even after all this time. The hairs on his chin had grown and his breath smelled just like Dad when he had been drinking for too long and had not tried to throw it all up yet. He smiled and wiped his eyes and smoked and rolled her one and then they smoked together. They blew all the smoke into the air and it swam around their faces and made the room blur and sway and it blunted all the sharp edges of the small things that he had not yet given to the needful and upset and tired people of the town. He smiled and his smile was not silver.

Do you like it here? he said.

Oh yes, I do.

It suits you.

What does?

I don't know. Outside. This place. Here. Living.

Does it?

Yes, I think it does. I think it makes you happy.

I like being here. I like you. I like Tick.

I'm glad you like Tick. I'm glad that when you go outside you seem happy. I don't think you know how much you've changed since we first met. You've soaked it all up. Me. Them. Life. You've soaked up all those people on the outside and you've soaked up living and I didn't think that would happen. When I go outside it makes me miserable. I bet you didn't know that. It makes me miserable and angry but I do it because I have to. I don't know. There's so much out there that I wish I didn't know and so much I wish I could change. Sometimes it's better to have walls around you so you can't see the world every day. Windows are good. If you have to see the world it's better to see it in little square pieces one frame at a time rather than all at once.

I don't know what you're saying.

A lot of people don't. I don't either.

Do you want a cup of tea?

Let me just sit awhile.

I'll stay with you.

Does my son hate me?

Mostly. Not all the time.

That's good.

He lay back and she lay back with him and he made a pillow with his hands and she made a pillow with hers and they lay like this on their sides facing each other. He talked and she listened. He talked about wanting to die when he was her age and asked her what she thought of that. He told her that he had tried to kill himself over and over and nothing ever worked.

The last time I tried to do it I decided that I wanted to die in the middle of the road. I picked a bus and got myself ready and waited for the bus to come but it didn't turn up. It was strange because I really did try but someone up there didn't want me to go. I can't get out even if I want to. I waited for the bus but it never came because someone planted a bomb on it and it exploded a few streets back. What do you think about that?

He was beautiful. Ugly. She leaned closer and scratched her neck and twisted the skin of her little finger and leaned back and closed her eyes and pushed her lips together for a kiss that didn't come. When she opened them again he was looking at the ceiling and blowing tusks of smoke from his nose and thinking on. She didn't know. Somewhere outside Dorothy was singing. In the other room the boy began to bark like a dog in the lap of his mother.

I'd say you were Lucky, she said.

He laughed.

That's what they all say.

Sweet Street

SWEET STREET WAS a place for.

On Sweet Street it was dark. All the lights had been smashed with rocks and everyone had to use the neon bright reds and greens from shop signs and windows to pass through and to find whatever it was that they were looking for. The street was on the black road between the town and the estate where all the buildings were old and everything was left to crumble. Tick had woken her up in the night by standing over her and stroking her hair back to her ear and she looked at him and looked at Lucky who had fallen to the left and into his own hands and he told her they had to go to work. Here, put my hoody on. Put the hood up. You look.

Cool.

The night was black glue. Sweet Street was a place for children. Sleepy-eyed and odd-socked. They stood on corners and in shop doorways and on the end of the street watching out for flashing lights and uniformed men all the way down that long black road and back up again. She had never seen so many children in one place and she had never seen so many that were not playing and not singing and not looking into the dreamy places beneath the pavement and in the air that whipped cold and fresh about their ears.

The children were working. They took small clear packets out of their school bags and pockets and socks and pencil cases and handed them to the men and women who lurked from the damp and dark and the keep-away-from and the do-not-enter and killed the itches on their raw bodies and held their crumpled money out and said mercy and bless you all the way back to the dark again. Tick didn't talk to the other children and they didn't talk to him. A man came and took something off a girl who was chewing on a sugar necklace and he gave her money and squeezed her face.

Fucking perv, Tick said.

They stood together on their own corner and she had the sweets in a red backpack that matched her shoes. Tick took the money and they waited for people to come and when they did they worked and when they didn't they watched the pavement or the road or the sky and didn't talk.

She took out a packet and looked at the white rabbit and she thought on Dad and on rabbits and how he went out every day looking for an hysterical high that came and went so fast it was like digging for stones in a sand pit with the rain coming down quick and heavy. She looked at Tick and looked down that road and she was sick and crying and she didn't care who saw it. She wiped her nose on the back of her hand.

I think my Dad came for these rabbits.

Probably. Does that upset you?

Yes, but not nearly enough.

Two small children played with a ball on the other side of the road and when a car came and drove straight through the street they left the ball roll to the kerb and ran to the grassy bank on the other side and hid in the dark. When the car had driven off they came back again and rubbed the wet leaves and sticks off the rubber and played with the ball again. The children were small and the ball was the only one she had seen that hadn't been broken or deflated and left to collect rainwater in the paths and cracks of the estate. The little girl with the touchable face called to the smaller children and said Mum will kill you if you get grass on your clothes, and she looked at Tick and scratched her head and looked back at the boys and then down at her shoes that lit up when she walked and into her own head that was full of.

It was cold. She looked at Tick and watched a man come from nowhere and he stood in front of her and swayed and held his hand out for balance and took hold of a drainpipe that was rusted and barely clinging to the wall. He gave her money. She gave the money to Tick and then she looked at the man and gave him a little white rabbit in a little clear plastic pouch. He took it and smiled and muttered and looked to the fat sky and the fat of the world that steamed up green and fantastic from the hard streets below. He went off again with the rabbit in his hand, staggering along the places where no one walked but him.

Tick slipped the money into the front pocket of his hoody and jerked his chin and said fuck over and over and waited for someone else to come. She sat on the kerb and watched the children with the ball and forgot about the rabbits in her pocket and forgot about the moths in her head. The children practised throwing and catching and then they sat down and rolled the ball back and forth between their legs and the children standing along the pavement in the neon lights of after bedtime watched them and opened their mouths and closed them again. They rolled their eyes back as Simon always did.

The ball rolled away and the small boys laughed and the smallest one stood up and went into his pocket and pulled out a dummy and put it into his mouth and sucked the rubber end. He picked up a stick and held the stick out and ran after the ball that rolled away beneath his feet. She laughed. They were lovely. Small. Terrible. Quick. Upsetting. Good. The boys ran the way she learned that all young boys do. They twisted their hips forward left and right and leaned over with their elbows pushed like wings out to the sides. Everything, all the momentum coming up from the groin which points at first out to their mothers, and then everlastingly out to the world.

Dad and the moths and Tick and the big black dog on the wall were all talking but she wasn't listening to any of it. She watched the little boy. She thought on TV until the TV went black in the back of her head and then she wiped her eyes and laughed long and hard at all the people trapped there inside the box. She laughed at the men she couldn't see. She laughed at the women she couldn't hear. She laughed at the children she couldn't feed and she laughed at Lucky who nailed himself to the pages of a blank book. She laughed for the woman in the bed, the boy and his little bag of rabbits, she laughed for all the people of the estate and she laughed the longest for the ones who buried themselves behind big curtains, turned the lights down low, looked deep into mirrors, and worshipped.

Any spare change?

None for you. Now fuck off.

The boys played and she watched and then she watched Tick who was talking about how he could drink so well for his age and no one ever congratulated him for it. The ball came from the other side of the road and rolled on the wet concrete and hit the lip of the pavement near her feet. Tick could drink even better than Lucky who sometimes didn't even try. The boys came and stood in front of her and pointed to the ball and played with themselves and wiped their noses with their sleeves and whispered. She picked the ball up and looked at it in her hands and it was shiny and deep red in one light and green in another and covered in the debris of the road. She crouched on the pavement and put the ball down and rolled it to the boys who watched it come and then scooped it into their hands and looked at all the other children who watched from their corners. Tick stepped back onto the pavement. The boy with the dummy chucked the ball onto the ground and kicked it towards her again and she caught it with her feet and stepped off the pavement and kicked it back. She watched the boys as they laughed and turned and ran in their clambering swarms to catch it. Tick stepped away further into the dark and into the womb of a boarded shop that had been closed for years and years and would not open again while the street was sweet.

A moth came to suck at the light that fizzed inside the tubes of the neon sign above the pavement where she had been standing. It slipped pure white beneath the greens and reds and in and out of the dark. She played with the small boys and the night grew cold and turned into smoke. The rainwater on the black road gathered the light where it could and mirrored it and inside the puddles was the rushing sky.

The boys kicked. The ball rolled and spun. She kicked it back and laughed and one of the other boy children who had been counting money rolled the money in a band and slipped it into his back pocket and dropped the pencil case that had been full of white rabbits and he came into the road. She kicked the ball to him and he stopped it and kicked it into the air and balanced it on his forehead and dropped it down and kicked it back again.

The smaller boys laughed and clapped and kicked it to her and she took it into her hands and watched all the other children that dropped their sweets and ignored their money and came to stand and play in the middle of that burning street. Those that had talent remembered it and those that didn't watched, saw, and tried to learn.

She called to Tick who stood somewhere away from the noise and light and he didn't come and she called him again and he stepped into the glow and looked up and down the road as though he couldn't find them where they had gone. As though they had stepped into a place that was too far from where he was then. Somewhere over the. She shouted again and caught the ball and threw it to Tick who opened his arms and caught it and unrolled it from his chest and looked at it. He looked at it underneath the green neon light surrounded by curls of autumn smoke. She called to him and he called back and said fuck over and over and stepped from the pavement and dropped the ball by his feet and rolled it underneath his heel and kicked it into the air and threw it onto his back and forehead and knees and elbows and scored a goal that no one kept.

She hadn't disappeared. She was more in that place than she'd ever been before and the children looked at her as though they had not seen her before then. She kicked and laughed and watched for skill and triumph and everyone was the same when they were raised into the green light. Children who had not been there before poured into the road from the cracks and hollows of the estate and both dark and pale men and women who had been looking for rabbits forgot what they were hungry for and came instead to play and to forget. There was no time behind them and no time in front of them. They kicked and called and followed the red ball and so did she and so did Tick and so did all of them good and bad and hungry like her. They didn't concern themselves with money or the anger of their mothers or the fear of their fathers or the men who came to knock on the door looking for money and clean bones. Being was remembering. Playing was forgetting.

Sometime in the middle of the night or the middle of a dark morning a silver car came slowly down that stormy road. It came slow, parting the rising smoke and stirring up the swirling orange puddles and breaking through the threads of green light that all at once fell to the children's feet.

She felt her heart bump against her chest. The face of the passenger looked out. The car was bigger than she remembered and its front lights lit the road and burned all the colours away. The children stood still and quiet and then moved aside when the car came close and the two young boys went to the grass and hid their faces and some of the children held hands and others stuck their hands into their mouths and sucked. The car stopped in the middle of the shrinking crowd and it kept its engine running and kept its windows drawn up.

Tick watched the car. The ball was in his hands. The other children had moved further back. He looked at her and she didn't know what to say. A dog barked. The night had no temperature at all and the rain existed only in the beams that shone from the front of the car. She felt something move in her fingers and she looked at her hand and saw a small girl standing next to her trying to hold on and she took her hand and looked at the child and the child looked at her with large absent eyes.

Tick whispered something into the driver's window. Then he went into his back pocket and pulled out something small and flicked it up and it beamed the light from eye to eye. It was a small silver knife.

He looked at his hands and then he stuck the knife deep into the ball and held on until the rubber began to collapse. She felt it. The knife. Deeply. She shook her head and so did the children who at first started and then held their fingers against their faces and looked on at the slow death. The little girl was crying. Tick whispered again and then he crossed the road and threw the ball past the grassy patch and over the wall that had no other side.

A game, Tick said. This is all just a fun. Game.

The car began to move again, slowly. She saw Dorothy return to the path in front of her and make rude gestures to the blackened windows and side mirrors and doors. The car drove away and turned around a corner and faded into other business on other streets.

They didn't talk as they walked back from Sweet Street. Tick was too much in his own head and didn't say fuck and didn't jerk pretty and wild.

In the park the dog on the wall was laughing as she approached with the boy just in front of her looking at his own boots. The dog looked at them and searched the ground for something that was buried and he barked and fixed his eyes on them as they approached. The boy stopped and sat on the swing and played with the money that was in the front pocket of his hoody.

Can I tell you something? she said.

He looked at her but didn't speak. She sat down next to him and handed him the five white rabbits that she couldn't sell that night and as he counted them and pocketed them she talked.

I want to tell you something that's true about me.

He looked at her.

I want to tell you that I'm afraid of small spaces because my Dad kept me locked inside until he died. He died a few weeks ago. A month. I can't remember. Everything is different now. It could've been years ago but. At the same time I can still smell his aftershave all mixed with death when I close my eyes. And sometimes I think I'll go to sleep and I'll wake up and I'll still be there. Where the walls are too wide and the wallpaper is giving way to rot and so many insects. I can't sleep because I'm thinking about it all too much. It's not in my memory anymore. The museum. It's not back there in a crumbling building. It's in my head.

I have moths in there too that I know aren't real but I can feel them chewing everything up and I can hear their wings and sometimes it sounds like talking and sometimes it sounds like buzzing and it gets so loud I think I'm going to smash my head in. My Dad was a mess and sometimes I don't know whether or not to blame you for that. Mum. She's just another memory. When I was little she went away but I have a secret about that. It's a big secret that I keep right back in my mind so deep that sometimes I can't even find it. Not even Dad knew. Can I tell you what it is?

She swung gently and kicked the stones under her feet.

My Mum murdered me twice. She murdered me by going away when I was four. Dad and I needed her more than. Then she murdered me a second time, when she came back. That's my secret. My Mum came back. It was years after she first went away. I was maybe ten or eleven. Dad doesn't know. If he did he would probably hate me. He said he was always looking for her and he didn't know where she went. I was alone. I heard a voice through the letterbox and I knew it was her. She called my name. I'm sorry I'm crying. I know. She said Anna, Anna, Anna. She told me she'd come back and wanted to be my Mum again and wanted to be with my Dad. I was so.

Tick held her hand.

I only remember thinking one thing. I remember thinking

that Dad always said he loved her so much. What if he loved her more than me? What if they loved each other so much that there wasn't enough room for me? I couldn't fit in there. I didn't like small spaces and my parents were always so loud and fantastic and I was so small and sick and there would be nowhere to put me. She asked me to open the door. I panicked. I shut my mouth and stepped back into the dark and she called me over and over and I put my hands over my ears. Dad would leave me. I would be alone. Dad loved her more than he loved me. I was crying but I dried my eyes and cleared my voice and I talked. Do you know what I said?

What did you say?

I said Anna's not here.

Mum said who's there now?

Not Anna. Anna moved away a few years ago with her Dad. They don't live here anymore. They live on a farm. My parents are going to be home any minute. They don't like strangers and neither do I. Please go away. Your family's not here. They're gone and I don't know where they are. They're not here anymore.

She told me she was sorry through the door and I covered my mouth because the words tasted like wax in my mouth. I saw her on the other side of the glass. She was just standing there. Then she told me she was sorry again and I told her to go away. I said fuck off. I said the word fuck over and over and sometimes I hear myself saying it now. I heard her crying. I made up a story in my head that Dad was behind me telling me not to open the door but that's not true because he wasn't there. I was alone in the house and I could've let her in but I didn't. I didn't open the door. It was my fault. I told her to fuck off and she did. She went away and didn't come back and then she died. And so did Dad. Everything that happened to me is because of me. Everything that happened to them is because of me. I'm so. I'm just bad.

They sat in the quiet and the dark and Tick kissed her hand and the night grew loud and the moon vanished behind the fog. She wiped her eyes and listened to her heart slowing down. They walked and Tick didn't speak. They walked and the sun began to come up on the other side of the world and the towers were golden and the panes of glass mirrored the light. She thought on Mum and Dad and she thought on the beautiful life that she had lost because she had been too afraid to open the door.

Tick held her hand and smiled and when they got to the house he watched her face and stood in front of her and set down two bricks beneath his feet that had come loose from the wall. He stood on them and raised himself up so that he was as tall as she was. He balanced with his arms out and when one brick wobbled and he was about to fall he laid his hands on her shoulders and smiled and flashed all the silver in his mouth and he closed his eyes and leaned forward. He kissed her. He kissed her on the lips. They stood under the black sky and in the light of all those lovely windows where people cried and laughed and spat and fought and were real. He kissed her and she let him do it. She let him stay there for a while without moving or talking or spoiling the time. His lips were wet and fat and her lip touched the tracks along his bottom teeth and his face was squashed against her glasses and she leaned back and pushed her lips together and it was like those black and white films. She closed her eyes and sank away from time and thinking and bad weather. She went away. She didn't know where. She was somewhere where there were no walls and no doors and the world was folded into a paper plane that glided along the grey green sky. They kissed for a long time. The boy pulled back and looked at her and she looked at him. She laughed. His cheeks grew roses. He stepped down from the bricks and took the key out of his pocket and looked at his boots and his tee shirt that had no Jesus on it that day. He turned from the door once more and held her hand and looked at her.

You're not bad, he said.

She looked at the little speck of shining glass that twisted in his eye.

You're just no good, like me.

There's No
Place Like

TIME WAS A BASTARD. It took Tick back to school and
exhausted Lucky and upset the woman in the bed who
looked into a little mirror and cried. It turned children into
shadows and left her alone sometimes for hours and hours
and for days and the TV was no help and neither was Plastic
Jesus who sat on the desk, pointed his finger and wept. She
rubbed her face. Dorothy twisted her hair into knots in the
corner of the room. She took Plastic Jesus into the living
room and he bobbed his head to nothing but the sound
of the rain and the noise of howling dogs and car radios.
The mad bird called. He flashed his doll face and kept them
all in the hour fifteen and the fifteenth hour shifted to the
fifteenth day and the fifteenth day became the fifteenth

275

week and everything drove on much quicker than it did when she had been with Dad.

She watched the woman in the room sometimes. Watched that long lovely back stretching in the fiery dust and silver plated light. The flat was emptied of furniture and small things more and more each day and Tick hid everything he owned in a safe in the back of the wardrobe and she kept her video in a slit in the mattress with her lipstick and a packet of lemon chewing gum that she had stolen when she was on her own and wandering through the concrete world.

Tick didn't talk much. She watched him from doorframes and corners. He went away and came back again with another stack of money that he kept in a box beneath his bed and sometimes she went out with him and sometimes she stayed at home and sometimes she sat outside the school gates and waited for him to finish and they walked home together and swore loudly into the open windows of cars that drove through town and turned onto thin roads that were not black.

Lucky spoke to Tick in the evenings when they were in front of the TV eating pie or chips or both with tomato sauce. He asked Tick how he was doing at school and what are you up to now and have you seen your mother today and the boy answered fine and nothing and no and Lucky took something from the kitchen and went out again.

She saw Lucky less and less and. She went with Tick to Sweet Street sometimes and then back to the passenger's place where Simon waited for them on the floor in the room full of rabbits, some fine and some almost alive or newly dead and still warm. She didn't see the man again. Only in the stories or actions of the children who vandalized and chewed and molested the whole of the estate and sent their mothers and fathers into misery and thoughts of chasing rabbits.

Any spare change?

Fuck. You.

She couldn't sleep. She looked out of the window where the moon was high and fat and listened to the sound of the boy who was asleep and barking loud in his own bed. He barked louder and louder and sometimes he howled and his mother began to cry asleep or awake in the room next to his. She listened to the boy and the woman and looked at the video that Plastic Jesus guarded and she looked at the cover and turned it around and looked at the back where the scenes were cut and glued back together and she read what she could of the shapes that were written down. Wizard. Oz. Green. Lion. Road. Dorothy. Yellow brick. Dorothy. Dorothy. Lion. Farm. Fifteen. Fifteen. She met the hour with a rolled smoke.

She went out onto the balcony and took off her shoes. She had fallen asleep with the sun on her face when she heard the front door open behind her. She looked back and saw Lucky walking down the hallway and she wiped her eyes underneath the green lenses and stood up and followed him into the hall and closed the door behind her. The sun had got into her eyes and made everything on the inside so dark she struggled to see him standing there.

I was just learning to read. I didn't get far.

Lucky stood in the doorway where the light was bright.

Why do you look at me like that? she said.

Like what?

I don't know. You look at me strange sometimes.

What do you mean?

I don't know. You stare at me. Like.

Like what?

Like work that needs to be finished. Like I'm a dog or.

Or.

I don't know.

I'm sorry. I don't mean it.

It makes me feel so.

I know.

Did you know my father?

No.

He stood for a while smoking and then he turned away and took off his shoes and scratched the hairs on his cheek and went into the living room. She followed him from the living room and into the kitchen where he opened the cupboard doors beneath the sink and brought out a bottle of whisky or rum and came back to the settee to look at the ceiling and drink. He rolled her another cigarette and they smoked and he sank into the chair and she looked at him as he talked.

Do you know that there's a woman who lives on this estate who gets dressed up every day in a suit and wears that suit when she cooks and cleans and takes the kids to school and picks them up? Did you know that?

No.

Do you know why she does it?

She doesn't have anything else to wear.

She does it because she thinks that if she wears a suit every day then she'll look important and if she looks important enough then someone will give her a job. She only has the one suit so sometimes she stays up all night and washes it and dries it and irons it just so she can put it on again in a hurry and listen to the sound of the phone not ringing. What do you think about that?

I don't care much.

He laughed and drank from the bottle and laid his head back to look at the ceiling and she moved closer to him on the settee. He talked and she listened. Lucky was like the sky turning and changing and falling into dark and that made him sadder than death and debt because he would be around forever without wanting it. He drank and she listened to the sound of the bottle filling him up. He drank and.

The curtains were gone from the window. Outside it was cold and it was wet. When the lights from the street came on she saw herself in the glass and when they went out again in flickers and tantrums she saw the wall and the sky and the stars above dotted like a rash. Sometimes she wondered if the sky was just the sea turned upside down. She wondered this and other things while the ugly love tightened in her throat and swelled so big she thought she would choke, and Lucky told her all the reasons to hate him.

I'm so bad. I'm broken. I can't think. I can't see. I still want to die. I don't know who I should help. I think maybe I shouldn't help anyone. I'm punished. I don't know how I can sit here with you. I don't know how I can do anything. Look at my hands. Look at my hands. Aren't they the hands of someone who does such terrible work?

He talked and she stopped listening. She held her film in her hands and looked at the letters again until she saw a word untwisting. Wizard. She stuck the video down the side of the chair and moved closer to Lucky who had already fallen asleep and she took his arm and wrapped it around her shoulder and turned his hand up in her palm and kissed the tips of his fingers. He was like a wizard. She looked at his face and she kissed his cheek that had not been shaved or cleaned that day or yesterday. He moved in his sleep and said something that she couldn't hear and he turned and let his head drop near her face and she watched him sleep. Only she could see him. Only she knew him. She pressed her lips together and took him by his hair and closed her eyes and kissed him. She kissed him on the mouth. She kissed him for a long time. She touched his hands. Kissed him again. Felt herself falling into his skin and into his bones and into his blood that warmed them both up.

The kiss was finished and she pulled her head back and opened her eyes and she looked at Lucky. His eyes were open. He was looking at her. She wanted to speak but her voice had been lost all the way into his mouth and into the back of his throat and she couldn't find it again. His face changed. He turned from the wizard she knew into one she didn't. He doglooked her. She sat up and moved away and he pulled himself back and looked at his hands again. He breathed through his nose and looked at her and sat up in his seat and she wanted to say something but she couldn't. She leaned against him and he took her by the shirt and his face was twisted and his eyes were wide and he shoved her.

He pushed her hard.

All the breath went out of her as she fell backwards off

the end of the settee and she landed on the TV remote that stuck into her back. She looked at him from the floor and she sat up and coughed into her hands. Her breath wouldn't come back. He sat with his fists over his mouth and then he wiped his eyes with his knuckles and laid his head in his fingers. She coughed. She could still feel his shock in her ribs. Her chest was raw and her throat had shrunk to the size of a cigarette. She couldn't get her voice back and she cried about that and cried about everything and she wiped it all with the I hate Jesus tee shirt that Tick had given to her the day before.

They were quiet. The light that flashed on and off had broken sometime after the kiss or sometime after he had pushed her away or perhaps it had broken a long time ago and she hadn't noticed until then.

Outside a bird sang. When she felt alone everything was bigger and colder and noisier and everything was more somehow. There were more doors down those long aisles and more pieces of rubbish that were piled up and carried away on stretches of wind that dragged everything back through the railings on the bridge. There were more steps to make her legs ache and there were more ways to get lost and stay that way. The alleyways were darker and longer and the towers were tall and wide and neither the dogs nor the tribes would ever go to sleep. It was not the place she dreamed about when she first dreamed of something else. The lights were like the roses that bloomed on Dad's arms and legs. Bloody. Raw. Broken.

You can't do things like that, Lucky said.

She looked at him. He was sitting with his fists open and his elbows on his knees and he was opening and closing his hands and looking at the pads on his fingers as though he had not seen them until then. His face was red but he had stopped crying. His eyes were wet and sad but they were lovely and she still thought it even after she knew that he didn't love her.

I love my wife, he said.

Can't you love me too?

I can love you in a different way.

Like Dad loved me?

Yes.

I don't want that. It's too much.

What do you want?

I want that ugly lovely love.

I can't give you that.

She smoked and looked out of the window and she didn't look at Lucky because he wouldn't look at her the same way. He moved away when she sat next to him and he watched her when she got up to go to the toilet and she stayed in the bathroom and thought about big white rooms with closed doors and quiet windows. She took off all her clothes and waited with her arms around her knees and her back against the cold toilet seat but he didn't come for her. The bathroom was warm and wet from the last shower and the black garden that had started to grow into the clear curtain was now trailing along the walls and the tiles and the ceiling. She sat on the toilet and pissed and then she. Lucky knocked on the door but he wouldn't come in.

Go away then, she said.

No. Talk to me.

I can't.

You need help.

I don't want help. I want you to.

You don't want me. You only think you do. You're so fucking young.

Stop talking.

He was silent. Then.

How did you know? he said through the door.

She flushed the piss away and wiped her eyes on the flannel that was lying dirty and wet on the side of the bath and she went to the door and rested her face and shoulder on the wood and warmed her breasts under the yellow light. She listened with her hand against the wood just like she'd done when he had been on the other side of her front door. She felt him press himself against the wood. He talked. She listened and heard. He cried and she listened to that too. Then they were quiet and so was everything else.

I knew your father, he said. You knew it, didn't you?

She raised her hand to the door and closed her eyes.

I couldn't tell you before because I was ashamed. Guilty. Afraid. I knew your father and I knew your mother and I knew you too when you were a little girl. I think a part of you remembers. Maybe. You were so sweet and lovely and you were so smart. You know that? You were smart as anything. Smarter than any of us. We were all friends like you and Tick. We lived on the same block and we went to the same school. My wife and your Mum went to Art College together. Your Mum helped me take care of myself when my father died. I think you probably remember me because I was there on that day. When it happened.

He smoked and drank. His voice got rougher.

Your mother was clever too you know. She looked like you. She was clever and she used to paint these pictures of us and she used to illustrate these little stories for you. She painted the ocean on the living room wall. Do you remember it? Your Dad was great at music. He could sing. He could sing so well they wanted him to sing in front of people. He was like Jagger or something. They were my best friends, you know? I miss them. I miss them a lot.

Another drink. Another break. She wiped her eyes.

I'm sorry too. For you. I'm sorry all the time. I always think it was raining when it happened but it must've been hot and clear because we had just come back from the beach. Do you remember that? I can still remember the way the air smelled. It was salt and vinegar and sugar cooking in wells of fat. We left early. Your Mum was sitting next to you in the back seat and I remember that you kept telling us you were hungry because we didn't stay long enough for food. You were always hungry. Your Mum was in the back and your Dad was in the front and I was driving. I remember you looking at me in my mirror. Your Mum used to say you liked my eyes. I can't see why. You just kept looking at me. I looked at you too and I made faces like you're supposed to do with kids. Your Dad wanted to get back and I was driving too fast. We were young. When you're young you think you'll be someone. You think you'll make a difference and people will know you and your life will mean something but it can all end in a minute. It can become nothing so damn fast. I was driving and you were hungry and crying and your mother took your seatbelt off so you could reach back and get some food and I took my eye off the road for a second and then. That's all it was. It was only a second. God must've taken his eye off the road too. Don't you think? And sometimes I think it was on purpose. Sometimes I think he's not really there and it's only me just wishing he were real. Putting a boss in the sky is easier than thinking that you're in charge of it all. Imagine that, there's only you and this life, it keeps me awake some nights. I try to talk to God about it and sometimes I think he answers but most of the time I think I'm talking to a dead TV character and trying to get a reply. There's no answer. There was no answer that day either, because I hit him.

He drank. She could hear the bottle.

I hit him, Sweetheart. I. I. I hit the little boy. I didn't mean to do it but none of that matters. I fucking did it. The kid ran out into the middle of the road. He was this flash. This little white outline was there in front of my damn car before I could think about doing something. I remember his eyes. They were blue but they turned to white in the light. I could've counted his eyelashes. I know the shape of the scar on his chin and I know the colour of the ball he was chasing and I know the sound his head made when it cracked the window. I know the sound your Mum and Dad made too, Sweetheart, when you were flung from the back seat and flew out past us and went through the window yourself.

It was an accident. It was one terrible second. Then everything was different. There was a before and an after and this life, your life, this house, the kids, the man who sits in the car and watches us, my wife, Tick, it's all the after. The boy had chased his ball from his parents' back garden and he ran into the middle of the road and that was it. I was driving too fast. I looked at you. I had the radio on too loud. We shouldn't have come back early from the beach. It was my fault. It was the worst thing in the world and it was me. I did it.

He stopped. She heard the last of the bottle emptying.

It was our fault. I mean we were in the car, weren't we? We were on the road that day. My hands were on the steering wheel. Your Dad was screaming next to me and your Mum was screaming behind me and you were lying in the middle of the road in front of the car and the boy was lying behind us. Broken. It was my fault because I was driving and it was your Dad's fault for talking so loud about bullshit and it was your Mum's fault for mothering you in the back seat and it was my wife's fault for deciding to visit her mother instead of driving us there. It was my fault. Yours. Everyone.

None of it matters though. You can tell yourself you weren't to blame but you can't take yourself out of the car. You can't drive a little slower. You can't decide not to get up. You can't stay at the beach a little longer. You can't change anything. That's your life. That's what you did and it's never going to change. You'll always be the one who did that one terrible thing. You see, Sweetheart, the reason I've tried so hard to die isn't anything to do with Luck. I know people don't understand. I know Tick hates me for it and you

288

probably don't understand either, but maybe you should just sit down and think about it. What can you live with? How much can you take? That's what life is, for me. Fingers constantly pointing at a kid's messed up face half-buried in blood and glass. Saying look there. Look what you did. The thoughts go round and round and they splinter and stick in me like nails. Look at what you did. Think about what you did. Drums. Drums. Banging on. Think about it every minute of every day. Remember. Every damn day. And I can't forget. Not even while I'm talking to you. I see his face. Even now. He's lying on the carpet right there next to the front door. Staring at me. One shoe off. Foot crushed. Little blue eyes looking at nothing. I can't ever forget. I see him. Always. Now you tell me, does that sound lucky to you?.

She was quiet. After a long time she stood up and collected her clothes that were draped over the side of the bath and she slipped her head through the hole in her tee shirt. She put on her knickers and jeans and did the zip and button and she looked at herself right there in the mirror. Her face. Eyes. Lips. Shoulders. She stared at herself for so long that her face became distorted and blurred. She was a stranger.

After the accident, Lucky said, I was frozen behind the wheel. Your Mum and Dad got out of the car though. They had to. They picked you up and looked at you. The boy had broken the glass on the way over the car. He smashed himself on the window so that by the time you were flung off the back seat you didn't have the same impact. When you went through the car and landed on the bonnet all you had was a graze on your neck and a few missing teeth and a nasty bump on the head. Your parents went to you first. I still remember the screams. I went to the boy. I got out and went behind the car and stood over him and I just looked at him. He was like a doll or something. He didn't even look real. His eyes were open but he wasn't there. His arm was bent right back and the bone was sticking out of his wrist. His back was crushed and his legs were twisted up so bad they looked like rope. I just stood there looking at him. I remember feeling the wind on my face and listening to someone's TV talking from an open window. There was blood. Mess. The boy was gone.

I expected to see someone running for him from a back door or something but there was nobody around. There was no screaming mother or father leaping over the garden fence to tear into me. The boy had nobody and nothing changed. Nothing stopped. Everything carried on and I heard children playing in the park behind the tower and a dog barking and music from my own radio that I hadn't turned off. I still remember the song that played. I can't listen to it but I know what it is. It was White Rabbit by Jefferson Airplane. Such a messed up song to hear while the boy was lying there dead. I couldn't do anything. The only thing that was different that day was us. I even looked different after that day. Your Dad too. I didn't like who I was. I didn't like the smell of my own skin. I'd always be the guy who drove too fast and I'd always be someone who killed a little kid.

Your mother came and grabbed me. She stood in front of me and turned my face away from the boy and then I was looking right at her while she was talking and I didn't hear a damn thing she said. She was shouting. Her mouth was so wide and her eyes. They were. I'll never forget her eyes. She was pulling my face and she was screaming and she was pointing back down the road. I turned away and looked there and your Dad was standing with you in his arms. He was looking down at you with his hands right in front of him. Your mother was pointing, screaming, frantic and all I could hear was that damn song. I looked at your Dad standing there with all that blood on his hands and then I heard everything all at once. Your Mum told me the boy was dead and she screamed at me to take you to the hospital. We'll come back, she said. We can't stay here. I turned and took you out of your father's arms and laid you down on the back seat and I told your mother to get in the car. She got in and held your head on her lap and your Dad went into the passenger seat still looking at the blood on his hands. I opened my door and got in. I stopped. My hands were shaking. Your mother was still screaming at me to drive on. In the mirror I saw a little foot that stuck out from behind on the road. I wanted it to move. I wanted some sign that he was still alive, but he never moved. So I started the car and I drove away. We got you to the hospital and we sat in the hall in the children's ward and nobody spoke. We didn't talk and nobody said anything about the boy and we didn't talk after that day. We weren't the same Nothing was. I think we all sort of fell into our heads. I'm the only one left now. That's my punishment. I sat behind the wheel and then I drove away and I'm the one who God's never going to let go. We all learned later on that the little boy hadn't died. There was a newspaper spread about it. We made everything worse by leaving and we couldn't go back after that. We couldn't confess. The boy was still alive. I found out later that his mother was a junky and she'd been asleep when it happened. The boy's father was in work. I found out that the boy had been lying there like that for ages. I didn't go back and the boy stayed on the ground, looking up at the sun, for hours.

He fell against the door on the other side and she listened to him breathing slow and deep. She closed her eyes and saw the blood on her mother's face and the open hands of her father and Lucky's eyes that were framed in the black edged mirror. She remembered the painful snow, that broken windscreen that she saw falling down around her and the horror in the voices that stayed with her all the way to the hospital room. Lucky had been young and so had Mum and Dad though she couldn't imagine them like that. Young. Happy. They were a little older than her, and their lives were split in two by the sea and the sand and by dangerous games inside fast cars. She wiped her eyes and let her cheek rest on her knees.

Simon, Lucky said from the other side of the door.

The boy's name was Simon.

Fly My Pretty

LUCKY TALKED FOR hours.

Something happened to the estate after that, he told her. The whole estate was different. It changed. Something hung over everything and drained the colour out of the sky and people sometimes stand outside for hours at a time and look up as though they expect to see something there. Simon's mother moved away and didn't want to be found. I've seen the father though. I'll never forget the look on his face in the newspaper. He doesn't know who I am and he doesn't know what I've done. I see him all the time. He's a tattoo between my eyes. Right here, on my memory.

There's chaos on this estate. Punishment. Suffering. Judgement. Sometimes Simon's father comes to the middle of the park and he holds his finger up and points from balcony to balcony and he shouts out. Screams. Howls. He tells us that we're all guilty. He knows it. We're all judged. We're all at fault. Cowards. Thieves. Reptiles. We're the wretched cunts of humanity. I listen like a coward when he comes, I hear it all, then I crawl away and hide.

If you and Tick ever see a man in a silver car you should stay away. Don't go near him. Don't talk to him. Men who are hurting are dangerous. They'll stamp out everyone and everything just to try to stop the pain. I don't want you or my son to ever have to suffer him. Can you promise me that? I don't want you to have to suffer that. What one man does to another should be kept between them. The suffering should be mine. Not yours. Not Tick's. Sometimes I imagine putting a gun in his hand. Sometimes I imagine a lot of things when it's dark and the darkness feels like fists in my eyes. I think about it all the time. His hand. A gun. My head lies between the barrel and the cool concrete. I close my eyes and then.

She didn't speak. After he finished talking she heard him shuffle and rise and open another bottle and zip up his coat and she felt him lean once more on the bathroom door before going off down the hall. Then she heard the front door closing. She felt the cold of the outside rushing in, and he was gone then into the night. She stayed where she was a while longer, the weight of everything pressing her so low she thought she'd fall through the floor. She imagined being pushed through the tiles and then through the ceiling of another room, another floor, another ceiling, all the way down to the concrete steps and then the cool earth where the mud was like butter. She knew the faults of her father and the faults of Lucky and Mum and Tick and everyone who had lived and died in those rows of concrete. She knew herself. Whoever she was. Small. Bad. Alone. Ugly. Pretty. Lovely. She had turned eighteen behind a bathroom door, talking to a beautiful wizard, and one who had drained the last ounces of magic from the world.

She had not seen Lucky for a long time. Weeks. Months. Maybe. Time went different since she knew how to count it. The mad bird reminded her that fifteen was fifteen was fifteen and there was nothing she could do about that. Lucky was gone since he. The woman cried and Tick turned from uncaring to angry to upset until he panicked about his father and showed it by punching walls and doors and trying to set fire to the school. He was home after that. Home to worry and to think and thinking was worse at home, he said. While they flew and raged and spat words out like sour pips she didn't say anything and the winter ended in grief. Then the days were warmer and the road was hot and the heat lifted to her knees and she could smell the burning of the tarmac as she walked on the road. The schools wouldn't keep the children during those hot weeks so they walked the road in their special groups and wrote their names on the high wall and sold their rabbits and ran when tall men came and handed money to the passenger who sat gazing out from a rumbling silver car. She didn't play with the children again. The last of the balls had been broken and none of the children asked for another. There was a red balloon that came and floated low in the air and then began to rise up next to one of the towers and off towards the fat sun. A pale boy stood looking there and then his eyes moved beyond it to the swirling green clouds and then beyond that where there was nothing but the blue air. The boy looked deeply, as though trying to remember something that was pushed too deep to dig up. Then the balloon lifted, floated high, swung around cables and drifted to the tops of the clouds until it was too high to see. The boy watched it go, and then he looked back to the road again, then to his feet, then to his hands as though for a moment he had not been himself.

On the way home from Sweet Street Tick took all he'd made and divided it into three parts and slid one part into his back pocket and one part into his front pocket and gave her the rest. She had been collecting her money but she had no reason for that. She didn't know what she could buy and she didn't know what she wanted apart from cigarettes and lipstick and fairytales in books that Tick taught her how to read. Tick told her to save it for something big.

I don't want anything.

Nothing?

No.

Everyone wants something.

I don't.

Well, what's the point in making money?

What's the point in anything?

In the night she worked on the cuckoo that was still mad and had not released her or anyone else from that long fifteenth hour. The bird flew at her and smiled with its doll face and stared at her with its sugary eyes as she worked it to the perch. She got it trapped and screwed it tight and pushed it back into its house and kept her hands on the door until the bird was still and quiet. She thought of Lucky. Then the bird bashed its head against the doors one more time and stopped.

Let's go out, Tick said when he came out of the bathroom.

Do you want to look for Lucky again?

No, I'm done with that.

He's coming back.

He might not.

He's coming back.

Stop it. We can't think about that. I have to be the one now. If I say we're going out, we're going out. I'm in charge. I have to be. I have to make more money if I'm going to take care of everything here. That's natural. I was just looking into the bathroom mirror and I realized something. I looked into my eyes and I thought that my eyes were the eyes of a man. Do you understand? A grown up. An adult. In that second I grew up because I decided it. It doesn't matter if I look like a boy because I'm not a boy. Not anymore. I have to be the one now. I have to take care of you and Mum and that's just. That's just how it is.

Fine, she said.

The boy was right. He had exploded and raged from the funny boy to the serious and silent shadow of what once there was, one that could sink into the alleys or fill up the room with hot white light. Since Lucky left he had taken care of the woman in the bed and he had taught her things in books and he had not talked about jokes or games and he no longer balanced on the edge of a bridge. His eyes were tired. The skin beneath was swollen. Sometimes he had bruises. Cuts. Burn marks. He would come home and his face would turn away or look into the fabric of a chair and chew on thoughts that she couldn't see. He was disappearing. Stripped of flesh. Hollow like an iron rail, beaten into the ground.

Let's go to the park first, she said.

What's the point?

The swings. The slide. The.

We'll go to the park, but not to play.

What else is there to do?

They dressed in their dark hoods and Tick put on his boots and tied the laces around his ankles and she put on a pair of thick socks and a scarf that Tick had stolen from a rich kid, and they both went out. It was dark. Cold. The days were hot but as soon as the sun went down and the moon came up everything froze. She could see the moon, her mother's right eye, which was working to arrest her where she stood. She looked up and set her hood over her head and pulled it just above her eyes and looked back towards the sky street with her head and sight darkened.

The concrete bridges seemed to last forever when it was night. They stretched out in the white glow of the moon and the orange glow of the streetlights that flickered and made the bridges seem like they were moving. Breathing. The estate was like a lung and the black streets were veins and the concrete grew thin as the slit of moon above them and everything unfolded brick by brick to fill all the cracks and broken bones of the world. Tick walked quickly with the hard rain coming down and soaking into his hood. She yawned. Lightning in the sky cracked her eyes awake and for one half second it lifted the estate into day before sending it all back to dark again. Everything was different. She missed Lucky. She wanted to be bad and she wanted to follow Tick to the end of everything that had been good before.

Rain tinked and tanked off a satellite dish and a curtain closed and opened and a door slammed and the noises of sex came from a window that was part opened. She stopped to listen and to be aroused and then she looked at Tick who sped over another bridge in front of her. She ran to catch him. The boy was a quick shadow. The light made green paths in the rainwater that fell all along the narrow corridors of the estate. She shouted for no reason. Mum's eye beamed down and Dad's face was set in all the windows. She ran and Dorothy ran in the windows beside her.

She was a shadow and she disappeared in a patch of dark and the boy stopped and looked back for her and she was not there. He called her name and walked slowly back along the bridge and called her name again and said this isn't funny and he said the word fuck over and over quiet and afraid. She watched him through the railings of the bridge and when he was close enough to touch she sprung up and shouted and the boy spun around and clutched his chest like she had killed him. He looked at her.

What are you doing?

I'm playing a game.

Don't.

Remember when you used to.

Don't.

She had climbed over the railing of the bridge and onto the other side where there was a thin concrete perch. The boy jerked his head and grabbed hold of her arms and she looked down at all the darkness that had fallen to the bottom of the world and she looked at her own red shoes and her thick wet socks that were standing in the middle of it all. She clicked her heels together and knocked stones off the bridge and she watched them fall down and down and. She was up so high. The rest of the world was down so low. The streetlights were like little silver fish and she moved her foot off the bridge and drew a circle in the air. She couldn't tell which way was up and which way was down. She clicked her heels once more and said home is no place.

The boy grabbed her arms and she started and took hold of his shirt and felt the wind toss her backwards. She pulled herself and used his arms to lift her body over the rail and step to the inside of the bridge and when she was safe again he held her hand and held it to his face.

Don't do that again, he said.

Why not?

Just don't do it.

It doesn't matter.

Why doesn't it matter?

Nothing matters.

You're crazy.

I should be dead.

What?

I think I died already after the accident. I think I died on the road.

You're crazy.

I know. So are you. We're both long gone.

His ears were red and swollen from where the rain and cold air had got to them and he pulled his hood up and held his hand out but she didn't take it. She stood in front of him and took his hood in her hands and blew down the side of his face and warmed his ears. Somewhere a dog barked and Simon laughed and in another place there were people all huddled and they were hungry and sorry and there was no redemption for anyone.

This is the first time I've done this, he said. It's okay. I'm okay. I'll be fine. I'm doing it for my Mum and I'm doing it for myself. One day I'm going to take us both away from here before it's too late. When I was seven I learned that one day my Mum will die and I decided to do something about that. I don't want my Mum to live and die in this place. I want her to die somewhere beautiful.

What about Lucky?

He can die anywhere he wants. I'm taking my Mum to Australia or Vietnam. I'm taking her somewhere warm. Where there are gardens and beaches and mountains. I'm leaving and I'm never coming back and my Mum won't be miserable all her life and she'll get out of bed to come with me. That's what it means to be older. A man. If she knows she's going somewhere beautiful she'll get up and get dressed and she'll come with me.

I think she will.

Do you know how to keep a secret?

I'm good at it.

Then keep it. Or kill me.

She held him by the sleeve of his hoody and they took the stairs and not the lift that had not been safe since that time when. They held onto the railings and went down the stairs and for a moment he was a boy and then in another instant he was gone again. The moon shone and then became dull. A man shouted and then grew quiet. She knew how to keep a secret because she was a secret. She looked into the shine of a metal handle and she told him they should both feel guilty.

He looked at her and didn't speak. They went through the big heavy doors at the bottom of the tower that still smelled like piss and eggs and she sang Somewhere Over the Rainbow and Tick looked at her and said that the film wasn't real.

Don't say that.

It's true. Not real.

It is.

Dorothy is called Judy and Judy is dead.

You're lying.

It's true.

Judy who?

Judy Garland. She was an actress and she died of.

Don't say it.

All right.

What did she die of?

What do you think?

She couldn't think. Some of the rabbits had got into her head and now they were jumping all around and making a mess. They went into the park where the bad dog waited on the wall and began to bark and howl as soon as they came close. The dog looked at her with his one big eye and snapped at the place where the wall was broken in two and he turned around and around and watched them both where they walked and didn't play. Tick told her to wait where she was. Hide yourself away. There. Go under there. Don't make a sound. Watch and learn. This isn't a game, not anymore. There are no games. There's only this. There's only me and you and what we're here to do.

Are we supposed to be doing this?

No, and the passenger doesn't know.

Will he find out?

Only if someone tells him.

What will you do if he finds out?

I'll die. I'll get hurt. I'll not last the week. Be quiet.

She hid underneath the slide and looked at the boy through the slats in the ladder that she had climbed the night before to spit at insects. The bars were rusted. When she wiped her hand across them they flaked a red dust that blew back over her face when the wind caught it up. She chewed a good piece of rubber that she had torn off the end of the handle of a kid's bike that was left to rot on the bank of the muddy river that ran alongside Sweet Street. Tick picked up a brick and chucked it at the dog on the wall and the dog moved away and snapped at the air where the brick had been swung. He picked up another and another.

She told Dad to shut up inside her head and she killed the itches on the inside of her wrist and rubbed her stomach where there was a knot that was tightening more and more as she watched the boy. Tick jerked his head and stamped his boots and tugged on his tee shirt and flashed all the silver in his mouth and said the word fuck and kept his eye on that place where the wall was split in half and the dog watched her as she rubbed the red dust from her face. She wasn't hungry. She hadn't been hungry for a long.

She was not. She was not. She was not.

Two shadows that were moving outside the lime green burn of the sickly buzzing streetlight came through the crack in the wall and stood on the opposite side of the park. The shadows were small and they were watchful and they stood hand in hand and warmed themselves in the light that did not give warmth. They lit their eyes beneath it. She could see the right eye of one and the left eye of the other. Burning.

The shadows looked at Tick and he looked at them and he stood still with a rock raised up in his fist. He barked and spat. They came in each other's arms into the patch of broken stones that spewed from the open mouth of the wall and made them stagger when they tried to walk over them. Tick dropped the stone and waited for them as they made their way into the light that stuck to the fog and sat in the middle of the park.

The rain got heavier. She could hear it typing something on the lid of the discarded freezer that Tick once pissed in.

The shadows were children. They were sisters with the same face. They came chewing gum and blowing fat white bubbles. They held hands and stretched black ties around their hair that was gathered into a tight tail at the back of their heads. They were talking that look-at-me talk. Walking that look-at-me walk. They were older than Tick but not by much and she looked at them long and hard and decided that they were fourteen or fifteen. They were using their hands to talk and talking loud and stretching their words and laughing and making faces that were lipsticked and unkind.

Oi you, the right sister said.

You got something, yeah? the other said.

They stopped in front of the beautiful boy who had spiked his long hair up so high that day that not even the rain or the hood could pat it down. She tried to see them better and she slid from the ladder and over to the swings that had not been swung for some time and she lay down on her belly and watched them with her chin in her hands. The dog on the wall snapped and grunted at her and she told it to hush so she could watch and listen and it growled and tossed the dirt with its nose and the girls pointed at the boy and spat into the rain and said I'm talking to you.

The sister who stood on the left laughed. She moved forward into the light and twirled her hair around her fingers and drummed her fingers on her belly that stuck out like a full balloon beneath her school shirt. She rubbed her hands over it and watched the face of the boy who looked at her and then looked down at her belly.

The girl on the left laughed long and mad at something her sister said and she watched the boy from the corner of her eye and she sucked on an aluminium can. She drank it all down and laughed high and loud and long and then she chucked the can into the fridge that was still open. The can dunked into the water that had been filling the fridge since the rain started.

Her mother came into her head and began to sing songs that she didn't understand and she could smell the sea and hear the water and feel the cold rocks beneath her feet and then it was all gone again.

What's that? the boy said.

He pointed to the belly of the laughing girl.

What do you think it is? Pregnant, aint she? the other sister said.

The boy pulled something from his pocket. It was one of the white rabbits that he had kept back from Sweet Street and didn't return to the rest of the pile that he kept in an old biscuit tin beneath his bed. The little rabbit lay flat in the clear packet that Tick would not give over to the right sister when she opened her hand.

Who's going to have this then? Tick said.

He was taller than he used to be. She was the same as she'd been before. The sisters snatched at the packet that the boy held over his head and then behind him and they came forward as he stepped back. She played with the twist on her finger and then looked up again. Tick pushed them both back and slipped the packet into his back pocket and

Plastic Jesus looked out from his tee shirt with the word fuck above his head and he didn't try to help. Tick was so much taller than he used to be.

Who's going to have this? It's not going to be her.

We're gonna share it, the right sister said. We'll share that and we'll share dinner and we'll share the baby too when it comes out of her fanny.

She spat into the mud and nudged her sister and the left child looked at her but she didn't laugh. She rubbed her belly and twisted her sleeve around her thumb and the boy looked at the belly and stepped back once and then again and he didn't look behind him as he walked because he knew the path through all of the junk that had been tossed without pity into the park.

You're not having it if you're going to give some to her, he said.

The boy turned and walked away. The sisters whispered together like fairytale witches and the boy shouted back and said what the fuck is wrong with you. The girls plotted and planned and seized the time and held hands and they looked at Tick and then they ran at him.

The rain got in her eyes and she took off her glasses and rubbed her face and she breathed small and quiet. The boy fought to keep the rabbit from the girls. There were sirens. A dog. Traffic. There was a car that came past along the black road. The wind. Another dog. Smashed glass. Fire. Music. Fighting. Everything was loud and all at once. She put on the glasses again and she watched the two girls as they rushed at Tick and knocked him to the ground.

The dog on the wall barked and snapped at the children as they fought and they fought so hard that they didn't see her as she stood up and came from beneath the rubber of the swinging seat. The boy took the packet from his jeans and held it in front of him and the girls knocked him down and he lay facing the ground with the mud in his eyes and the dirt turning into dust from a bag of cement that had been dumped and left to peel away over the mound inside it. The boy turned grey as he struggled. He said no no no no no no and then he said hut hut hut when the girls kicked him in his side and all the air that was in him blew out.

She came from the swing and went around the concrete that kept the iron in the ground and her fists were pumping and her breath was short and the moths were a gale of wings. The right sister pulled the boy's hoody and pinched his pale back and he put his hand there and rolled over and she slapped him in the eye. The sisters were laughing and so was that damn dog on the. She spat at him as she passed. She walked quickly and didn't make a sound. The right sister snatched the packet from the boy. Little wanker, one of them said. Fucking this. Fucking that.

Little shit. Boy. Shit. Piece of. Grubby little.

The right sister laughed and waved the white rabbit above her head but it was the other sister, the one with the big moon belly and the wordless mouth, who did it to him. The boy was breathless on the floor and his eyes were pinched shut and he was holding his guts with one hand and rubbing his back with the other and one sister whispered to the other and they both laughed and then the sister with the belly stepped over the boy and stood above his head with her legs wide apart. She lifted up her skirt and slipped her thumb through the crotch of her knickers and moved them to one side until her private lips were showing. She squatted down. A little lower. Fucking this. Fucking that. Then she did it. She pissed.

The girl squatted down and pissed on him.

The boy didn't move at first. He looked at the girl in that place and watched as the piss came to him and then he stayed there for seconds longer and then he cried. He cried hard. He closed his eyes and tears collected in his lashes. He rubbed his face. Spit collected between his teeth. His nose ran. The girl told him he was thick as shit. Your family is shit. Your Dad is dead and your Mum is mental. Little prick with a little. Prick with a little. The girl pissed and cursed and she cursed him and she cursed his Mum and she cursed his Dad and his grandmother who had moved to the estate to become a whore, they said. The boy cried.

He turned on his side with his hands on his face. She had stopped somewhere around the dog because Tick had told her not to interfere no matter what happened. He was a man and he could take care of things himself. He told her that things could go easy and he told her that things could go hard and he told her that things could go violent because that's the way it was with kids. There was always violence that was built up underneath like roots growing thicker and thicker until one day something bursts. She felt them inside her then. There was a root for herself and there was a root for Mum and Dad and Simon and Lucky and there was a root for the grandparents that she couldn't remember and those she had never met and on and on for many mothers all back in the past. She felt them. They throbbed. Like hearts.

The girls walked away from the boy with the prize in their hands and they tossed it from one hand to the other and then into the air where the light chased the packet in the air. They laughed. They walked along the wall that was peppered with the names of a hundred children that were still living and a hundred others that had died when their bodies had grown old. They came to the stones that had rolled down from the break in the wall and they stopped to look at the white rabbit and to smoke.

Tick was on the floor and the moon burst from behind a travelling silver cloud and she looked at the two girls who laughed and. And she ran. She ran. She ran. Fast. Faster. She ran in those shoes that were bright red and too small for her feet until she reached the sisters who turned towards her as she came and screamed when she took bunches of their hair in her hands and pulled them back into the park.

She let go of the sister with the fat round belly and she took the other one instead and took her hair over her shoulder like a sack and yanked her down from the stones. The sister with the belly screamed and the dog on the wall howled. She twisted the hair up in her hands and she yanked it hard one time and brought the girl down to the ground and then she dragged her backwards along the dirt and mud that pressed around her shoulders. The girl snatched at her hair and dug her nails into her hand and into her fingers but she had no feeling there. The girl pulled her little finger but there was no feeling there either and she couldn't feel anything but the cold and the shape of the no-nail twist on the end.

She cursed the girl and spat. The sister with the baby inside screamed on the edge of the park with one hand on her belly and the other on her face and she didn't stop while her sister was being dragged. The one in the dirt offered up what she had stolen and she stopped dragging her and she took the white rabbit and looked at it in the light. She let go of the girl and she put the rabbit into her pocket and she took hold of her by the collar of her school uniform and she looked at her crying face that was swollen and green through the lenses of her glasses and she slapped her. She slapped her once. She slapped her hard in the face and the noise of it was like a firework. The slap bounced off the towers then it disappeared somewhere above the estate.

The girl looked at her.

The dog was quiet then. Everything was.

She stood up and let the girl go and watched her stumble through the dark and through the hole and out of the park holding onto her hair and her cheeks and everything as though she was afraid it would all come away. The dog on the wall began to bark again but she was not afraid. She went over to Tick who had pulled himself onto his knees to watch her as she stole back the rabbit.

The muscles in her legs were still twitching from the long run across the park and her fingernails were still covered with red mud and she felt sick and it was a good sickness. Whole. Strong. She wasn't scared of anything, not the man in her head or the mother in her eyes or the twins who cursed and pissed or the moon in the sky or the fish in the sea or the silver poet or the root inside that went back a hundred years to a place she had forgotten or the museum she had forgotten or the men and women who loved that junk or the smell of gone off food or her own mind or the dark plughole or any of the days that were left or the face of

Plastic Jesus that could answer all the questions she didn't want to ask or the passenger or that lovely ugly love or the way the beautiful boy looked at her then.

Tick didn't have a voice and the hoody he was wearing had been lifted over his pale belly that was now red where the blood had rushed to the pinch. His eyes were red and his head was still dripping with the piss that came from the girl and had a bitter rotten apple smell. She sat down next to him and pulled his head into her lap and wiped his face with her sleeve and she rubbed his hair out of those spikes and she sang a song about Dorothy that came to her then.

She kissed him on the face and wiped the dirt out of his eyes and she told him he was good and kind and lovely. He cried into his hands and she watched him. He had grown since she met him. He was fourteen and almost a man and fighting against a boyhood that he had no use for, and he was too old for childish games and too old to be cut so deeply and too high to be brought down so low and too lovely to be broken. She thought that boys who claw manhood to their chests are all too easy to hurt, and what was worse was that he was not a man yet. He was still hers. The boy from long ago who took her out and showed her how to stand on the edges of walls. What was worse was that he loved her and what was worse than the others was that when the pregnant child had moved her knickers aside with her thumb, and

Tick looked up into that secret place, she saw it rise up in his jeans. She saw his private thing rise up in his jeans. She stroked his hair. He held her very tight. He cried.

It didn't go back down again until he learned to stop.

Boy Broken

THE WRITING ON the wall was all scratches and swears. It was slang and rude words and bloody pictures that had been spat along the walls by the young and impatient. Some of the children had gathered to look at Tick but they didn't point and didn't say anything. She stood the boy up and walked with him out of the park and over the hump of concrete and through the metal doors and out into the night again. She didn't speak. Tick didn't kick the football that stood in his path. The children stood aside and looked at the ground and wiped their tired eyes.

An old man slid his hand down the front of his jeans and played with himself in the concrete tunnel and looked at her breasts as she went past. In her head the estate had become like the darkest spaces of home. It was like the cracks in the walls or the soles of her mother's shoes still kept at the back of the cupboard. It was the back of her father's throat after he had taken his last breath. It was the sound of sirens. Dogs. Fast feet. Crying. It was a fresh howl down an old street or a layer of dust on a broken TV screen. She asked him if he wanted to try phoning Lucky once more and he shook his head and they walked without holding hands and without speaking through the grey everything. Tick stopped to tie his shoe near a newly closed factory. She stopped to rest her legs that still ached from the run. It took a while to get home. His feet were slow. So were hers. It was dark. Wet. Quiet. The dark got inside her and softened her bones.

They went through the front door and Tick stood in the hallway and didn't answer her when she said his name and asked him if he was feeling all right. He looked at the space three feet in front of his boots and then he looked at his hands that should have been full of money but were instead covered in piss and dirt. It was quiet all around. Quiet in her head. The noise of the estate had been blunted by the front door and his mother had tossed herself to sleep sometime during that lunatic hour and his father was outside drowning himself in sorrowful work or the black book or some other kind of horror. She and the boy were alone in the empty hall.

The dog on the wall had followed them into the flat. A siren sang and predicted their deaths. Once, twice, three times over. She said nothing. The boy washed his face in the sink and rubbed the suds into his hair rough and hard and he filled his hands with water and tipped it on the top of his head and let it run down his face and back into the sink again. He looked at her in the bathroom mirror where she stood behind him. The dog on the wall had disappeared when the sun began to come through the windows and through the segmented glass in the front door. The boy's eyes were different. Blunt. Sorry. They were drained of colour and spark and they no longer reflected her face back to her.

Can you talk to me?

He shook his head.

She turned on the TV in the living room and the boy came and sat in front of it with his knees drawn up to his face and the sunlight creeping over his back and his mind on things that were not with them in the room. She went into the bedroom and brought a pack of cigarettes back with her and sat next to the boy and lit one up and gave it to him and lit one up for herself and they sat and smoked together. On the TV was a man in a suit who hated the poor. He said so over and over. They were lazy and what was theirs was their own damn fault and the faults of their parents who should've known not to have children. They changed channels. On the other side was a girl with fine yellow hair who was told to shut up over and over until she cried.

She laughed. Smoked. She laughed and didn't know why. The boy smoked with her and said nothing and she watched him during the adverts and ignored him when something good was on and the smoke rose into the air above them and the sunlight came stronger through the window. Dorothy was on the TV. She wasn't an actress and she wasn't dead. She appeared in adverts for betting shops and in colouring books and in pubs where there was whisky and crisps but no singing. She changed the channel. The boy turned to her.

Have you ever been drunk? he said.

No. I've seen drunk people. I've never been drunk.

Tick stood up and went into the kitchen and stood next to the sink. He went underneath and there was a bucket and inside were two glass bottles half filled with clear liquid that she knew was not water. He sat down and faced her with his legs crossed and he gave her one bottle and he took the other and he opened his and took a drink and pulled a face and jerked his jaw. He drank again. He looked at her.

She looked at the bottle in her lap and she thought of Dad who had bottles just like this one emptied and stacked in a pile in his bedroom and underneath the chair in the living room and beside the Hi-Fi and in the attic where he used to drink because he didn't want her to see. Sometimes she heard him crying. She twisted the lid and smelled the acid and petrol that fed into the air and she closed her eyes and lifted the bottle. She drew her tongue back and felt the liquid running and she swallowed it and felt the sting of it at the back of her throat.

She looked at him and watched him lift the bottle to his lips and she watched his throat working to send it all through his pipes and into his head. She drank. Supped. The liquid poured cold and poisonous down her throat and into her stomach where it heated up and boiled and burned all the air out of her lungs. She took too much. Couldn't breathe. Her lungs jerked in fits and snatches and Tick laughed as she leaned over and sucked the air.

The boy drank again. They drank together until their throats and legs went numb and their bellies were warm and their minds were full of jokes and the edges of the room were blunt and their feet became fat in their shoes and nothing was bad and they didn't need air to live only the smoke and the booze and the good time and the Hey-Dee-Dee. She laughed but she. The TV twisted around the room and on the screen there was Dorothy and standing next to her was Dad who she had not seen for all those yesterdays gone and would not see for all those tomorrows that were yet to come. Dorothy held her little dog in her hands. Dad smiled. He had the most beautiful teeth. The loveliest chin.

The room shifted in the light that came thick through the

window. Her eyes darted to the patches of sun that spread along the edge of the TV and the microwave in the kitchen and the silver spoon that had dropped on the carpet next to the settee. She drank. The boy was somewhere. He was sitting far away on the end of the black road and so close to her face that she could smell the burning at the back of his throat and the smoke that huffed out of his mouth and the piss that remained on his hair and clothes. She couldn't find him. He was laughing mad and hysterical at something she couldn't see. She fell forward and snatched at the thick material of his hoody and the little speck of shining glass that had been born again in his eye and she laughed and wiped her face and thought on Dad who had always told her she was a good girl. The boy took her by the shoulders and leaned towards her and pushed his lips together and waited for a kiss that would not come. She looked at him and touched his lips with her fingers. You're so. She fell back and the boy rushed forward. He kissed her so fast and hard it hurt. The metal in his mouth was like. The kiss was heavy and his braces cut her lip and she bit the inside of her cheek and drew up the taste of blood.

It made her feel sick. She couldn't breathe. She pushed him away and he fell to the carpet and he punched the floor and wrapped his arms around his face. She stood up and found her way to the kitchen and stood over the sink and opened her mouth and stuck her fingers in just like she used to do with Dad when he was. She felt the retch and she threw it all up. She steadied herself on the sink edge and closed her eyes and felt the sun rising on her back. She thought of Lucky. The moths came sputtering. She drank a glass of water and wiped her mouth. She turned on the tap and pulled the hair out of her face and watched all the sickness go down the plughole. She cried, but it wasn't a lot, just enough to pass the rest of the drunk. She looked at the plughole where there used to be all these noises that she didn't know. Now she knew them. It was the groaning of home, and the sound of life. She knew it now, that tremendous agony.

She went to the boy who lay there far away and close and he said sorry and said it a thousand times. He wiped his face and drew his fists into his lap and he coughed and closed his eyes. He wouldn't look at her. On the TV there was a cartoon and the cartoon told them it was five or six or eight in the morning but she didn't know because she had lost time. The bird said fifteen. She looked at the boy.

You can't do that, she said. You can't just do that.

I'm sorry. I thought it was okay. I'm bad. I'm a bastard.

You're not bad.

I am. I hurt you. I'm so fucking. I'm so messed up.

No. You just made a mistake. You're a good.

Then.

Then what? Look at me.

No. No, I won't. I can't.

Then what?

Then why don't you love me?

They sat in silence. They watched cartoons and they drew themselves together on the carpet. The boy laid his head in her lap and she let him keep it there. They were both still drunk but sobering as the sun poured in fatter and fatter through the window. She had never seen the world drunk and through her father's eyes. It was so dream-like and different. All the edges were blurred and there was no feeling in anything. There were hundreds of colours more than in Dorothy's rainbow. There were sounds like the falling of water but it wasn't rain. She loved the boy. And she didn't love him. She didn't know who she loved. She loved them all. Mum. Dad. Lucky. Tick. She loved the woman in the bed with the long beautiful back and she loved the beggar who scrambled to the floor whenever he stood in a crowd and heard something drop. She loved them all. She loved herself. She loved them all.

She thought of her mother who painted oceans and yellow boats and she thought of Dad who told her more than once that her mother was a bitch and more than once that she was the best person he knew. Love changed with time. It was an ugly lovely thing that came up with the day and down with the night and lived deep in the bones of everyone old and young. She kissed the boy on the top of the ears and listened to him breathing deeply. She loved through her pores, and it was her father who taught her that.

She slept curled around the boy with the TV on in front of them. When they woke up she was looking at the boy and the boy was looking at her. He jerked his chin and spoke. She brushed the hair out of his eyes and looked at his face and she asked him what he had said and she licked the blood off her lips.

I don't want to work on Sweet Street anymore.

I don't think you should do anything you don't want to.

It's not that easy.

It is. You decide something and then it happens. That's how everything works.

Sometimes you decide something and because of that you get hurt.

In cartoons.

In real life too. Sometimes when you decide something it's bad. Worse. When you decide something it changes everything and sometimes they don't like that. Sometimes they don't like it and then they come to hurt you. And sometimes they hurt your family. Real life is so much more complicated than you think. My secret is much more complicated than you think.

She sat up. Tick sniffed into his hand and brought his knees to his chest and jerked his neck and hiccupped. His face was red and his freckles bloomed. Inside his eye the little speck of shining glass was dull again and it reflected nothing.

Are you scared?

Yeah. I am.

Tell your Mum. Find Lucky. Tell him.

I can't. I'm terrified. I'm scared all the time, Anna. All. The. Time. I can't tell anyone. None of us can. I want to leave but I can't do that because. I just can't do it. I'm stuck. We're all stuck. We can't do anything and we can't tell anyone about it and sometimes I wish I were as mad as my Dad. Sometimes I wish I were brave enough to swallow all the white rabbits under my bed at once. I wish I were as brave as him. Then I'll be done with everything. Then I'll be gone and I won't be scared anymore.

I don't want you to do that.

What's the point? Life is shit and no one will miss me.

I will. I'll miss you.

Will you?

I miss you now. I miss you even when I'm with you.

Surrender Dorothy

SWEET STREET WAS where the people came for pills and Lollipop Lane was where they came for something stronger. Tick was supposed to go to Lollipop Lane that night but he got dressed and went into the kitchen and made tea and sat down and told her that he wasn't going anywhere. He had decided.

Decided what?

To stay here. With you.

He looked outside at the black cat that had once again begun to purr and fuss on the edge of the wall. The cat jumped on a bird and the bird struggled and chirped and the cat sniffed and squeezed. There were feathers. Fur. Then the bird got between the cat's paws and opened its wings and flew off into the night. The cat watched it go, looked into the window where she was sitting with soup and cigarettes. Then it jumped back onto the wall and ran into the corner and disappeared into black ink. There were sirens. Again. Tick sat in a corner and closed his eyes when they sang and then he whistled to drown out the noise. In the world there was good and bad and sometimes there was both mixed up together and she couldn't tell which was which. It was all grey, like too much ink pumped into the same cup of water.

The boy was waiting.

What are you waiting for?

Nothing. It doesn't matter. Your clock is broken anyway.

Sometime into the night when the cartoons became bloody and perverted and the adverts were about gambling and meat, he went into his wardrobe and pulled out a small box with electrical tape wrapped around it. He unwound the tape while she stood over him. Plastic Jesus nodded and the cuckoo clock bashed his head against his broken house until he broke his neck and his head knocked sideways. She twisted the head back again and played with the video that she had kept with her for hours. Dorothy smiled from the cover and the Scarecrow said the word fuck over and over.

I've never watched this all the way through, she said.

But you watch it all the time.

I watch it, but not to the end. I watch it right through until that bit where Dorothy clicks her heels and everything goes into a dream. Then I stop it and look at it and I rewind it all the way back to the start and play it again. I do that because.

You don't want it to end?

And I don't want Dorothy to go home.

The boy looked at her. He took the cigarette out of her hand and pushed it between his lips and sucked on it. He gave it back and she smoked it too. But what if something happened to you? he said. What if you never got to see the end? It's your favourite thing in the world and you don't even know how it's supposed to go. It's stupid. You have to play it through. You have to know how everything turns out.

Why?

I. I don't know.

If you don't know then I don't either.

Fine.

Fine.

They played with a pack of cards that he had got from his grandmother who was now dead. The pack was new and unopened, and when she pointed to it on the shelf he took it down and unwrapped it and opened the box and pulled the cards out. They smelled like ink and bread. They were red and blue and green with shiny fronts that held the sun when they were turned to face the window. They played snap, and Tick looked up at the clock so many times that it was easy to beat him. She shuffled all the cards in her hand and looked at the cartoon faces painted on the front and back of each one.

My Gran got me those, he said.

They're nice. I never had games.

Not even when you were a kid?

Maybe I did then. I can't remember. Everything we got we sent back into the world again. I think I remember a stuffed bear or a stuffed dog. It's all just fog now. It's like something that happened in a story that I read when I was really young. And now I try to remember and it's all washed away. Do you remember things from when you were a kid?

Yeah.

What?

I remember Mum had a job but she finished early to pick me up from school. I think we used to go by the park and it was green then. It smelled good. You know? When things smell good that's what you remember. The smell. It was cut grass and dirt. Mum always let me play as long as I wanted and then Dad would come home and he would go to the park first because he knew we would be there. Mum would swing me, but not as high as Dad. We used to get chips.

With salt and vinegar?

Yeah. I remember that.

When you remember things it's like there's no time. I think of my Dad sometimes and then I smell his aftershave and listen to the sound of him sleeping or sitting down in his chair. It's like. It's like time is broken, but in a good way. There are all these pieces everywhere and you can take hold of one and think on it and then it's there. It's here. Now. I see my Dad, and then I'm smiling. Then I feel sad, but that's okay. I think it's okay to feel everything at once because that means Dad was real once. He was real, and sometimes he's more real than anything.

When they were done with the game she shoved the video underneath Tick's pillow and folded the blanket on top of that. There was a knock on the door that had come before they picked all the cards up. They were scattered in a pile in their pairs and when someone knocked on the front door they shoved them back into the box and hid the box away. The knock came again. Tick stood up and opened his mouth wide and she looked at him and knew that it wasn't Lucky.

What's wrong? Who's that?

It's them.

Who?

I've been waiting. I knew they'd come. They're angry.

You shouldn't answer. Let them think we're not here.

They know. They always know. I knew they'd come get

me. They know. They knew it as soon as I didn't show up to look after Simon. It's happened before. This is just like then but worse now because there's no coming back. They realize what I've done. They know now. It's so. It's. The cards were fun though. I forgot about them until last night. I forgot I even had them. I just wanted to be a kid again. I wanted to be a kid once more before I had to put those cards away. You can have them now. They're yours. You can be a kid too if you want. Time, like you said, it's just broken apart and if we want to go back we can.

You can too.

No. I can't. Not now.

She started to cry. Outside the day was cold and grey and the sky had sunk around the estate in a thick cloud and the world looked so much smaller then. There was no background. The sky was sharp and white and the moon was a thumbprint without edges. There were no hills that rolled into the distance. No feathering grass caught by the breeze. Everything had disappeared into a damp fog that hid the cracks and the streets. Tick turned away from her and sat on the edge of the bed. He pulled his boots on and did the laces and looked at the carpet.

Can't you just stay here?

No. I wish I could.

Stay and watch TV.

I can't. I'll go out and I'll try to settle things, but if I'm not back you should take all the money and you should leave here. You're the only person I've ever met who isn't really from anywhere. You're not tied here. You can leave. You can go away and get lost and you don't ever have to be found if you don't want to. All you need is money. Money is freedom. You can take it and you can go. You can go anywhere you want in the whole world and nobody would know.

I want to go where you are.

The boy stood up and shook his head and she leaped off the bed and pulled him to her chest and laid her chin on his head. His hair smelled like chemicals and shampoo, but there was something else there too. She closed her eyes. She squeezed him so hard he yelped like a dog and then became quiet. He smelled of grass and dirt.

The dog on the wall had disappeared and his mother had gone to sleep in the other room and the boy was spiking his hair back up in a mirror that belonged to the outside of his father's car. He jerked his chin and made little noises in the back of his throat. The knock came again. Then voices. They shouted through the letterbox but she couldn't understand what they said. It sounded like the barking of dogs. He took all his money and the white rabbits and everything else from underneath the bed and he took it all into his hands and he looked at her and she looked at him. He gave her the money and he kissed her on the cheek and he left the room. She looked at the money in her hands and listened to the sound of the door clicking open. The cold wind blew in. There was the sound of shuffling and then the voices of children. Tick's words were caught in the wind and then he too sounded like the barking of dogs. His mother called from the next room.

Is that you, Tick? Can you come here? I just want to look at you. I only want to look at you.

But the boy had already gone.

Tick didn't come home that night and he didn't come back the next day. She sat in the living room and smoked and watched TV and she rubbed her eyes and played with all the money in her lap. On the TV there was a cartoon and the cartoon was red. She stared at the TV for hours but she hadn't watched anything. Her sight stopped at the base of the carpet where her own feet were as still and useless as plastic toys that couldn't run or walk or kick or fight. She saw only the things in her mind that was swollen with bloody pictures and broken glass and hollow iron fences driven deep into the ground. Her feet wouldn't move. The red shoes shone. She hated them. Everything.

The cuckoo struck.

Shut up, she said.

The cuckoo was silent.

The front door popped and clicked open. Keys jangled and the wind came into the room and then went back out again. She stood up and let the money fall out of her arms and it caught on the breeze and rolled around the empty room like the moth wings in her head. Then it was all still. She stood up and wiped her face and waited. The boy was home. He was back and everything was good and lovely again. She played with the twist in her little finger and smiled for the boy.

I knew you'd.

She stood back. She felt her feet go numb again as the money rolled and covered the shoes in green. Her nose ran but she didn't wipe it. The boy had not come home. It was Lucky who stood in the doorway. He stood tall against the frame of the door with the keys in his hand and looked at her. He smiled at first but then his eyes darted around the room and he looked at the money that rolled like rabbits over her feet. He raised his hand to his face and then balanced against the frame. He steadied himself. His eyes were tired. His face was a rolling, sunken sheet. His cheeks were dirty and covered with yellow and grey hair. He stood in front of her and watched the shadows lean into the room, and he was both close and far away. He wiped the raw circles underneath his eyes and licked his dry lips.

What's happened? he said. What's going on?

She was quiet. She felt herself emptying. Crying.

He stumbled forward and looked at her. He wiped her eyes and then he fell onto his hands and knees and took the money in his fists and looked at it there. She came down to the floor and shook her head and he took her by the shoulders and stared deeply into her face. His lovely eyes rolled. That lovely ugly love was nowhere in the room and she thought that nothing would ever be good again. He didn't speak. He couldn't. He couldn't say anything. She wished he were the boy. The ruby shoes sat on her feet as useless as stones and she worked them into the carpet.

Tell me what happened. What the Hell is going on here? Where did all this money come from? Where's Tick?

You left, she said.

What?

You were gone and Tick was.

I'm sorry.

You can't just go. You can't just go away, Dad.

What?

You can't just.

She slapped him, and he pinned her arms to her sides.

She fought.

You can't just go away, Dad. Please. Please.

He pulled her to his chest and she smelled the ash in his clothes and the beer in his throat. She felt his heart beating against her cheek and the warmth of his body and she remembered what his eyes looked like in the rear-view mirror all those years ago. He said sorry. She let herself empty on him. Her mouth opened and she howled until there was no sound left. She was still. Her eyes closed. He said sorry. He said sorry, over and over. Sorry, for everything. For all he'd ever done and everything he ever was. I'm sorry. I'm just a man and I'm learning how to live with that. I have to try. I have to be different. I have to make things right again.

The sun peeked through the windows and warmed them both. The moon and sun shared the same sky and the fog broke apart and disappeared. She could see the hills again. The long towers in the distance and the black road. She could see a place that could've been her father's place, sticking up like a finger. Like the bad finger one person points at another when they're trying to be rude. She smiled.

I have to tell you something, she said.

Please, tell me everything.

She sat with the fallen man and she told him about Tick and about Sweet Street and the man in the car and she told him about the boy who had rolled over the top of the car and she told him that Tick had been gone for a long time. She talked about all the things that they had done and she told him all the things that Tick said he would do if he could. Lucky listened and he opened his eyes and he held his hand on the top of her head while all the moths came flying out through her eyes. She sank as the words came. He held her up. When she was done he braced himself on the frame of the door and pushed himself up. Every word seemed like a stone thrown hard against his back. He was crippled with the broken bones and the red marks that existed only in his heart and underneath the layers of scarred skin. He drew his hands to his face and held them there. He said something into his palms but his voice was too muffled for her to understand and then he brought his hands down and looked at them. He spoke again. She listened.

I'm his father and he is my son, he said.

She looked at him and she.

I'm the father, he said. He's the son.

I think they want to hurt him. He wants to hurt him.

No, he said. He doesn't want to hurt him.

Who then?

Not him.

Then he was quiet. All the light that had poured in from the sun had turned into streetlights and the red and blue of police cars. On the outside the world was dark and the darkness seemed to settle on his face. He stood in the doorway and she could see all the scars and the age and the wear that had crept upon him while he had not been there.

What are you going to do? she said.

It's him. It's always been him. He's my son and all this time I didn't see how much it mattered. I'm the father and he is mine. My son. My boy. I'm going to end this, all of it. I'm going to bring him home.

The woman in the bed had been listening. She shouted murder and rage from the other room and there was so much noise all around them but Lucky was calm. The woman cried, howled, barked like a dog and then there was nothing. There was silence. All the noise of the estate and all the noise of the other room were numbed into whispers. Lucky dried his eyes on his sleeves.

She shook her head. Don't go.

I have to.

I love you.

He laughed. I don't know why.

I don't know why everything hurts but it does. I don't know why people do things they don't want to do but they do. Nothing makes sense. You don't take care of each other and you don't take care of yourselves and things rot and you watch them do it because you're too scared of anything different. Everyone is afraid all the time, and nobody sleeps. Not really. You all lie there thinking you're asleep but you're not. I know you're not. All you are is quiet and still and thinking and doing nothing while the world rolls. Like tin people. You lie there awake watching everything like TV until the TV gets into your head and you can't see anything else. I can't sleep either. I'm awake all the time and it's bullshit. I didn't realise how bullshit it all is but it is and I don't know why.

That's just life.

Please don't go.

I have to go. I have to bring my son back.

I know. I wish.

You wish it could be different.

That's just life.

Yes.

He looked at her and she looked at him. She closed her eyes and she pretended to be somewhere else. She felt the walls recede around her and she felt the wash of the cold waves and the salt that dried her skin and the cool sand underneath her feet. She felt him standing there, the man who came. The first one there ever was who wasn't her father. She pushed her lips together and tilted her head back and she pretended to be. Then he kissed her. She felt him there. Breath. Lips. Eyes that saw who she had been and who she now was. He kissed her while she stood on that impossible beach. She felt the ugly lovely love rush over her and then she felt it sink away again. She opened her eyes.

I would've loved you, he said. Back then. Before I got into the car and before the world split into two. If I was a better man. I think I would've loved you, Sweetheart. If it had all been different.

Simon Says

LUCKY DIED SOMETIME around that fifteenth hour, or so they said.

It was all he'd ever wanted.

Tick came home one day later just like Plastic Jesus said he would when she took him in her fist and asked him if Lucky would die. She waited. She sat for hours and hours in the hallway looking up at the front door just like she did when she had lived inside the museum. It wasn't parcels or papers or a voice without a face that she was waiting for this time. It was the boy. Her boy. Her lovely wild friend who would not turn away from pain but drove towards it with furious certainty and a bright silver smile. She waited in the hall until bedtime and then she kept herself awake. Her eyes burned. The next day the door clicked and then opened and the boy stood in the hallway.

Tick came into the light. She stood up and looked at him with the sun showing all the difference that was made by those two days. The boy looked at the ground. She stepped towards him and pulled his chin up. He had a bruised eye that was punctured on the lid and specks of blood that turned the ends of his lashes into roses. His lip was swollen and purple. The white of his left eye was bright red and one of his teeth was chipped. The silver tracks in his mouth hung broken and crooked and it had cut the inside of his lip. His thumb was twisted. Body bruised underneath a school uniform that he hadn't needed on the day he left but told her it would help when they found him afterwards. When he was gone. He would be a doll then, he said. He would be a doll dressed in a school uniform and they would know where he belonged and his Mum would know what happened.

The cuckoo in the room struck sixteen and seventeen and twenty-one all at once and she held him to her chest until she felt him recede into despair. Then he didn't talk. Then he didn't look at her. He went to sleep for two days and woke up again hungry. He had wet his sheets. She changed them. When she took his clothes off he said nothing and when she washed his body he said nothing. She changed his clothes into what was fresh and clean and then he looked in the mirror. In the mirror the boy was different. He told her that his eyes had changed.

I look like Lucky, he said. My eyes. They're his.

Yes, they are. So much like his.

I never noticed before. They're the same colour.

Sometimes.

The boy began to cry. I lost my keys, he said. I don't remember losing them but they're gone now. I think they're somewhere around the estate. Probably on the grass or maybe they dropped down a drain or something. I'll have to find them. I'm not supposed to lose them. They're my only set and they cost a lot of money to cut. I'm such an idiot.

He cried long and hard in the bathroom and his mother began to cry from the other room. They killed him, the boy said. They killed my Dad. Anna. Anna. Anna. He came to get me and they let me go and they killed him instead. They killed him like he was nothing. I don't know. I just. He's dead. He's gone.

She held the boy.

Tick told her that Lucky had died somewhere on the black road. He had gone there to take his son home and to face whatever needed facing, and there was no way back from that. Lucky told Tick to run. That's it, boy. Run on home now. Run. Go that way. Don't look back. Don't you look back even for a second. Just run. So Tick turned around but he didn't run. He walked, slowly, and he felt his father standing behind him and he saw the shine in the windows and the young shadows that began to move in. Some were crying. He heard them all behind. Then he heard the passenger and saw all the people in the windows and all the people lurking down alleyways. Listening. Watching. Crying. Doing nothing. Lucky died and the whole of the estate turned out to watch, but silently behind closed doors and lovely little gardens. The passenger shouted after Tick. He said that's what you get, Son. You make me do these things. It's all on you. The boy didn't believe him, he said. It was all on him. All him. And nobody else.

Lucky was beaten until he was still and then he was dragged to the concrete and then to the dirt by a dozen children who cried as they took him there and didn't stop when the boy was over the rough mound of the park. She washed the boy's face with cold water and wiped it with a towel that had been warming on the radiator and she took him into the living room where the TV was playing and she sat him on the floor in front of it. The woman in the bed was. All this chaos came from behind her door and she threw down a cup and watched the water spin in the air and went into her room and looked at her where she fought with her quilt and pulled it into her mouth and tried to choke herself.

The woman cried. Wailed. Shouted. She turned in the bed and wrapped herself up and called for Lucky over and over until the name was chewed up like fat. She reached out and snatched the quilt and stood over the woman and watched as she looked up and bit the air like a dog. Outside there was no sound. The last of the day collapsed around them and tomorrow would soon come aching into now. The mad bird said. Dorothy was. She turned around and went out of the room and left the woman naked and crying on the bed.

I knew it. I heard it. I knew it, the woman said. I knew it wouldn't be long before he left us all. Good things die. Pretty things die. I knew it before he went out of the door. Let me sleep. Dear Dog in heaven let me sleep. She shoved the quilt into the bath and turned on the water and shut the door and got into the bath with the wet quilt underneath. She wiped her face. Closed her eyes. She turned to look at the toilet seat and then at the ceiling, and thought long and hard about all the things that were no longer there.

There were no more games. The next day the boy was silent but his eyes were wide and when she spoke they looked through her. Tick lay in bed but he didn't sleep and she lay next to him and slept even less and they didn't speak and didn't look at each other for hours at a time. She took Plastic Jesus in her hand and asked him if everyone has to die in the end and Plastic Jesus smiled and nodded yes, yes, yes. She thought about all the people of the estate. Good. Bad. Ugly. Fat. Lovely. Old. New. And she thought of Dorothy who would last forever in a plastic case and she knew that people were more than that. They were minutes long. Seconds. They screamed furiously into life and then furiously into death just as fast. They were the dreams that burned. Hot. Hungry. And she burned too.

She watched a film. It wasn't *The Wizard of Oz*. She watched the TV in the dark and she mouthed the words to all the songs that played in black and white but she didn't sing out loud. Outside the black road snaked and looped. She slept on the living room floor and she didn't dream and didn't think of Dad and she didn't think of Mum who she couldn't remember anymore. Then in front of her in a line down the beach she saw a hundred of her mothers all naked in a row and each daughter played with the hair of each mother and each mother played with the hair of each grandmother and so on and so on for hundreds of years back. They stretched so far she couldn't see. All blood. All of them connected. When she woke up she smoked and wore the dark green glasses and blew all the smoke into the air. Remember when you were a girl, her mother said in her head.

No, why don't you tell me.

She watched the flicker of the black and white fuzz where she had kicked out or hit out at the TV in the night and the cable had come loose from the back and broken off and the wires twisted like veins that didn't connect to anything. The bird in the back room called nine or six or eight. She didn't know because she wasn't listening anymore. She turned the TV off and she sat in the middle of the room staring into the black.

There was no blue beneath the paper on the walls that surrounded her. No yellow boat painted by her father to remind her that they had once been happy. She looked at the curtainless window and then she looked at the doorless frame beside the TV set and she watched the hallway where the woman in the bed was standing.

What are you doing?

The woman didn't answer.

Where are you going?

Silent still.

The woman didn't look into the room but walked through the hallway and past the frame of the door so slow, very slow. Then the woman was gone and she heard the front door open. And close. She stood up and went into the hallway and into all the warm light that came from the little window and into the cold artificial light that hung above them and she opened the door.

The woman stood looking out from the balcony. The wind caught her by the long hair and sent it in swirls behind, just above that long beautiful back. Her breasts were lifted over the wall. Her arms rested there. A flowerpot was on her left. There were poppies. Dying. She stood naked and unafraid and bathed in all that light that came from the moon and though she was bare her bareness wasn't strange. It seemed just as it should be. She joined her on the balcony and stood next to her and saw her tall and beautiful and pale before that lovely sky. The woman closed her eyes and the light caught her skin and the smoke rose around her. I forgot about this, the woman said.

What?

She smiled but didn't speak and stood looking at the sky and at the towers that rose like polished black stones in the distance. They stayed there watching the world with that close edge and the lights on the black road and the people that lived their lives in the rooms that were cemented together and cemented apart. The woman smiled but didn't speak. After some time she turned and looked at her and she bent down to kiss her face and the kiss caught the cold and stayed on her cheek awhile. The woman turned around then and went back inside. She followed her to the bathroom where she washed her face and put on makeup and she followed her into the bedroom where she picked out the clothes that she wanted to wear. She couldn't leave her side and couldn't take her eyes away as the woman who had drawn herself out of her bed had begun to resurrect.

The boy had been quiet for days. When she stood in front of him he looked at his feet or out of the window and when she offered him food he shook his head. He didn't jerk his head or bark in his sleep. That part of him was gone.

The woman who had once been in the bed went into the kitchen to sing and make dinner and to fascinate the room and the birds and the black cat that did not know her. When she was done there were potatoes and there was meat and there was cabbage and food that she hadn't seen before. Gravy. Pudding. Mint. The woman had woken early and gone out and taken the bus and she had talked to people who had thought she died when she had got married and she talked to others who didn't know her and she came back with bags of food and told her that she had been pushed into life and cooking. She couldn't help it. There were flowers standing in vases that grew towards the sun even though they had been cut and would die in days.

Have you seen those people, the woman said, have you seen all those people? There are some who grow old and scared and seek out forgiveness just before the end. There are some who play like they're worried the playing will run out. Have you seen the ones who claw through brambles and drag themselves to church to seek their posthumous reward? Why do they grow old? Why do they let themselves do that? I think I love them all. This meal is ours and when we eat it we'll think of them.

She ate and said nothing and when she was done she smelled the sleeves of Lucky's coat and went into the kitchen to clean while the woman stood outside and caught the rain in her hands. She took a plate into Tick who wouldn't eat and wouldn't talk and wouldn't turn to look at her when she came into his room. He stayed beneath his blanket and she sat with him until the sound of breathing turned into nothing but soft sighs and the word Dad, shouted over and over.

She went outside to throw stones at the dog on the wall and to sit on the swing that had been twisted all the way up to the frame. She smoked and looked at the light on the end of the lamppost above the wall and she looked at the old fridge that had been turned on its side and she looked at the whole estate through the green glasses that were now more hers than ever before.

A boy in black walked by and she watched him go. He climbed over fences in the rain and kicked the railing that was topped with razor wire and he broke through a door that had been locked and she followed him. She followed him across the concrete and as he went up the stairs and she stood on the other side of a wide space in the cold and the dark where the towers stood side by side and there were no bridges between them. She called out to the boy and the boy turned around.

Where are you going, Tick?

He didn't answer.

Can you come back?

He jerked his head and grabbed the back of his neck and in the driving rain and the light that cracked in the sky she could see the shape of his face and she could look deep into the mines of his eyes. He mouthed something but she couldn't hear it and he shook his head but. He turned around and went through another door and he was gone.

She found a staircase and she ran down it and she found a corridor and went through it and she tried to follow him but she didn't know where he had gone. In the park there was a child and she asked him if he had seen Tick but he just covered his face and cried. She went on. The world was grey and green and black. The boy and his shadow were drawn up onto the walls and she followed one and then the other as they rose and fell. She coughed and threw down her cigarette. She ran.

She went where the light didn't want to go and she looked up and saw the edge of that blackened building where there had once been a fire that was started by a child. Below the blackened edge where the walls of the building fell there was a small girl who stood with her hands together in prayer and her face looking up. She stood beside her and turned the child around. The child looked up.

What are you doing?

The boy has come again.

What boy?

The one who burns.

The girl nodded her head like Plastic Jesus. She pointed to the open mouth of the building and she pointed to each blackened floor and she pointed to the top where a boy stood looking down.

She climbed through the blackened room at the bottom of the estate and went through the door that was not there and she went into the hall where the smoke had not gone and junk had been left to pile up along the walls. She climbed the junk as she had before. There was a brick that wedged a heavy door open and she opened the door and kicked the brick away and went through and closed the door after her.

She went up the familiar stairs and down the familiar corridor and she stood outside that familiar door that was wedged wide open with a stone just like the door downstairs and it all looked different because nothing was green. She went through the door and into the white room and Simon was not inside and neither were the rabbits. The TV that played on the ceiling was broken and projected only the black and white static that fizzed and growled like a monster. She turned it off.

In the hallway the rabbits were running. She looked towards the end and saw the ears of one and the tail of another and the shadow of all of them cast upon the wall and she followed it as it turned the corner. At the end of another hall there were three rabbits and around another corner there were seven more and they were all going in the same direction. She followed them. They jumped and stopped and jumped and stopped, all travelling forwards and back towards where she had already been. The corridor turned black and became burnt and twisted and the cold air drove through and the rabbits began to leave little black footprints and stretched the burn to the untouched white that she left behind her.

The black corridor became a black room that had lost its door and part of the floor and its entire back wall that had been ripped out and scattered all over the estate below. There was a wide opening. As though she was standing in a black mouth. The wind blew through and caught her hair up in twists. The white rabbits were dirty and they lined up along the walls and refused to venture near the long drop.

The door was on the floor and she fell over it as she stepped into the burnt room. She pulled herself up again. Junk was everywhere and it was sodden and broken and falling apart just like the junk she remembered that ate up her Dad and ate up her memories.

On the edge of everything was the boy. He stood with Simon on the folds of floor that broke off into nothing and he looked down at the world under his feet. The wind swept the ashes into black powder that stained the corridor behind her and the boy stood back from it and held Simon by his wasted arm and twisted hand and his body that was tilted to the left. Simon made a noise deep in the gutter of his throat and Tick held him closer. The wind did not touch the boys. They were suspended. They were stones tilted on the edge of a wall that would soon crumble beneath them.

She stepped into the middle of the room and called their names.

What are you doing? she said. She walked closer, her red shoes gathering dust and changing from red to grey and into black. She held her hands out for balance and moved slowly around the battered furniture turned on its side and she went around the back of the TV that had been hollowed out and she stepped over the films that were burned and melted into stacks and she stood apart from Tick and the boy who gurgled and smiled and pointed at her. Tick drew the boy to him and held him tightly by the arm and looked to the edge of the room.

Please, can we take him home?

Tick wiped his eyes with the sleeves of his coat and shook his head.

Let's take him back.

Simon clapped and smiled and laughed at the birds that began to sail in the air beside their faces. Her red shoes were caked in black. Her black shoes were.

Let me take Simon home.

It's too late.

It's not. I can take him back and we can go home.

I can't.

You can. I'll help you.

It's too late. The other kids already saw me.

The cold air caught them again. The boy pulled Simon closer. She clung onto a fence that had been put up and then pulled back down again. Her body twisted in the wind. The dog on the wall growled at the moonless sky. She steadied herself and stood between the bricks that had once belonged to the room. Underneath the old TV was an old video player that was still plugged in.

We can run away.

Then they'll win.

Who?

Everyone else.

I don't understand. I'm scared.

That's how they like it.

The boy cried into his sleeves and she tried to move and she couldn't do anything because her feet were stuck and her shoes would do nothing to help her. She was crying too. She cried for the boy and she cried for herself and she cried for her mother who couldn't help her and she cried for Dad who helped her only once. When the crying was done she looked at the boy once more and reached out.

I want to go home.

I can't go there now. It's too late.

It's not.

Simon made a noise and Tick pulled him by his pyjama top and he looked at her and he smiled. Everyone said he couldn't die. Don't you know that? Everyone said he couldn't die and everyone said he was their friend but no one helped him when he needed them. He killed him and it was because of me. He was my Dad. He wasn't like me. He was good and kind and he prayed for good things to happen and sometimes they did. I saw it. He was better than me and now he's gone. I'm still here and it's my fault. Everyone is scared all the time and I'm sick of it. I'm scared too and I'm sick of it. I can't. I can't. I'm me. I'm me. I'm me and this is all there is. This is all there'll ever be.

The boy cried and Simon cried too and rubbed the dust out of his face. The rabbits dived madly around the room and some of them jumped over the edge and into the drop. The boy turned Simon to face him and Simon looked at Tick who was not as tall. Tick wiped Simon's face with his sleeve and he wiped his own and he smiled and he said don't you know that it's all a game, Simon? Don't you know that it's so much fun? Everything. Look at that and that and that there. Look at Anna. Don't you know that it's all a mad game?

She stepped forward with her hand out and her shoes slipped and she couldn't take another step again and she held onto the TV and the cable that was still plugged into the wall socket. The wind came. Dad was in her head and Mum was in her shoes and she couldn't move because she was weighed down by thoughts of falling. Tick looked at Simon who pointed to the ground and clapped.

Let's play a good game, he said. Let's play Simon says. You like that game, don't you? You like playing Simon says with me. He looked at the boy and the boy looked at him.

Simon says clap, he said.

The boy did.

Simon says nod your head.

The boy did.

The boy looked at Tick and Tick looked at the boy. Simon looked below him at the long drop down and then he looked back up. Tick stepped away from Simon who balanced on the edge of broken bricks and crumbled floor and iron bars that stuck out broken like Tick's braces. Simon laughed and tried to hold onto Tick but Tick was pulling himself away and crying.

Simon says jump, Tick said.

Simon gurgled.

Simon says jump. Jump. JUMP.

Then Simon smiled. And jumped.

She lunged forward from behind the TV and grabbed the air and got hold of him and caught hold of his pyjamas and held herself back on the TV cable that was still attached to the wall. The boy clapped wildly. He moved up and down. She held him as tight as she could while he shouted and laughed. She twisted her arms around his waist and felt the pull of her muscles. Tick stood back with his hands on his face. He watched them like they weren't there. Watched them like TV. What was happening was far away. Not there. Not to her. She couldn't. She pulled and Simon kept jumping over and over again and he leaned out of the gaping mouth and laughed into the wind that caught his voice and sent it shooting out between the towers. The TV cable pulled tight and whined and the last rabbit watched them from a dirty chair. She kicked off her shoes and she planted her feet and pulled Simon back from the edge and he jumped and pulled himself forward again and she cried and held the TV cable as tight as she could. Tick looked at the rabbit. Her. Simon. The edge.

Help me, she said. Tick. Help. Help.

She lost her red shoe down the long drop. Tick wiped his eyes and opened his mouth and then he came forward quickly. He bounded over the upturned concrete and over the broken sheets of wallpaper and past the rabbit that watched him as he split from his terrible dreaming. He came fast and took Simon by the collar. He shook his head and pulled Simon back but the boy kept jumping over and over. Stop, he said. Stop. Stop. Stop.

They were close to the edge now. They held onto each other and each felt the wind that came up from the bottom. They couldn't hear each other, only the hearts that beat fast and heavy under their clothes. There was grass in the air. Cold water. There was the smell of cooking and the smell of dogs. There were no sirens but there was talking from below. There was the sound of a million other TVs. Closing doors. Music. Mess. Home.

Stop, Tick said. Simon pulled.

Simon says stop, she said, Simon says stop.

Simon stopped, and they pulled him back.

They didn't know until then that the passenger had been watching them while they. She could see that his shadow had darkened the room and she could see in the eyes of the boy that he had come there. The passenger stood behind them and called out in a rage when he saw Simon held unsteady above the fall. She couldn't turn to look at him as he came, but she watched the fear in Tick's face and she felt the footsteps and she didn't turn because she couldn't let any of them go. The passenger came and he came too quickly. She heard him stumble and fall. He tripped on the cable that she held in her hand and he went into Simon who laughed and smiled and clapped his hands as his father danced around the edge. She held onto Simon and Tick held onto her and the man stumbled all the way over the edge.

She saw the man and she followed him down as he twisted black and terrified in the cold air. She watched him fall all the way down, and she held onto Simon who wanted to follow. She pulled him away from the drop and pushed him back into Tick's arms. Simon giggled and clapped and Tick sat down with him and put his arms around him and he said Sorry. Sorry. Sorry.

She looked at the man who was broken on the black street. He went down and didn't rise up again on the folds of concrete there. There was blood. There was a cold breeze. He was broken on the slabs below and he was dead. Gone in blood and anger. Dead. And surrounded by the bodies of six white rabbits that had fallen sometime before.

Simon cried and Tick held him and she came to hold them both. When the sun came up the dog on the wall turned his tail around and disappeared and would not come back again. She kissed Tick on the face and Simon laughed and she kissed him too and Tick wiped his mouth. She pulled the TV cable up and looked at the last rabbit as it turned from them, jumped from the chair and darted down the hall. She sat with the boys in the decay of the world and she drew Simon's head to her lap.

They went slowly down that long corridor and down that long staircase helping Simon along and she took them both out into the street where the people had begun to gather with their hands on the shoulders of their children. She turned Simon's face away from his father where he lay bloody and dead on the slab and they stood in the middle of the people who had come to make sure the passenger was gone. Simon laughed. He laughed at everything. Anything. He looked at a bird that came and sat on a fence in front of him and he held his hand out and pointed.

We're sorry, Tick said.

She looked on and held Tick's hand.

One of the women stepped forward with her son's hand in her own and she looked at her where she stood and she didn't doglook her. The child was still and silent and the woman laid her hand on his head and she spoke.

I didn't see you up there, she said. I didn't see you go up there. I only saw Simon's father go up there. I saw him go up there and I saw him throw himself off the top and there was nobody else with him.

A man stepped forward with his daughter in his arms and he told her that he saw the same thing. I saw him jump, he said. He was up there and he jumped off and I didn't see anyone else there. I saw him go up there alone.

Another came forward and then another and she watched them all as they told their own truth and their children held onto them and they each took their turns and the children didn't have to speak for themselves.

And You Were There

THE CHILDREN PLAYED.

She heard them as she slept next to the boy who had cried for hours and hours at first in the arms of his Mum and then in the dark alone. The wind blew in through the window and the woman warmed the boy's school uniform on the radiators and the sound of the children came in with the warm air and she went to the window and watched them all below. They played their games in the light of the street and in the light that came from their own front doors. They picked up their bikes and rode them through the concrete tunnels and down the concrete stairs and through their concrete childhoods that were just as lovely as any on the greener grass. They chased balls that were thrown into the air. A girl whispered to another and ran. Kids were caught and chased and they fell and raised themselves up on the wet dirt.

A woman in a dress sent Simon to live with his mother who had not disappeared entirely from the world. She lived far away, but not too far that she couldn't bring the boy along every once in a while to look at the birds and the buildings and to play in a garden that had been laid some months after his father's death. Anna saw him there often, and she was allowed to play with him and so was Tick when he wasn't in school.

Tick's Mum raised him up early in the morning and cooked them all a fat meal and made them shower and dress and stood by the door to kiss Tick as he went out dazed and driven by complete surrender. She walked with him to school and told his Mum that she would fetch him home again and she did this every day until the boy began to talk and eat and sleep without crying. The boy talked about what he learned and then he talked about where his life would go and she listened and told him it was all a good idea.

She took a walk down Sweet Street one night while the boy was at home helping to wash dishes and talk and fix the TV that had been broken for a long time. The road was black but the lights were fixed and she could see into all the corners that had been hidden before. The moon was high and so was the sun. A girl walked through the street with a red backpack and yellow hair and she stood outside a shop that had been boarded for some time. A moth came to land on the window and it flew off again and fluttered around a light that was bright and milky. The girl looked up as she came close and stopped.

My Mum just bought this shop, the girl said.

Why did she do that?

She sells books.

Will she sell them there?

Yeah. It's a dream.

I think it will be.

She smiled at the girl and then walked along the black road with Dad in her head. There were no more moths after that, and no more twist in her stomach. She had seen the faults of her father and he had seen the faults of his daughter but that was all there was to love, seeing and then looking beyond to that little speck of glass that still shone brightly even after death.

She climbed the stairs of the fallen tower and went along the corridors and into the black room where the passenger had fallen. The room was the same. The walls were black and pictures hung in jig-jags and stuck corners and there were scraps of furniture and wet wallpaper all shoved into the middle of the room and blue police tape over the edge. On one wall was the TV and she wiped the black soot off the screen and off the top of the video player that was underneath. She kneeled down and pulled Dorothy out from her bag and opened the cover and took the tape in her hand and she slipped it into the player. The thing chugged and the machine spun and whirred and remembered what it once had been. She pressed the power button on the TV and hit it on the side and then pressed it again. The TV fizzed and sputtered and then it came on. In the black room the TV was lit and her body was grey and then full of colour. She sat watching the film play. She listened to all the songs. Dorothy looked out from the TV and the music drowned out the quiet that had stayed too long in that part of the world.

She watched the film. The light burned into all the corners and shone brightly from the room and lit the darkest part of the estate. She watched the film all the way through, until Dorothy stood in the middle of the Emerald City and said her goodbyes to the phantom men and women who would miss her in the end. Then the film ended with Dorothy in her bed, the credits rolled on the screen and then the video clicked and purred and another film rolled. She looked up. She crawled along the floor and placed her hands on either side of the TV. On the screen was a film that she hadn't expected. It was a recording of life as it really was. Past. Old. It was something from long ago, a small rolling picture. She raised her knees up and held them tight. On the screen was the face of her mother.

It was taken a long time ago, long before Simon and long before the creeping habit and the walls that wouldn't let her alone. Her mother sat leaning against a wall with a round belly, singing Somewhere Over the Rainbow. She clapped her hands to her face and listened as her mother's voice filled up the estate.

She watched it again and again, all the way through.

She walked along the black road and looked at all the places she had played with the boy and all the places she had driven with Lucky and she came into the park and sat on the swing. The boy would finish school soon. He would come to the park and he would talk about everything he had learned and then she would learn it too. They would look at books. They would swing and they wouldn't smoke. She swung and looked at the wall where the dog used to be and was now gone. A man came up to her and scratched his face and held out his hand and she gave him money and he smiled and went away again.

Some time later Tick came to sit with her and Simon came after and they were allowed to take him and stand next to him while he swung. He shouted and made little noises and they swung him higher and higher because he wanted the feeling of flying or of letting go or the same feeling he got when he was flung over the car and changed forever. And maybe he thought he could jump. And maybe he liked to fall. Tick talked and she listened. Everything was beautiful. Ugly. She looked at the moon as the boy swung higher. Tick talked about school. English. Science. Music. He talked about all the things that filled up the world and made it bigger. Infinite. She listened as Tick's voice filled up all the spaces that had been empty in her mind, and it grew above the background of the estate and ate up the noise from the streets and the noise of the women with thick arms and pink tops singing songs and hanging up their washing on the thin black lines. Their voices mattered more than the noise of the angry crowds that gathered and shouted near the river that sliced the town in two, or the crackle from the TV that was not the same, or the calls from men who knocked on doors and wanted money or furniture or children for unpaid bills, or the moths in her head, or Lucky carrying boxes and talking about Jesus, or Dad and his rabbits, or the one rabbit that lived wild in the estate. That nobody could catch. And her. She was louder than all of it. Louder than that nothing from the other side of the wall, and the men and women who were children once who came dazed and thoughtful with their hands outstretched, and the long lovely back of the woman who was no longer in bed, and the children who saw fear in the eyes of their parents, and that good ugly love, and everything, and everyone. Line them up and make them shout and hear how they make no sound at all.

Acknowledgements

I would like to acknowledge the support of Dominic Richards, Jayne Canciani, Christian Canciani and Louise Canciani, without whom this book would never have been written.

I would also like to thank Will Francis, Helen Francis, Jennifer Edwards and Angela Morelli, who offered constant encouragement and the best advice.

I'm forever grateful to Linda Ruhemann, Phillip Morris, Samantha Harvey, Leyton Tanner and to all the incredible teachers and mentors who helped me along the way. You made the difference.

To the teachers and staff at Bryncethin Primary School during the 90s, you told me I could write, and I remembered. Thank you.